THE
AVICULTURIST

By

Ann Smythe

For Nick and Harry
(even though they probably won't read it)

'Don't believe what your eyes are telling you. All they show is limitation. Look with your understanding, find out what you already know, and you'll see the way to fly.'

- Jonathan Livingston Seagull, Richard Bach

CONTENTS

CHAPTER 1

Thursday, 17ᵗʰ June 1971

Soft laughter floated up from the girls' hiding place in the tall grass. The sisters lay on flattened, dark green blades, their arms and legs spread wide from making grass angels, watching a few clouds scudding by in an otherwise bright blue summer sky.

'You can't always see them,' Lily said. 'Except for maybe a tiny dot, but you can hear them.'

'How do you know that?' Alice asked, squinting upwards.

'Joe told me. He knows everything about birds.'

The skylark's twittering abruptly stopped as the unseen bird dropped like a stone, swooping on some unsuspecting snack below, before once more ascending, bobbing and singing somewhere overhead.

For the girls, the afternoon slipped by in a haze of chatting and laughter.

'I wish it was tomorrow,' Alice sighed.

'Hmmm, and how old will you be?' Lily teased her younger sister who had spoken of little else for the past two days.

'Six, silly!' she giggled. 'Remember? I'm having a party and all my friends are coming.'

'Oh yes, I forgot!' Lily grinned. 'Come on, we should get going. I promised

1

Mother we wouldn't be too late.'

They picked their way along the edge of the field, heading towards a familiar gap in the hedgerow, before stepping through into a large meadow. The girls ambled through a mass of swaying ox-eye daisies and buttercups. Earlier, bees had hovered and flit among the flowers, the air vibrating with their soft drone, but now the sun lay low on the horizon and the only noise was a soft breeze whispering through the grass.

At the far end of the meadow, flanked on the left by dense woodland, lay Penwyth House, beyond which open fields sloped upwards to the unseen cliffs and sea beyond – its waters, for now, calm and subdued. The Gothic mansion loomed up ahead of them, grim and silent, its silhouette dramatic against the pink-tinged sky. Oddly out of place in such a setting, it was still a wondrous curiosity. Tall, leaded glass windows towered either side the heavy oak front door like royal sentry boxes. Numerous spires rose shambolically from its vaulted roof casting long, thin shadows that crept across the lawn, beckoning to the girls like fingers.

As they drew nearer, Lily looked for her father's car on the drive. Not there. Relieved, she turned to Alice.

'Come on! I'll race you!' They half skipped, half ran the rest of the way home, screaming and laughing as they collapsed against the door. Lily banged on the big old brass knocker as hard as she could.

'Mother, let us in!'

Their mother greeted them with open arms before shooing them upstairs to wash and change for supper. Outside, an unseasonal cool breeze blew in from the sea, whispering down the house's old chimneys like a warning.

Friday, 20ᵗʰ January 1995

Windscreen wipers working overtime, the young woman strained to see the narrow lane ahead. Storm clouds converged into a marauding grey mass stampeding inland, while an off-sea gale pummelled and shook her little red Ford Fiesta. It was 3.00 pm – it felt more like midnight.

The car's tyres struggled to find traction as the lane gradually deteriorated into a rough, uneven track and sheet rain ricocheted off the car bonnet as she tentatively drove down the steep cliffside. Panic threatened to well up inside her – not due to the storm or the driving conditions, although they weren't helping. Something more intangible was unsettling her and she felt her stomach constricting like a tourniquet that was slowly twisting and twisting ever tighter.

She forced herself to focus on the track ahead, which to her relief finally began to widen before opening out into a small parking area. At the far end, she could just make out a farm gate and, beyond it, through a few scrawny trees – Kleger Cottage. As confirmed, a dark blue Land Rover, with *Seaward Lets* painted in white on the rear door, was waiting for her. She pulled up next to it, feeling slightly foolish driving such a 'townie' car in the near off-road conditions, and waved at the man in the driver's seat, barely visible through the torrential rain. The figure looked up and waved back before pulling his hood up and entering the fray. Taking a deep, still shaky breath, she grabbed her denim jacket off the back seat and, raising it above her head, also took the plunge.

'Hello!' the man shouted through the storm, ushering her through the gate. 'I'm Adam. Shall we get in first?'

'Lily. Lily Sanders,' she replied, offering a soggy hand, struggling not to lose her coat in the gale. Adam gave the aged, wooden door a shove and gestured for her to go in. The traditional low-beamed kitchen had a wide, slate-tiled floor and, to the left, a huge inglenook fireplace dominated the room. It was, as stated in the *Seaward Lets'* brochure, '*a quintessential Cornish holiday home*'.

'Welcome to Kleger Cottage,' Adam said, stooping slightly to enter.

'It's lovely, very cosy. Especially right now,' Lily smiled, shaking off her denim jacket and glancing at the small kitchen window, where fingers of rain tapped insistently.

Adam pushed wet specs up his nose. 'I'm glad you like it,' he said, in a soft West Country lilt. He had an easy manner. Lily trailed behind him, whilst he showed her the downstairs rooms, all of which had the same low-beamed ceilings and slate floors covered with thick, warm-coloured rugs. Small wooden windows housed deep sills, through which she snatched glimpses of a dark, volatile sea.

'Why don't I leave you to have a look upstairs?' he suggested. 'I'll wait in the kitchen for you, okay?' Lily nodded and made her way up the steep, narrow stairs to find two charming bedrooms, one with a small en suite. A furious wind rattled eerily through the eaves. She peered through the tiny window at the writhing black mass of water crashing into the cliffs: land versus sea.

'Everything's great,' she said, back in the kitchen.

'Good,' Adam smiled. 'That just leaves for me to give you the keys. Oh, and there's some information about the cottage and local numbers in that folder,' he added, nodding at the kitchen table. 'If there's anything else I can help you with, just give me a call.'

'Thanks, I'm sure I'll be fine. I'm only here a few days.'

'You just down from Bristol for a bit of a break, then?' His question threw her slightly.

'Yes, that's right. I used to come here as a child with my family and have always been meaning to return,' Lily lied, fiddling with the keys. 'Hopefully, tomorrow I can do a bit of exploring.' She smiled weakly as the wind whipped even harder.

'Storms do come and go quite quick round here. Fingers crossed for a bit of sunshine,' Adam grinned. 'Oh, and if you want to try a decent pint of Cornish ale, there's always the Black Dog Inn at the far end of Tresor Bay. It's a nice place if you prefer traditional. Most holidaymakers head for the newer bars near the beach. Though, this time of year things are pretty quiet.'

'I'll bear that in mind,' said Lily, 'and thanks for braving the weather to come and meet me.'

With Adam gone, her initial relief at finding Kleger Cottage began to wane. She dragged her case from the car, getting wet all over again. Night descended quickly. Lily had changed into warm clothes, but the cold soon crept in even through the thick, stone walls. After a few practice runs and half a newspaper later, she managed to light a fire using the generous stack of wood and kindle stored in the inglenook. She pushed the old couch nearer to the flames and curled up with a glass of local wine from the welcome pack. Fatigue finally set in from the day's events. She felt herself relax, submitting to the fire's warmth and the numbing effect of the wine. Outside, the storm raged and the wind relentlessly pummelled the cottage on into the night.

CHAPTER 2

Lily awoke suddenly from a dream in which a huge, aqueous claw wrenched Kleger Cottage clean off the cliffside and plunged it deep into the black water below. She blinked the images away... *silence*. The storm had finally blown itself out and pale sunlight filtered through the tiny window. Quickly throwing on some old jeans and a sweatshirt, she ventured outside. Yesterday's roughshod sea had transformed into a panoramic expanse of shimmering calm water. To her right stretched uninterrupted coastline, to her left, behind the headland and nestled into the cliffside, she knew, was the seaside town of Lostmor. Closing her eyes for a moment, she enjoyed the warmth of the winter sun on her face. Seagulls spiralled overhead. Their familiar sky-call spiked childhood memories of herself and Alice laughing, running through the sand dunes, of ice cream and fish and chips by the sea. She watched the gulls disappear beyond the headland, heading for richer pickings in the bay.

A low-pitched, guttural sound made her swing round suddenly. Perched on a rickety old table, just inches away from her, was a huge seagull. She hadn't seen or heard it land. Mean-looking yellow eyes observed her as it shifted closer. Taken aback, but fascinated by the bird's sheer audacity, Lily stayed very still and, for a few moments, they eye-balled each other. Then, the gull lifted its head skywards and let out a long, undulating call before huge, powerful wings raised it high over the cottage and it wheeled out of sight behind the clifftop, still hollering.

'Nice of you to drop by!' she shouted after the errant gull, half expecting it to swoop back down for another look, but it had gone as quickly as it had appeared.

Back inside the cottage, Lily sat at the kitchen table, rereading the letter that had instigated her return to Lostmor for the first time in twenty-four years. She took a deep breath and dialled the solicitor's number.

'Mr Walker? Hello. This is Lily Sanders, Elizabeth Sander's daughter. We spoke on the phone a few days ago.'

'Ah yes, Miss Sanders. I've been expecting your call. Once again, I am so very sorry for your loss.'

'Thank you.'

'I am grateful to you for travelling to Lostmor especially, but it is in your best interest to be present for the reading of her will. When would be a good time for you to drop into my office?'

'As soon as you like. I'm renting a cottage for three nights, but can come today if you have time.'

Ever since leaving Lostmor, Lily's home had been in Bristol. Over the past seven years, the early onset of Alzheimer's had slowly ravaged her mother's body and ruined her mind, leaving her a sad, paper-thin version of her former self. The woman she had loved more than anyone in the world was lost to her long before death had taken her. *And now this*. Just days after the funeral, a letter from a solicitor in Lostmor, requesting her presence for the reading of her mother's will. A solicitor and a will she knew nothing about.

When she could no longer care for her mother, Lily reluctantly had to sell their home to cover the costly nursing fees and, as far as she knew, the house had been her only asset. Mr Walker agreed to meet her at 2.00 pm. The sooner the will was read, the sooner she could go home.

A walk along the coastal path to Lostmor looked more appealing than driving, but she needed a few supplies and decided to tackle the cliffside road once again. To her surprise, manoeuvring her car back up to the coastal road proved much easier, thanks to the dryer, sunnier conditions. The views, hidden by a wall of grey the day before, were stunning. Lush pasture rolled inland and grassy verges were dotted with yellow gorse. Beyond the cliffs, the sea, still bathed in sunshine, was a golden strip below clear pale blue. A few miles on, the coastal road descended and widened until the whole of Tresor Bay came into view. A tumble of houses spilled down the hillside, bejewelled windows sparkling in the sunlight. Residential houses appeared either side of the road, gradually giving way to restaurants, shops and pubs, all crowded in together and jostling for prime position along the seafront.

Lily parked a few streets back in the bay area. Still a little early for her appointment, she meandered through the quaint cobbled streets, glad of the distraction. The place was quiet, just a few couples and dog walkers enjoying the winter sunshine. The small inlet was no more than a 100-metre stretch of sand, dotted with deserted covered-up rowing boats. As she sat on a bench and gazed out, the bay looked different. It seemed less impressive now, smaller and strangely less colourful than she remembered as a child. The small horizon was very nearly enclosed by the dramatic, looming headland on both sides.

Her mother had sometimes taken her and her younger sister, Alice, for a picnic at Stoney Point, which had meant climbing the seemingly endless steep steps hugging the cliffside to her left. Beyond that, about four miles east of town, was her childhood home – Penwyth House. She wondered who might be living there now. Maybe it had been turned into some sort of country retreat or hotel? She had lived there, with her family, until Alice's sixth birthday. Then her world had fallen apart. A familiar knot was forming in her stomach. Her hands trembled and a cold sweat prickled her forehead. She closed her eyes and saw Alice. *Alice giggling… her fair hair golden in the sunlight. The two sisters hiding together in the long grass, whispering little-girl secrets.* But the image swiftly dissolved. A blackness cleaved through Lily's consciousness, trying to reach her, to draw her into something she did not want to see. Lily's eyes sprang wide open.

CHAPTER 3

Mr Walker's office was above a souvenir shop in a terraced Tudor-style house at the far end of the bay. Lily climbed the narrow spiral stairs to his office, her thoughts racing. She had initially worried that there may be outstanding debts she knew nothing about, but the solicitor had not hinted at any such thing. Perhaps it was just a matter of signing some overlooked documents. She wasn't sure how these things worked.

'Timothy, Timothy Walker. It's so nice to finally meet you, Miss Sanders.'

They shook hands and he gestured for Lily to take a seat. Originally an attic space, the office's sloping roof and book-lined walls made the room even tinier. Folders and papers were piled high on every surface. An ornate wooden desk was positioned under a small skylight and, behind it, an aged leather studded chair. She wondered how he'd got the furniture up the stairs. Mr Walker squeezed his generous paunch in behind the desk and unbuttoned his ill-fitting suit jacket.

'It's a little snug in here,' he apologised, searching for his glasses amongst the documents strewn in front of him.

'It's fine,' Lily smiled. 'Your letter did come as something of a shock. I didn't know my mother had made a will. We were quite close, so I'm wondering why she never mentioned it. Did she write it some time ago? She had suffered from Alzheimer's for many years.'

'Yes… she did,' replied Mr Walker. 'In fact, before you and your mother left… when you were just a child. Is this the first time you have returned to Lostmor since moving to Bristol, Miss Sanders?'

Lily nodded. 'After the accident... well, perhaps you know? My mother wanted to start again.' She stared down at her hands, her voice not much more than a whisper. 'It was a terrible, terrible time... for my family...' *And I don't want to talk about it, now or ever*, she thought to herself.

'Indeed, indeed,' he regretted asking. 'I am sorry, I do not mean to intrude or cause you any upset. I'll get to the point. The reason you are here is that I was instructed by your mother, Elizabeth, to keep this document safe.' Mr Walker unfolded the will, the existence of which had remained a secret from Lily for so many years. He peered over the rims of his glasses at her, knowing the life-changing impact his next few words would have on this young woman. 'Your childhood home here in Lostmor, Penwyth House, was never sold.'

Lily looked up, eyes wide in disbelief. 'But it was sold,' she said. 'Not long after we moved to Bristol! Mother was too upset to return to Lostmor and we needed the money to buy a house and, well... to start over.' She twisted her hands in her lap, wishing she was back in her apartment, in her studio, surrounded by her beloved jumble of canvasses, paints and brushes.

When they had first left Lostmor, she had felt responsible for what had happened. Just weeks after her father and Alice's funerals and still reeling from their loss, she had been dragged from her home in the dead of night, distraught and confused. It had felt like they were running away; and, to make matters worse, her mother refused to discuss the accident or explain why they had to leave. It had felt like they – no, *she* – had done something wrong.

To this day, Lily could not recall that tragic night, those last moments of Alice's life when she had fallen to her death, along with her father. Images that came to her, on nights when sleep was impossible, teetered at the edge of her thoughts. Snapshots of a scene, rerunning over and over in perpetuity, that never quite played itself out. She distinctly remembered a storm raging. Her father stood, statue-like, in the darkness, his skin white, drained of all pallor, whilst behind him flashes of lightning scuttled like spiders across the night sky.

Lily would see her young self, time and time again, afraid, watching Alice, so little, running through the storm to their father... He picks her up. Lily hears her mother calling from somewhere. She clambers back down the narrow stairs from the roof and, inexplicably, a dark, mask-like face appears. It has mean, narrow eyes and bony features that move ever closer to her... then she would wake, gasping for breath and her heart racing.

She forced herself back into the present. To listen to the words coming like white noise from Mr Walker's mouth, instead of the voices in her head. He noticed how pale she looked. The shock of his news, he presumed.

'I'm sorry, this is a lot to take in, I know,' he said kindly. 'Would you like a glass of water?'

'No. No, thanks,' Lily replied. 'Please continue, I'm fine.'

Mr Walker regarded her with concern and spoke in what he hoped was a gentle tone. 'I don't fully understand why your mother wanted to keep the house all these years, but she left the estate in the care of the groundsman – Joe Newman. Perhaps you remember him?'

She nodded, trying to take in this further revelation. Joe. Of course, she remembered him. But she had not thought of him for many years, just another lost face from her childhood.

'The house itself,' Mr Walker continued, 'has not been lived in since your family left, but the grounds, as you will see, have been well cared for. Joe's tried to keep up with a few minor external repairs to the main house, but the place has stood empty for decades. The roof is, I'm sure, in disrepair and I just don't know the condition of the interior… Your mother left instructions that no one should go inside, and no one has.'

'Why?' Lily asked, feeling beyond shocked. 'I can't believe that, after all this time, the house remains practically as it was when we left twenty-four years ago. And, to cap it all, the former groundsman, Joe Newman, is still working there!' It was too much. 'When we were little... Alice and I...'

She realised she hadn't even uttered her sister's name in years. She swallowed down a sudden wave of emotion threatening to surface and knew that, in her heart and her mind, she had never really escaped this place. She struggled to keep her voice even.

'We used to follow Joe around the grounds. He was kind to us. He used to keep us busy in the summer holidays, giving us little jobs to do. He taught us about the plants and herbs in the old Victorian glasshouses. And he knew about birds. Mother had an aviary and he took care of that, too.'

'I'm glad you remember him so fondly because, unlikely as this must all sound to you, Joe is still living on the estate… at Edhen Cottage,' said Mr Walker. 'Shortly after you left Lostmor, at your mother's request, I asked him if, in return for lodgings and a modest income, he would stay on and tend the grounds and, you know, keep an eye on things. He agreed. I kept waiting to see if your mother would contact me, but she never did. The years went by and not once did Joe ask me about your mother, whether I had heard from her, or if I knew why she had asked him to stay on. I can only guess that, maybe, to him, he was just continuing the job he had always done and enjoyed. In the early days, I used to drop by to see him, but nowadays I think he prefers his own company. He rarely answers the door at Edhen. Occasionally I see him in town, coming in for supplies, and he'll give me a nod.'

'I don't know what to say,' said Lily. 'I thought maybe this would be some final request, but this? Our home not sold, sat empty all these years? Why? Why would she do this?'

'I honestly do not know, and it was not my business to ask,' the solicitor explained. 'What I do know is that, before she left with you, back in 1971, Elizabeth granted me power of attorney over her affairs regarding Penwyth House until you inherited it. So, as requested, an account was set up to pay Joe a monthly wage and an annual sum towards the general upkeep of Penwyth's twenty-acre estate, including Edhen Cottage. She also advised me that, in the event of her death, l would be notified. Until recently, I presumed she was still alive and well and that she had built a new life for you both. Then, about a month ago, Meadow Heights nursing home in Bristol, a place you must know well, informed me of her passing. The owners, Mr and Mrs Charles, explained to me that Elizabeth had arranged this with them over eight years ago – I think when she first moved there. So, that is why, all these years later, I have contacted you and asked you to return to Lostmor. It is what she wanted. For you, Miss Sanders – her daughter – to inherit Penwyth House.'

'But if, as you say, Penwyth was never sold, how did she afford our home in Bristol?' asked Lily. 'I was still young, only nine, and she was at home looking after me. Any jobs she had were just part-time casual work, nothing that paid very well.'

'Your mother was once a very wealthy lady. Back in the day, a lot of people around here presumed your father owned Penwyth House. But it was hers… How much do you know about her parents?'

'Alfred and Jeanie?' said Lily. 'I knew of them, but they died before I was born… in a house fire. My mother was only in her twenties when it happened. She never talked about them very much… I think it upset her.'

'It must have been a terrible time in her life, but it was shortly after their deaths that she got in touch with me,' replied Mr Walker.

'She had had an offer accepted for Penwyth Estate and needed a solicitor to handle the purchase. At our first-ever meeting, she mentioned the fire. I think she had since been renting, perhaps deciding what to do next. I remember her saying that her father had been teaching her all about the family business and that she had enjoyed learning the ropes. Being their only child, she may even have taken over the running of it one day. But, after losing them and the farm so suddenly, she had wanted a fresh start.'

'Hendra Farm, wasn't it? That was where she grew up?' Lily asked.

'That name vaguely rings a bell, yes,' said Mr Walker. 'I think it was only about half an hour up the coast. I don't know if she received insurance money, but I do know that her parents had already set up a trust fund for her and deposited large sums into it ever since she was born, because she asked for my advice on how to access it after they passed.'

'I still don't quite understand how they accumulated so much money,' said Lily. 'I mean, for her to have a trust fund and be able to buy Penwyth Estate, which even back then must have cost a small fortune. Weren't Alfred and Jeanie farmers?'

'Initially yes, they were,' replied Mr Walker, 'and I presume worked hard to build up a reasonable living. But then they diversified. They wanted to be the first Cornish family to produce a single-malt whiskey in over three hundred years.'

'Alcohol?'

Mr Walker nodded. 'Built their own distillery and even grew their own barley. It started small, but over time it became a hugely successful company, much more so than they ever dreamt of. I don't think your mother knew how profitable the business had become until she inherited the proceeds. Her parents were shrewd; they had several other savings accounts, all of which contained large sums of money. So you see, although it must have been the most difficult of times when she lost them, she also became rich, more or less overnight. She had enough money to buy Penwyth Estate outright and still have a large chunk of her inheritance left, which I must say she invested wisely. Later, when she married your father, she opened a joint account that she regularly paid money into, but she also kept several other accounts in her name only. She also left a trust fund for you, the details of which you can read for yourself.' He passed Lily her mother's will.

She read the document, trying to focus on the words in front of her and not the thoughts ricocheting around her brain. Her newly discovered trust fund had over five million pounds in it. She placed her mother's will on the desk, before leaning back in the chair and meeting Mr Walker's eyes with a steely gaze.

'I think I really could do with a drink, after all,' she said. 'But maybe something stronger than water?'

Perhaps Miss Sanders was a little more resilient than Mr Walker had first thought. 'I don't have anything here,' he said. 'But the Black Dog Inn is just around the corner?'

She gave a little smile. 'Believe it or not, I have heard of it and that would be splendid. It's been a strange day and I still have so many questions – but only if you have the time, of course?'

'You're my last appointment of the day, Miss Sanders, and it would be my pleasure.'

'Please, call me Lily.'

CHAPTER 4

'Afternoon,' the man behind the bar smiled and nodded. The pub was quiet. They had just sat down with their drinks when, very appropriately, a black Labrador wandered into the bar. In full-body wag, Horace made a beeline for the solicitor.

'Something tells me you've been in here before, Mr Walker?' Lily leant down to stroke the dog's broad, soft forehead.

'Timothy, please,' he smiled. Horace wandered over to Timothy and rested his head on his ample thigh, large liquid brown eyes imploring him. 'You've given my regular frequenting of your pub away, you know!' he said, giving the dog a friendly pat.

Lily laughed, despite herself. 'Who am I to judge your drinking habits, when it seems I've just inherited the proceeds of a distillery? You know, I don't understand any of this,' she added, sipping a welcome glass of wine. 'Have you any idea why my mother has chosen to keep so many secrets from me all these years? I presume you knew her reasonably well at the time. As she had not planned on selling the house, why did we have to leave it? I mean, I understand how distraught she was – how much we both were at the time. But surely, we could have returned there one day, if only to sell it? Did she not leave me a note... a letter, anything?'

Timothy shook his head at Lily's many questions, whilst wiping the froth of his ale from his untamed moustache.

'No, no letter of any kind, I'm afraid,' he replied. 'I wish I could be of more help. I knew your mother, yes. Apart from acting in an official capacity for her, our paths crossed from time to time, at the odd annual fete or local wedding. Lostmor is a small place, after all. But, it is kind of an unspoken word that I don't intrude on a client's privacy more than is necessary. People often have to share information with me, things that they don't necessarily want other people to know about. Understandably, your mother wanted to keep our relationship on a purely professional level.'

Lily looked around and lowered her voice. 'Five million pounds? I realise most people would be extremely happy to be in my position right now, but it just doesn't seem real, any of this.'

'Well, it is real. And you, Lily, are now a very wealthy woman…' Timothy sighed in exasperation. 'Perhaps when you go to the house you may find some answers. I think your mother left some of her belongings behind. Over the years, I'm afraid it has become something of a shrine – everything covered up with sheets, and… well, almost frozen in time.' He regarded her with kind eyes. 'What will you do next? Can you stay in Lostmor a little longer, or do you have to get back to Bristol?'

'It was supposed to be just this weekend,' she replied. 'But yes, I think I can stay for a while. I run a small art gallery. Just a rented shop, really, but I could take a week or two off right now. I'll have to go back and sort a few things out. Oh, and speak to Adam at *Seaward Lets*. When I booked Kleger Cottage, he'd told me that there were no other lets until March, so I don't think it will be a problem to extend my stay.' Of all the scenarios she could have imagined, perhaps a last request to scatter her mother's ashes, being bequeathed the family estate and millions of pounds, were not amongst them. 'As far as the estate is concerned, I don't know where to start. Before I can even think about selling it, I guess I'll need to go through the contents of the house, and I've no idea what to expect…'

Her stomach lurched. The thought of returning to Penwyth, especially knowing now that it would be almost untouched since she had left it as a child, filled her with dread. She felt as though something, almost ethereal, was creeping up on her… as if glimpsing a dark shadow or movement from the corner of her eye…

She drained her glass.

'And what do I do about Joe?' she asked. 'Edhen Cottage has been his home for decades, since he was a young man.'

'I'm sure that he will be pleased to see you after all these years,' replied Timothy. 'He's a good man. Talk to him. If you plan to sell the estate, maybe you could consider keeping Edhen Cottage? It does lie near one of the estate's borders. Perhaps you can come to some sort of arrangement with him?'

'It's more a matter of *when* I sell, than if,' Lily smiled weakly. 'What would I do with it all? My home and my work are in Bristol.' She was going to add the word 'friends', but that wasn't strictly true. The few close friends she'd had had moved on themselves. Patsy, her best friend and one-time roomy at art college, was happily working as a theatre set designer in London, and Archie, a former flatmate, had fallen in love with a French man and moved to Nice three years ago. Over time, other friends, including several disillusioned boyfriends, had drifted away. She had been so busy building up her gallery, and loving every minute of it, that her personal life had fallen by the wayside.

She felt suddenly weary. Grateful though she was to talk things over with Timothy, now she just wanted to drive back to the cottage as quickly as she could, curl up in front of the fire and try to process the day's events. Horace, bored with their conversation, sloped off to a nearby table where food had just arrived.

'Well, if there's anything else I can help you with…' began Timothy. 'If you need financial advice or even just someone to talk things over with, you know where I am,' he joked, gesturing around the pub's cosy little bar. 'Sorry,' he frowned, noting the young woman's tired expression. 'I'm being insensitive. This must all be a huge shock and I didn't mean to be flippant.'

'Not at all, I'm grateful for your time and it was my idea to come,' she smiled wryly. 'It's just such a lot to take in. I think I should probably be heading back.'

'Well, my office is where I usually am if you need me,' replied Timothy. 'Here, please, take my card, my mobile's on there too. In the meantime… these are yours.' He fished out a large, heavy envelope from his briefcase. Lily looked quizzically at him.

'These are the keys… for Penwyth Estate.'

CHAPTER 5

L ily drove back to Kleger Cottage, the day's brightness stultified, the sky bleached white. Her thoughts drifted from her mother to Alice and her father, to Joe and Penwyth House. Up ahead, by the side of the road, was what looked like a small white boulder. However, as she got closer, she could see it was a little dog, a Jack Russell. She slowly pulled up. He sat quite still, his head slightly cocked, the tip of his tail moving from side to side as she opened the door.

'Hello! What are you doing all alone?' She could see the dog had no collar. Getting out, she scanned the remote horizon, hoping that someone might appear. The dog, clearly pleased she had come along, acted not at all lost, but instead ran to the open car door and promptly jumped across to the passenger seat as if he'd been waiting for a bus. There were no houses anywhere in sight. Lily got back in and dialled Adam's number.

He answered promptly. 'Hello, Adam speaking.'

'Hello Adam, I am sorry to bother you. It's Lily Sanders here.'

'How are you, Miss Sanders? Is everything all right?'

Yes, fine thanks. I wonder if you could help with something. I was just coming back from Lostmor when I found a dog all alone sitting by the roadside. There doesn't appear to be anyone around and there are no houses in sight. I just wondered if you might know who he belongs to? He's a Jack Russell. He doesn't look like a stray, but he has no collar.'

'Let me see,' said Adam, 'there aren't that many places along there, apart from another of our lets, but that's empty. There is a farm about a half a mile past Kleger, the Blighs' place. You could try there. Otherwise, there's only one vet in town, on the main high street. Dr Morgan. Her number's in the information folder. She might be able to hazard a guess.'

'Ok, thanks,' replied Lily. 'I'll try the farm first. Oh, and can I get back to you tomorrow about extending my stay?'

'No problem, Miss Sanders. Give me a call whenever suits you.'

Back in her car, with the dog riding co-pilot, Lily followed the meandering road that gradually headed inland. Grazing pasture gave way to open agricultural fields. The turning for Bligh Farm was signposted. She drove up the track leading to a low-squat, stone farmhouse with a small front garden surrounded by a tumbledown dry stone wall. Several battered corrugated barns stood further back. The property was surrounded by fields that she guessed had lain fallow for the winter months.

As she got out of the car, the dog leapt past her, grinning wildly as it scrambled over the low wall and into the garden. *Well, he certainly seems at home*, Lily thought, pushing the rusty gate open and tentatively knocking on the front door. As she did so, the door slowly opened. She peered inside...

'Hello! Anyone home?' Nothing. 'Hello! Anyone home?' she repeated, casting her eye around the small, low-ceilinged room. There was a recently used stone fireplace in the centre and beaten-up leather sofas either side. The dog flopped down on a rug in front of the hearth. Lily sighed. He must live here.

'Well, bye fella,' she smiled. 'Be good now.' The Jack Russell looked up briefly, before closing his eyes for a well-earned snooze.

'Can I help you?' said a gruff voice behind her.

'Oh!' Lily jumped. 'I'm sorry to bother you,' she said, feeling like an intruder. 'I'm Lily. Lily Sanders.' The man filled the low doorway. He ignored her proffered hand.

'Um… is this your dog?' she asked. 'I found him about a mile away up on the coastal road.'

The man, whom she presumed to be a 'Bligh', wore dirty old jeans and a faded checked shirt. He looked her up and down, unimpressed. He nodded in the dog's direction, who now looked as if he'd been asleep for hours.

'That's Flynn,' said the man. 'He knows his way around. He doesn't need rescuing.'

'Well, I didn't like to just leave him…'

'I really am very busy, so if you don't mind,' the man said, cutting her off mid-sentence whilst guiding her through the door with his hand. Outside, he swung round to face her, his dark eyes studying her. 'Look, I know you're trying to help, but I have to get back to work.'

Lily tried not to show she was slightly rattled by his behaviour.

'I'm going!' she raised her hands in exasperation.

The man yanked the door shut behind them and marched up the path, before tramping off round the side of the house, wiping his brow with one sleeve. He didn't look back.

*

The next day, Adam dropped by and agreed for Lily's stay at Kleger Cottage to be extended. He didn't seem particularly phased by her lame excuse of wanting to spend more time exploring. Having already told him she was there on a weekend break, it was easier to continue the pretence. *Lies beget lies*, she thought, hoping two weeks would be long enough for her to at least clear some of her family's belongings out of Penwyth House.

In truth, Lily did not know where to start. She could just sell the property straight away, whatever its condition. After all, money was not now an issue for her. However, despite her apprehension about returning to the house, she was already thinking that she could at least clean the place up and make it more presentable, even if she wasn't planning on any major restoration work. She was not sure how her mother would feel about her selling their childhood home, having gone to so much trouble to keep it all those years. On the other hand, her mother's will had not stipulated either way. So, Lily chose to believe that her mother would have wanted her to decide for herself and that the reason she had kept things a secret from her daughter for so long was simply that she could not face dealing with Penwyth House and its distressing memories, even decades on. Perhaps she had always meant to one day tell Lily, or take her back home, but the longer it had gone the harder it had seemed to go back.

Lily would probably never know. However, as the only surviving member of the family, the least she could do was to breathe some life back into the house, to honour her family's memory. Perhaps she would also find some answers. Reluctant as she was to return to it, the creeping possibility that she might better understand the events leading up to Alice and her father's deaths gave her hope. It was a chance to finally be free of her strange nightmares and the feeling of dread that crept over her whenever she tried to recall what happened on that terrible night.

CHAPTER 6

Lily always felt restless whenever she was away from her painting for too long and was relieved to be back in Bristol, if only briefly. She checked her answer machine and sorted through the usual junk mail and bills. Her rented two-bed apartment in Clifton, a leafy and affluent part of the town, was on the first floor of a big, Georgian house. The rooms were large and airy with traditional corniced ceilings and tall, sash windows. She used the second bedroom as her art studio, where dozens of canvasses were stacked against the walls and more filled every conceivable surface and space. Art was her passion and this room her haven, her most favourite place to be in the world. She was a perfectionist and treated each painting with equal care and attention, no matter if she was painting for herself or, as was more often the case, a commissioned piece.

She collected up her palette, paints and easel and carefully packaged a small, unfinished seascape using pushpins and foam board to transport it back to Lostmor. It would be a welcome distraction in the evenings if her days were to be spent at Penwyth Estate. She walked the short distance to her gallery, *The Blue,* recorded a message on the landline, apologising for its temporary closure, and left a note on the door saying that it would be closed for two weeks. She reassured herself that she would soon be back and, if needed, could return to Lostmor at weekends. She also hoped to enlist the help of Timothy in eventually overseeing the house sale.

The next morning, she packed a large case and set off once more for Lostmor. She spent the three-hour drive flicking through the radio stations, trying not to think about the fact that she would shortly be returning to Penwyth House, but with every mile that passed, she felt more anxious. She knew she was being irrational – after all, what was there to be afraid of? Yes, she reasoned, she did sometimes have flashbacks and nightmares, because she had been a child at the time and was traumatised by losing half of her family. But that was twenty-four years ago. *Time to move on, to close this chapter of my life…* she told herself, gripping the steering wheel so hard her knuckles turned white.

Later that evening, back at Kleger Cottage, she sat at the kitchen table picking at a ready meal and scanning a local paper she'd picked up on the way back. She flicked through the news items covering such things as council cuts and poll tax increases. Lostmor's first luxury dog kennels was soon opening on the outskirts. There was a picture of the owner, a slim lady wearing jeans, a wax jacket, and wellington boots. She was kneeling next to a sign that read 'Fern Retreat - a home from home for dogs' and hugging a springer spaniel. Beneath that, a smaller heading read 'Parrot Pandemonium!' It was a curious story about three green and yellow birds spotted by a surprised family whilst eating fish and chips in their car parked up at nearby Penny Cove.

'Time to stop distracting yourself,' she sighed. The thought of being solely responsible for a crumbling mansion was daunting, but she reluctantly turned her attention to the Classifieds. Casting her eye through the various local traders, she circled the number for Lostmor Antiques who offered appraisals and house clearances. It was a start.

Outside, a sharp wind was building, whistling through the cracks in the cottage walls. Lily listened to the fat raindrops splattering the kitchen window. She cupped her hands on the glass and peered through; it was inky black outside. The rain began to beat down harder and she heard the first low rumble of thunder in the distance. Drawing the flimsy gingham curtains against the brewing storm, she lit a fire, quicker this time, then pulled up a seat in front of the small easel set up in the far corner of the kitchen and tried her best to ignore the menacing wind that shook the front door so violently its hinges rattled.

She familiarised herself once more with her half-finished painting and focused on the canvas and the seascape before her. Waves of deep royal blue rolled into soft silver sand. The sky was ablaze; a spectacular sunset of coral, violet, and turquoise. She worked the colours in from her palette, smudging the edges of the fading light into a fiery orange, creating a stunning scene. She painted late into the night, losing track of time and paying no attention to the altogether different seascape outside, where the ocean raged, tempestuous and unforgiving.

CHAPTER 7

The next morning, Lily stood looking out at the sea, breathing in the smell of fresh rain. Steam rose from the ground and she felt the damp, warm grass between her toes. Pale sunlight started to filter through static clouds and she had a sudden urge to paint the ever-changing scene spread out before her; what had, only hours earlier, been a wild, roughshod sea, was now innocuous and benign. But she had no time to paint this morning. Today, she had other plans.

A little later, she was heading east on the coastal road, out the other side of Lostmor. On the passenger seat of the car was the large envelope of keys Timothy had given her. She drove on, her lips set in a hard line, for once oblivious to the changing landscape. Could returning to Penwyth explain her strange nightmares? Were they actual memories, distorted and fragmented over time, or were they just her childhood imaginings – a reaction to the trauma of losing Alice and her father?

She recognised the turning and the large, rusty iron gate that looked as if it had been wedged open many years prior. Tall grass had grown up through the gate's fretwork, which hung off one of two lichen-covered stone piers. These were topped with fierce-looking eagles, their weathered wings raised and dark expressions watchful. The drive up to the house was long and meandering. Lily drove through lush green meadowland and apple orchards whose rows of cropped trees stood dormant, patiently awaiting their spring revival.

The narrow road levelled out and the familiar lawns and side view of Penwyth House with its strange collection of spires came into view. Lily's stomach took a nosedive and she gripped the wheel as if she were lost at sea and clinging to a lifebuoy. She pulled up on the drive, her heart pounding. There were no other vehicles and no sign of Joe Newman. She got out and stood, gazing at the familiar meadow where she and Alice had spent so many happy childhood hours playing, then turned to look at the old house. It dawned on her how out of place the building looked.

It was rumoured to have been built in the 1800s by an eccentric gentleman who spent over a decade creating his Gothic vision, only to sell it two years after its completion. Nobody knew why, but locals suspected his romantic ideal had not quite lived up to the harsh reality of long, bitterly cold winters in a draughty mansion house. In time, it was updated with running water, mains electricity and, finally, central heating. When Elizabeth had laid eyes on it, several hundred years later, she had instantly fallen in love with its dramatic façade, its quirky steeples and spires and its proximity to the sea.

The keys were labelled. Lily slid the largest one into the lock, turned it, took a deep breath, and pushed. Her legs felt heavy and rooted to the floor. Surprisingly, the old oak door swung open easily. As her eyes adjusted, she could see the familiar grandiose staircase that rose majestically, sweeping up either side of what was once a formidable hallway.

The house was dull and airless. Dust particles, suspended in long, thin shafts of light, filtered down from a glass dome in the ceiling above the intricately carved oak staircase. Lily stepped across the threshold and a slight breeze, the first for decades, sent dust swirling around her. She pushed the door shut, the noise echoing around the large space. Through the gloom, she could see the eerie shapes of hidden furniture covered in sheets. She gazed up at the swaths of cobwebs that hung like draped curtains from the ceiling and connected to the arched walls and leaded glass windows. More tendrils swooped and clung to a once beautiful French crystal chandelier above her.

She dug into her envelope of keys once more and found one labelled 'Breakfast room'. Another layer of dust swamped her as she struggled to push the double doors inwards. She closed her eyes, tried to steady her breathing, then opened them, and saw her mother. She was sitting at the long breakfast table. Young, beautiful, her long blonde hair swept up in a ponytail, smiling and gently beckoning for Lily to join her and Alice, who sat on her lap, giggling and grappling with a piece of toast.

Lily shook the images away. She stared at the vaguely familiar shrouded shapes of dressers and shelves lined with dust-covered books. Floor to ceiling, leaded glass windows with stained-glass panels above, once proud and beautiful, were now cracked and broken. Thin rays of light seeped through chinks in the panes, the rich colours of which were blunted by decades of neglect and weathering. Beyond, lay the Gallery room. She swiped away more cobwebs as she entered. Down the entire length of the galleried wall hung large, heavy-framed paintings, which someone, perhaps Joe, had managed to cover up with more dust sheets.

In the centre of the gallery was an imposing wrought iron fireplace, over which hung another, larger painting. Lily gingerly pulled at the edge of the material covering it. This one she remembered well. She had been a little afraid, but also intrigued, by it as a child. The sheet fell more easily than she expected and she only partly dodged the cloud of dust that came with it. Coughing and blinking hard, she slowly raised her head. Her eyes met those of the painting. Her father, sitting in an armchair, in front of the very same fireplace. One ankle resting on one knee, he had a whiskey in one hand whilst stroking a pale-coloured Labrador with the other. She remembered this dog now. He was a gun dog that, in fact, her father had never allowed in the house, much to the girls' disappointment. Instead, he had been kennelled in the grounds near the old stables, along with several other harshly treated hounds.

The painting had darkened with age, but still those fierce eyes looked down at her, angry and accusing. As a little girl, it had seemed that, wherever she stood in the room, his intense gaze had followed her. But she was no longer a child and, although seeing her father's face again made her nervous, she felt relieved. Lily knew that if she was ever to recall what happened, being here could help. And now she had done it, taken the first steps, walked right back into Penwyth House and nothing bad had happened.

Unlocking room after room, she familiarised herself once more with her childhood home. All around were the dusty artefacts of lives lived then hastily abandoned. Books, dolls, a marble chess set laid out for a game never played. The dank basement kitchen was a time warp of long-forgotten brands, neatly stored in cupboards and piles of once gleaming porcelain plates stacked on units covered in fragments of damp plaster. She found a broom in a tall kitchen cupboard and used it to clear cobwebs as she went.

There were two ways of getting upstairs, the central staircase or the narrow stairs in the west wing previously used by the staff. She climbed the staff stairs leading to the upper hallway that she and Alice had often used when playing hide and seek in the mansion's many rooms. At the top, she stopped. For a moment she was a child again. Alice was standing waving from halfway down the landing, beckoning her to follow. Lily's vision swam. Alice smiled, then ran away from her, past the central staircase and disappeared into the east wing.

The long passageway seemed to stretch out into eternity, with doorways and heavy stone arched windows twisted and distorted. She steadied herself with one hand on the wall until the spinning stopped. Determined to keep going, she moved slowly forward, pushing open bedroom doors to long-forgotten rooms, most of them never used apart from occasional guests. In some, dark stains spread across the ceilings where water damage had seeped through from the porous roof above, first rotting out the attic space then dripping unfettered onto rank-smelling carpets and furniture, turning once richly coloured damask wallpapers into peeling strips of brown.

Luckily, the east wing, where the family bedrooms were located, had fared better. She hesitated when she reached Alice's room. She couldn't face it. Not yet. Instead, she slid into her own bedroom opposite. Most of the furniture was covered up. On the shelves, between storybooks and a faded pink jewellery box, was a neat line of teddies and dolls sitting patiently waiting. On the floor, a few comics and clothes were scattered about, a child's pair of silver sandals thrown hastily in the corner. Lily looked around at her old bedroom. How sad, her childhood room frozen in time. She felt sorry for the little girl she had once been. Twenty-four years ago, not only had her family been ripped apart by tragedy, but they had completely abandoned their home. They had fled as if this estranged old house were to blame for everything.

The door to her parents' bedroom opened with a sigh that made her shudder. Like hers, it looked to have been left hastily. She felt, as she always had when she'd entered this room, like an intruder. She remembered terrible arguments behind these doors. Her father's raised voice, usually in a drunken rage, and her mother sometimes crying or begging him to leave her alone. She lifted the sheet from her mother's dresser and ran her fingers over the cool glass of scattered bottles of perfume. A faint smell of jasmine permeated the air. The musky fragrance reminded her of her mother. Even as a little girl, Lily had noticed how men had behaved around her mother. She had emanated an aura of femininity and yet she had seemed completely unaware of the effect she had on other people. The atmosphere would seem to lighten whenever she entered a room; men and women alike just wanted to be around her. That was, unless her father had joined them, then more often than not the atmosphere would sour and lie heavy with an unspoken mood.

Sweeping dust from the dresser mirror, Lily was struck by another recollection. Her young self, sitting on her parents' huge bed, watching her mother as she sat brushing her hair, her reflection smiling back at her. Unlike Alice and her mother, who had the same heart-shaped faces framed by long blonde hair, Lily's face was narrower with higher, more distinctive, cheekbones and long dark brown, wavy hair that refused to frame anything. She winced at the wild reflection staring back at her; threads of spiderweb were trapped in her hair and dust plumed off of her when she tried to brush the filth away. Lily felt weary and in need of a hot shower. She must have been wandering around the house for hours and had not noticed the light beginning to fade, even though it was only 3.30 pm. She had a sudden urge to run out of the house and never come back.

Turning to leave the room, she saw her mother's wardrobe looming large. The door was hanging slightly open under its shroud and she remembered how it had never quite shut properly. She pulled off the sheet to reveal shiny dark ornate wood. Inside, a few of her mother's long, floaty dresses still hung on padded wooden hangers, now timeworn and musty. On the upper shelf was a large cardboard box. Lily struggled to pull it out and on to the floor. Inside were books, which, at a glance, looked to be detective novels. On top of the books was a small silver-framed black and white photo. Lily studied the faded grainy photo. Alice sat on her father's lap. Lily sat next to her mother, everyone smiling. She decided to take the box with her and have a look through it later, back at the cottage. Maybe there were more photos, even an album, anything to connect her to her family.

Lily locked the front door on her way out and stored the box in the car boot. She knew she should try and see Joe, even though she was now in no mood to make conversation. Coming home had taken the wind out of her sails, but her conscience got the better of her. She left her car on the drive and walked through the wood to Edhen

Cottage. The small thatched house looked the same as she vaguely remembered, low slung with tiny windows. To the side of it was a huge pile of logs neatly stacked in a wood store.

She knocked on the door and shouted Joe's name several times, but the place looked empty. The curtains were drawn and there was no vehicle anywhere in sight. Perhaps he was in town, she decided, or working somewhere on the estate. In hindsight, she realised she should have come here first; she had been so anxious when she had pulled up at the house that she hadn't thought things through. She needed to let him know about her mother's passing and explain about her inheritance, but also to thank him for staying on so loyally all these years. Lily didn't want to leave him a note, it seemed too flippant. '*Hi, it's Lily, just thought I'd drop by...*'

After waiting ten minutes or so, Lily walked back to her car. She vowed to come straight to Edhen Cottage on her next visit and, if Joe wasn't home, she would track him down, even if she had to search the entire estate for him.

CHAPTER 8

Lily drove home under a low winter sun that had released its tenuous grip on the day and, now, was fast descending behind a grim line of foreboding charcoal clouds.

Please don't let there be another storm tonight.

Up ahead, she spotted a movement. A small animal, half lying, half sitting on the grassy verge. As she drew nearer, she could make out the small, toffee-coloured splotches on Flynn's torso. His sweet face lowered, eyes half shut. He was shaking, whether due to the cold or through shock she was not sure. She slowly pulled up alongside him, praying he had not been hit by a car. It seemed unlikely, as vehicles were so far and few between.

'Hi, Flynn. Hi, fella,' Lily spoke softly, kneeling in front of him. He managed one wag, then nosed his leg. It didn't look swollen. She gingerly lifted it a little and could see then that he had a deep cut in the soft pad of his paw, which was caked with dried blood. She opened the rear passenger door and gently lifted him in, all the while talking calmly, trying to soothe him. This time, she had been approaching Tresor Bay, so she decided to take Flynn to the vets on the high street. It seemed a better idea than returning him to the bad-tempered Bligh, especially as he had let the dog roam once again and now, she thought crossly, he was injured.

'Can I help you?' asked Dr Morgan, who had come out to reception to greet her. The waiting room was small with a few dog-eared posters advertising worm treatments and reminders for pet vaccinations.

'Yes. Hello. Sorry to just turn up like this.'

'No matter,' the vet replied, grinning at Lily and Flynn. 'As you can see,' she gestured at the empty row of orange plastic seats, 'things are quiet right now. You are my only customer this afternoon, apart from a lady who brought in an injured cockatoo that she'd found in her garden.'

'Oh, I see,' replied Lily. 'Is the bird okay?'

'Yes, it will be. Just a minor wing injury,' Dr Morgan smiled. 'Anyway,' she said, turning her attention to the rather forlorn-looking dog in Lily's arms. 'You're Flynn, aren't you?' She gently began inspecting his paw. 'Are you a friend of Oliver Bligh's?' she said, looking up at Lily.

'No,' said Lily. 'Well, more of a neighbour... temporarily. I'm staying at Kleger Cottage. It's a rental not far from his place. I picked Flynn up by the side of the road. It's the second time I've found him roaming, but as he is injured and I was nearer to here than Bligh Farm, I thought I'd bring him in.'

'Oliver will be grateful, I'm sure,' Dr Morgan said whilst adeptly cleaning Flynn's wound.

'Oliver? Dark curly hair? Grim personality?'

'That's him,' the vet smiled knowingly.

'He certainly seemed anything but grateful when I returned Flynn from his first walkabout,' said Lily frowning.

'Don't be too hard on him,' said Dr Morgan. 'It hasn't been easy for him lately, what with his mother recently passing. I used to visit the farm, back when they had livestock. Megan was a lovely lady and Oliver has a good heart. I expect he's busy with the farm and sorting his mother's affairs out.'

Lily shrugged. 'It's really not any of my business.'

Dr Morgan laughed, a little embarrassed. 'It's me. I'm running off at the mouth again. That's what happens when I only have two customers all day.'

She fell quiet for a while as she tended to her patient. 'There you go, Flynn,' she said, taping a fat bandage in place. 'It was very good of you to bring him in…' She noticed for the first time that the young woman's clothes were dirty and her hair speckled with dust, and what looked like cobwebs. 'If you like, I can drop him back to Bligh Farm. I'm leaving shortly, anyway, and I live in that direction.'

'Thank you, I appreciate that,' said Lily with a sense of relief. 'It's been a bit of a long day. My mother also passed away recently and I've just come from the family home.'

'Oh, my condolences, I'm sorry for your loss.'

'Thank you.'

'Well, I hope everything works out okay, and don't worry about Flynn here. It will give me a chance to catch up with Oliver. I haven't seen him since his mother's funeral.'

Lily gave the dog a gentle goodbye hug. 'I'm hoping I don't see you again too soon. No more running away.' Flynn sat up, ears tucked back and eyes as big as saucers, clearly astonished at such an accusation.

'It was nice to meet you,' said Lily. 'Dr Morgan, isn't it?'

'Yes, that's right,' she beamed, offering her hand.

'I'm Lily. Lily Sanders. How much do I owe you?'

'Nothing, I wouldn't dream of it. I see a lot of injured paws; dogs getting caught on barbed wire fences and such like. All I've done is clean the soft pad up a bit, and I'm not sure how long he'll keep that bandage on, anyway.'

Later, having showered away twenty-year-old grime and changed into a thick, warm jumper and leggings, Lily sat at the kitchen table sorting through the forgotten box of old books. It made her feel closer to her mother as she looked through the various Agatha Christie and Nancy Drew mysteries. She smiled at the memory of her mother sitting on the front lawn in the sunshine, with her trademark floppy hat and large sunglasses, deeply ensconced in a book, whilst she and Alice had played hide and seek in the meadow. Back when their days were long, sunny, and carefree. Before it all went so wrong and things had gotten so dark.

Disappointingly, apart from the framed photo on top, there were no albums or hidden diaries. She uncovered a book that she instantly recognised, *The Enchanted Wood* by Enid Blyton. She wondered how her book had ended up here with all her mother's novels. In her young hand, on the inside cover, she had proudly written, 'Lily Sanders, 8½ years old, 2nd September 1970'. She smiled at the memory of her favourite story, full of charming characters that had inhabited a huge magical tree. Best of all, she had loved the incredible lands waiting to be discovered at the top where its branches disappeared into the clouds. As a child, Lily had often walked with her mother in the woods next to the house, hoping she would find such a tree. Wishing she could climb it and visit some fantastical world where there were giants and fairy tale castles.

The book felt strangely bulky and she could feel a large paper clip on the back cover. Concealed inside the jacket were some folded pieces of paper. She tipped them onto the table and spread them out. Most were grubby, the paper torn and the writing smudged in places, but each had a partial date scribbled on the outside. She flipped open the earliest, dated 2nd May.

CHAPTER 9

Janet Morgan had known the Bligh family for many years. She missed dropping in for a cup of tea, regaling stories from her practice to Megan who, in turn, would recount the latest happenings on the farm. It was only a year ago that she was diagnosed with terminal cancer at the age of sixty-one. Her health had quickly deteriorated, during which time Janet had become a frequent visitor. Whilst Oliver worked on the farm, she would sit with his mother whenever she could. Megan always greeted her with a smile and enjoyed hearing of her latest animal encounters. She never complained of the pain or discomfort she was most assuredly in, but the relentless and brutal disease continued to unfurl inside her. Towards the end, Janet and Oliver took turns to sit, holding her hand or reading to her from her beloved book of Charles Causley poems. She slipped quietly away in her sleep just a few months later.

Oliver Bligh stood in the window, watching Janet's station wagon pull out of the drive and turn into the lane. Flynn sat on the padded window seat that doubled as his lookout point. The dog offered up his bandaged paw as proof of his injury. Oliver gave Flynn a reassuring rub behind the ear. In truth, he regretted his rudeness towards Lily Sanders, especially as she had now twice rescued his dog. Janet had explained how she had found Flynn and brought him to the surgery, and he could tell by Janet's raised eyebrow that the young woman had said something to her about his brusque manner. She had also dropped into the conversation that Lily was renting Kleger Cottage. It was a hint, he was sure, for him to go and thank her for helping Flynn and, perhaps, a silent intimation to apologise.

'Okay, Flynn', he said, giving his dog a sympathetic stroke. 'I think you and I need to pay someone a visit.'

The day Lily had turned up at Bligh Farm, Oliver had just had an altercation with a farmhand he had recently taken on. Douglas Holt had replied to his advert in the Classifieds for casual labour needed. He'd explained to Douglas that he needed someone reliable who would turn up on time. The young man assured him that he was and that he had previous experience working on his uncle's farm. So, Oliver took him on and, for the first week, things worked out okay. The lad didn't seem to know as much as he had suggested, but he turned up on time and followed instructions. He wasn't much for talking, either. Oliver wasn't surprised, as he'd hired farmhands before. They usually kept to themselves and, as the work was seasonal, moved on quickly – so long as they got the job done.

However, by the second week Douglas began turning up late, jobs were half-finished and farm equipment was left lying around. On this particular day, Oliver had found him leaning against the barn smoking a roll-up. Oliver was angry and asked him why he had left the tractor out instead of housing it in the barn the day before. Douglas had become sullen, glowering at him, tight-lipped and unapologetic. When Oliver told him he would have to let him go, Douglas had grabbed the pitchfork he'd left lying around and hurled it at him. Oliver had easily dodged it, but was shocked at the farmhand's hostility. Then, before he could speak, Douglas had launched himself at him, swinging a wild punch that missed its target completely. The younger man was powerfully built, but easily outwitted. As Douglas lunged at him, Oliver restrained him from behind before pushing him away. He stumbled and fell backward.

'You'd better get out of here right now before I really lose my temper,' Oliver had said.

Douglas struggled to his feet and spat at him, a look of inexplicable malevolence in his eyes, before slowly turning away. Oliver watched him swagger off towards his van, slam the door shut and accelerate off, deliberately kicking up a cloud of dust behind him.

A few minutes later, having cleared up the mess left behind in the barn, Lily had shown up. She had been halfway into his house and suggesting he took better care of his dog. Okay, he knew he had overreacted. Not his finest moment. He would heed Janet's eyebrow.

CHAPTER 10

*P*lease, *I must see you again tomorrow 6.00 pm at same place x* the note
read. That was it. Not signed and no clues as to why 'they'
needed to meet. It sounded like a liaison − a secret liaison, Lily
thought, and her mother must have kept this and the other notes for
sentimental reasons.

She picked up the next note dated 12th May. The paper felt grimy.
Some of the letters were dirty, as if they had been left outside —
outside, in an arranged place where only her mother would find
them. They surely couldn't be from her father. Unless it was before
he was living at Penwyth House, perhaps a game they had played…
However, Lily couldn't imagine her father playing such a game. On
the other hand, she reasoned, he could have been a much younger
and more sober man when the notes were written. Her mother had
once said how romantic and utterly charming her father had been
when they had first met, but that theory went out the window when
she read the next note:

*Dear Elizabeth, I will watch for his car leaving and wait for you here, please
come if you can x*

She had to concede, the notes were probably written to her
mother when she was already married and the car referred to was her
father's. Lily could hardly believe it. She read them all. They were all

deliberately brief, arranging a time and place to meet. The dates became further apart, some by several months. She had no way of knowing when they were written, but the dated months indicated over a year and there could have been other arranged liaisons. She tried to remember her mother's friends, but it was such a long time ago. All she could recall were social gatherings rather than individuals. Evenings where people were milling about in the downstairs rooms, drinks in hands, swaying to music by the likes of the Stones and Dylan; albums stacked up on the record player. During the summer, she and Alice would sit on the upstairs landing, watching below as gatherings spilled outside. Groups of people sitting on the lawn, smoking, drinking and chatting, their mother amongst them, flicking her long hair off her shoulders, happy and at ease. They must have been good times for her, Lily thought, before her father's drinking had really taken hold.

The last note was dated in August, she supposed the following summer. It was another meeting at a place they had agreed, probably somewhere in the estate's grounds. Lily was frustrated; now that she knew her mother had had an affair, she had even more unanswered questions. She could guess why. Her father had not treated her well. But who was this other man? Had she loved him? Lily sighed. Perhaps it really didn't matter any more? It was all such a long time ago.

A loud knocking at the door shook Lily from her thoughts. It wasn't that late, about 7.00 pm, but she couldn't think who would be calling now. If it were Adam or Timothy, surely they would have phoned first or probably dropped by during the day? She tugged open the door, to be confronted with Oliver Bligh of all people. He was stooped in the porch, smiling and proffering a bottle of wine.

'Oh, hello. You're the last person I expected to see,' she said as Flynn trotted past her and hopped onto the couch in front of the fire.

'I'm sorry for disturbing you like this,' he replied. 'I just wanted to thank you for returning Flynn and… well, to apologise for being rude to you the other day.'

Lily hesitated, but as his dog had already made himself at home, she felt she had to ask him in. 'Um, well… of course, come in. Is Flynn okay now?'

'He's fine, thanks to you,' Oliver smiled. 'Janet, Dr Morgan that is, has given me strict instructions. I'm clamping down on Flynn's walkabouts, but I think I'm going to have to build a bigger wall and buy a new gate.'

'Yes, he does seem to be a bit of a Houdini,' Lily laughed, feeling a little awkward and exposed at suddenly having a strange man stood in the small kitchen space with her.

'You look busy,' Oliver said glancing at the scattered books on the table. She hastily pushed the notes to one side to make way for the wine he'd brought.

'Oh, it's nothing, just some stuff of my late mother's I've been going through.'

'I'm sorry to hear that,' he said uneasily. 'Is that why you're here? In Lostmor?'

'Yes, I've been to my old home today… the first time since I was a child, actually.' Lily half-smiled. 'It's a long story.'

Oliver sensed a fragility about her that he had not noticed before. *Too busy shouting at her.* 'Well, I don't want to impose. Come on, Flynn,' he said, making his way to the door. 'I really am sorry for the other day. That, too, is a long story. I'm not usually quite so obnoxious.'

She smiled. 'Your friend Janet said as much.'

Oliver laughed. She noticed his dark complexion from years of outdoor work and his dishevelled hair. He swept Flynn up, tucking him under one arm and paced off towards his battered old Land Rover. He turned once to wave before disappearing into the gloom.

CHAPTER 11

Penwyth House loomed large. Lily stood staring up at the two roof turrets, fifty feet above her. On her first visit, she couldn't bring herself to look up. This is where Alice and her father had fallen. She had to go up there, onto the roof. To try and remember what had happened that night. Her mother had always told Lily that she had been downstairs with Lily when it happened. So why did she have flashbacks of her father standing amongst the roof spires in the middle of a storm?

On the few occasions that she had managed to get her mother to talk about the events of that night, her explanation had been brief. Alice had gone to bed earlier, exhausted from her birthday party. Later, her father had come home blind drunk and in a terrible rage. Her parents had argued and her father had stormed off upstairs. Her mother had presumed he had gone to bed to sleep it off, as was usual after one of his all-day drinking sessions, but inexplicably he had gone up onto the roof in the foulest of weathers. Alice had woken, perhaps hearing her father's raised voice or the sounds of the storm raging, left her room, possibly just in time to see him climbing the narrow stairs to the roof. The girls had been forbidden from going up there, but Alice had not seen her father all day. Later, people surmised that she had wanted to tell her father about her birthday party. She may have been half asleep and it was dark, wet and windy. Perhaps she had been too near the edge of the roof, her intoxicated father might have slipped trying to save her, but tragically they had both fallen. No one knew for sure, but 'accidental death' was the verdict subsequently reached by the coroner.

'It was a terrible, tragic accident, Lily, and we must try to put it behind us,' her mother had placated. 'We have a new life now in Bristol and a new home.'

And so, Lily had put it behind her, or at least she had tried. The nightmares had become less frequent over time, but, like a festering wound reopening itself, they would always return, spewing forth the same terrifying images over and over. Inescapable, she thought, like this place. She turned away from the house and instead made her way through the woods to Edhen Cottage. This time, an old Ford Ranger truck was parked in front of the wood store. She tentatively knocked. The door opened a fraction.

'Who are you?' The man looked dazed. Lily imagined she was the first person to knock at his door in quite some time, maybe even years.

'Hello, I am sorry to intrude like this, but you are Joe, aren't you? Joe Newman?'

'I don't know how you know my name, but you're trespassing. I think you'd better be on your way.' He started to close the door.

'Mr Newman, my name is Lily. Lily Sanders. Do you remember me?'

'Lily?' He let the door fall open. 'I don't believe it... look at you! Come in, please.'

She sat while Joe made them both tea. He returned from the tiny kitchen with two steaming mugs. Neither of them had said a word since he'd beckoned for her to sit.

'Mr Newman,' she began.

'Joe. It's just Joe...' he said. 'Look, I'm sorry, I didn't know who you were at first. You took me by surprise. I didn't think you were ever going to come back.'

'It's been a very long time Joe, for both of us. Thank you for seeing me.'

'I always hoped that one day someone might return here, either you or your mother. How is Elizabeth?'

Lily felt tears pricking her eyes. 'She's gone,' she whispered, unsure as to why she was suddenly overwhelmed. 'She had been ill for quite some time. I'm afraid she died just a few weeks ago.'

'I see…' said Joe sadly. 'I am very sorry to hear that. Your mother was a lovely lady.' He had a kind face, etched deeply with lines and startling green eyes.

'Yes, she was,' said Lily. 'I miss her very much. It is also why I have returned now. Although my mother and I were close in many ways, I recently discovered that there were some things she never told me – some quite important things. You see, I thought Penwyth House had been sold decades ago. Mother said we needed the money to buy a house in Bristol. I had no reason to disbelieve her and I knew nothing of her asking you to stay on and look after the estate. It was only recently... after she had passed, that I received a letter from a solicitor, Timothy Walker, asking me to come to Lostmor. All I knew until a few days ago was that he thought it wise for me to be present for the reading of my mother's will. A will I didn't even know existed. That was when I found out that Penwyth House had never been sold and that my mother had left the entire estate to me...'

Lily looked apologetic. She felt guilty. Guilty for not wanting to keep the estate and guilty for the upset she was about to cause Joe. She looked away from those piercing eyes. The old man placed one weathered hand on hers.

'It seems another lifetime ago, doesn't it?' he smiled. 'You and Alice playing in the meadow and following two steps behind me round the gardens. You girls – laughing and chasing each other around – they were good times.'

'Yes…' Lily was still finding it difficult to meet his eyes. They were talking about things she had tried very hard not to think about most of her adult life.

'It was a shock when I found out that you and Elizabeth had gone,' said Joe. 'But you had suffered a terrible loss. Then that solicitor bloke, Timothy, came to the cottage and told me about a letter your mother had left asking if I would stay on. It just seemed the right thing to do. To carry on doing what I had always done. Look after the estate as best I could, and it meant I could stay here.' He gestured around him. 'Edhen Cottage is my home, Lily. I have never even thought about leaving.'

'Of course,' she replied. 'I understand and it must be very strange for you, me just turning up like this. You don't have to leave here, Joe. That is what I wanted to say. Edhen is yours as far as I'm concerned.'

The old man nodded. 'That's good to know, thank you… What will you do with the house? Are you going to move back in?'

'I'm afraid not,' said Lily. 'I shall probably sell most of the estate. My life has been in Bristol ever since leaving Lostmor and I'm settled there. I run a small art gallery now.'

'You're an artist?'

Lily nodded.

'That doesn't surprise me at all. You liked to create little scenes in the gardens and the woods when you were little and then draw pictures of them.'

'Did I? I don't remember that!'

'Yes, you would pick wildflowers and collect stones and feathers, anything that caught your eye, including a few things smuggled out of the house! Then you would find a nice spot and make a little miniature scene, kind of like a… what do you call it… a still life! Then you'd sit and draw it. Sometimes for hours or until Alice came looking for you.' He smiled, pausing. 'The pair of you were good at keeping yourselves occupied. If you weren't helping me in the gardens, you would be off on some adventure. Often, you'd be gone all day with a satchel full of sandwiches and lemonade from the kitchen. But look at you now! Grown into a beautiful and talented young woman. I'm sure your mother was very proud of you.'

Lily felt a warmth for this man who had always been so kind to her and Alice.

'I hope so,' she replied. 'I'm afraid she was kind of lost to me in the end. She suffered from dementia for quite a few years before she died.'

'That's a shame,' said Joe. He looked wistfully at her.

'You know,' said Lily, 'when we left, Mother always remained positive about our new life together and said what an adventure it would be. I hated Bristol at first and didn't want to leave everything I'd ever known, but she couldn't bear to stay here. I understand now, how much she must have been grieving too, but she hid it from me and gradually she picked up the pieces of her life. She never remarried, although I think she had a few proposals. And she had a lot of friends, too. I believe she was happy. I had a pretty normal childhood, went to school, then college, made new friends. As I grew older, it became easier not to think about how life was before and I found it harder to remember Alice and my father's faces... Everything became... kind of fuzzy and vague.' Lily shook her head. 'I am sorry, I don't know why I'm telling you all this. Perhaps because there is no one left now to remember — except you and me.'

Happy though he was to see Lily again, Joe felt a little overwhelmed. She had stirred long-buried memories, memories of a stormy night, and of Elizabeth running towards him screaming, her face full of fear. A scene he had tried very hard to forget for decades had just risen sharply back into focus. He rose slowly to his feet. Lily took his cue by standing also.

He smiled. 'I'm so glad you came back, Lily. It's good to know that you are okay after me wondering all these years.'

'It means a lot to me, too,' Lily replied. 'And I am sorry that I've sprung this on you.'

'Nonsense,' said Joe. 'You being here now… well, you've just brought some sunshine back into my life. But the sad news of your mother and that the house is to be sold, it's just a lot to take in, is all. Perhaps, though, whilst you're in Lostmor, you can come see me again?'

'I'd love to.' Lily wanted to hug this kind old man, but he looked a little unnerved, so instead she offered her hand. 'I am very grateful to you for looking after the estate all this time.'

As she headed for the door, she noticed a black and white photo on the windowsill. It was a close-up of a beautiful young woman, her head thrown back laughing. She looked so carefree and happy. It was unmistakably her mother.

CHAPTER 12

Thursday, 17th June 1971

A confusion of sounds woke Alice. First, a loud crack of overhead thunder had dragged her from a deep sleep. Frightened, she sat up, pulling the blankets tightly around her. She wanted to run and find her mother, but at the same time was reluctant to leave the safety of her bed. She heard her father shouting. Lightning flickered across the bedroom, transforming a row of dolls into pale little ghosts whose distorted shadows flashed across the wall, shortly followed by another huge explosion of thunder. She grabbed Hoppy, her favourite blue bunny, jumped out of bed, and ran into the hallway just in time to see her father disappearing up the stairs that led to the roof.

'Daddy! I'm scared. Where are you going?' she called out, but her voice was lost in the chaos of the storm. 'Wait for me, please!'

Barefoot, she ran to the bottom of the narrow stairs, but her father had already reached the door to the roof and flung it wide open to the elements. By the time she'd reached the top, he had vanished. For a moment, Alice could not see anything in the driving rain, but then she saw her father's silhouette as lightning streaked across the night sky. He was standing amongst the turrets, staring over the edge at the ground below.

'Daddy!!' she screamed. Vincent, shaken from dark thoughts, turned to see Alice standing in the small doorway to the roof. He watched in a daze as his little

girl, with nothing on but a thin nightie, ran through the squall towards him...

Wednesday, 1ˢᵗ February 1995

At first, Lily's bequeathment of Penwyth House had seemed an onerous burden. However, over time, she found herself surprisingly pragmatic about the task of going through her family's things. She was kept so busy that, after her first few visits, she realised that not only did she no longer dread entering the place but found herself strangely drawn to it.

Mr Carne, the owner of Lostmor Antiques, had already visited the house several times to label and record the more valuable pieces of furniture and objet d'art, including many antiquities her parents, in happier times, had brought back from their travels in Africa and Asia. He had suggested an auction in the local community hall. She thought it a splendid idea and informed him that she would be donating all proceeds, minus fees, to local charities. Not a man to miss a good business opportunity, Mr Carne also offered to organise the clearance of any remaining unwanted household items for disposal, including all the soft furnishings. No small task. Lilly realised how naïve she had been to think Penwyth House would be ready for selling within a few weeks. She accepted his offer of clearing the house once his team of staff had collected everything for auction.

Even with professional help, the size of her newly acquired home meant emptying it was a massive undertaking. And something else was dawning on her. The more time she spent at the house, the more attached to it she felt. Somehow, the process of airing rooms and boxing and labelling what she wanted to keep or dispose of became strangely cathartic for her. She sorted through her childhood possessions and cleared out her parents' bedroom. Strangely, nothing of her father's belongings remained, not even the odd piece of clothing or photo, apart from the framed photo of them all that she'd found on her first visit. Her mother must have got rid of it all before they left Lostmor. If it wasn't for the painting of her father still hanging over the fireplace in the gallery, one could almost believe he had never existed. Almost, except on restless nights when flashbacks of him standing amongst the roof turrets, gaunt and pale faced, still haunted her.

She had hesitated outside Alice's room several times. She wasn't quite ready to face this room. Instead, she threw herself into the task of packing up the house contents as best she could and the days sped by. Lily promised herself that, one day soon, she would explore the grounds. She should check the condition of the glasshouses and the old kennels and stables. For now, though, the tasks inside the house were more pressing.

One particularly blustery day she listened as the wind moved through the house, whistling down the chimneys and rattling windows. Just like her mother before her, Lily had always liked the sounds the house made. It was beginning to feel like home again and, even though it had been abandoned for so long, she felt its strength – its spirit. In places, the building was in desperate need of repair, but it felt solid and safe. It stood proudly defiant against the harsh sea winds and winter storms that had battered and tormented it for decades. A thought was forming in her mind. What if she were to do more than just clear the house? What if she restored it to its former glory? She had the resources to try. Perhaps by stripping away the decades of neglect she could somehow purge the place of its terrible past. She could still sell it, but just further down the line.

Joe was busy around the estate. He was doing what he had done for decades, tending to the grounds and gardens, fixing broken fences. An endless list of jobs, a bit like the house, Lily realised. On such occasions when their paths crossed, the conversation was light; an unspoken understanding. They chatted about what they had been doing that day, or sometimes he would reminisce. He would regale stories of some of the more flamboyant characters who had visited the house during her mother's famous parties, or 'soirees' as she liked to call them.

On one such occasion when Lily had stopped at Edhen Cottage for a cup of tea, he seemed thoughtful.

'Is everything alright today, Joe?'

He gazed steadily at her, his sea-green eyes as intense as ever. 'I wondered if you'd been to visit Alice's grave since you'd been home?' he asked.

Alice had been laid to rest under a cedar tree on a secluded hill that overlooked the sea and which lay only five minutes' walk from Joe's cottage. When Lily shook her head, Joe had looked at her sadly. She couldn't easily explain it to him, but she wasn't ready to visit her sister's grave yet. It was important for her to try and remember what had happened to Alice first — to try and get her head straight.

Towards the end of her third week of daily visits to Penwyth, Lily climbed the central staircase and walked towards Alice's room. Would seeing Alice's childhood things help? Even though she was frightened by the possibility, she knew she had to try. And she wanted to see her sister's room again; to feel closer to her.

In the end, there was no sudden recollection, just another child's room frozen in time – much like her own. For Alice, however, there had been no second chance, no new start. Gazing around in dismay at the hastily abandoned doll's house, the dusty pink chest of drawers with teddies and dolls left piled on top, Lily felt herself crumble. She sank to her knees and wept, overwhelmed by sadness for her little sister. Poor, poor Alice. Her Alice.

Lily was unsure how long she'd sat there, surrounded by the remains of Alice's short life, but when she stepped out of the room she felt strangely calm. She headed for the stairs leading to the roof. She would see for herself where Alice and her father had fallen from, but as she began to climb the steps she suddenly felt gripped by panic. A wave of nausea hit her, bile rising in her throat, and she thought she would vomit. She could hear voices, as if she was trapped in one of her nightmares. At first, her father shouting her name. Then, up close, she heard her father whispering in her ear, as if he was standing right next to her, 'Why did you run away, Lily?'

Shocked and terrified to her core, Lily ran back down the stairs, through the hallway and threw open the front door. Outside, she fell to her knees, gasping for air. After a minute or two of trying to calm herself down, she turned and looked back at the imposing entrance hall and sweeping staircase. She was afraid to go back in. She had heard his voice so clearly. It wasn't a dream, it had been real. She shut the heavy oak door and walked to her car. Driving off at speed, she watched in the rear mirror as the spires and chimneys of Penwyth receded. She breathed a sigh of relief when she had turned the corner and the house was no longer in sight.

Back at Kleger Cottage, Lily was so shaken by the day's events that she changed her mind about the house. What was she thinking? She wasn't sure she could even face going back there now, let alone attempt to renovate it. No, instead she would return to Bristol and ask Timothy to help manage things in Lostmor. He had already offered to help and she knew she could rely on him to oversee any payments for repair work carried out. Besides, she had to leave the cottage in a week as Adam had a booking. It was time to go.

CHAPTER 13

After a restless night's sleep, Lily busied herself by packing her newly finished seascape. It was 9.30 am and by this time of day she would have left for her daily visit to Penwyth. A loud knock at the door startled her. Adam, maybe?

'Oliver. This is a surprise. No Flynn?'

'No, but he's fine,' Oliver smiled wryly. 'A little put out by the newly repaired wall and secure gate he now has to contend with.'

'A new challenge for him, then,' she said, returning his smile.

'I hope you don't mind me dropping by again,' he began. 'Last night, I drove past on the road not far from here. You didn't see me, but you looked... well, to be honest, you looked like you'd seen a ghost. Is everything okay?'

Lily ignored his last comment. 'I'm sorry, I must have been on autopilot. I was a bit tired. I'd been at Penwyth House all day. It's even bigger than I remember and there's such a lot to sort out.'

'Well, as long as you're okay,' said Oliver. 'I hope you don't think I'm being some kind of nuisance.' He studied Lily's face. She seemed different, downhearted. 'It can be a lonely place here, especially in the winter.'

'I'm fine, honestly, and you're not a nuisance.' Lily took a step back. 'Why don't you come in? I'll put the kettle on, if you like?' She could do with some company. Even though she felt worn out at the end of most days, she had hardly spoken to anyone in weeks apart from Joe.

'Okay, great,' replied Oliver. 'Thanks.'

She pulled a kitchen chair out for him and moved her newly packed painting off the table.

'Did you say Penwyth?' said Oliver. 'Penwyth House?'

'Yes, that's right.'

'I've heard of it, I think... Is that the place where there was an accident... years ago?'

Lily instantly wished she hadn't let the house name slip. He probably remembered it being on the news. Now he would be curious and want to ask questions. Since yesterday, she had felt uneasy about things again. She had awoken with a start last night, her mother's voice ringing in her ears and a darkly grinning face with spiteful eyes filling her vision. A familiar creeping dread had taken hold of her. Oliver was right. She had been scared while driving home.

'Do you mind if we don't talk about it?' she asked. 'Sorry, it's just that it's been quite unsettling for me returning home after all this time.'

'No, of course. I honestly didn't mean to pry,' Oliver said, taking the mug of hot tea from her. He glanced at the box of brushes and easel on the kitchen floor.

'You're an artist?'

'Yes,' she replied, relieved that he'd changed the subject. 'It's my passion and, luckily for me, my job.' She smiled. 'I sell artwork in a little shop called *The Blue*, back in Bristol. I've had to close it for now, but I'm heading back in about a week or so.'

'That's a shame,' said Oliver. He was disappointed – just when he'd finally managed to see her again, she was about to leave. 'I mean, that you're leaving so soon.' He leant forward, lightly touching her arm. 'Why don't you let me take you out for a drink before you go?'

He spoke softly, his face close to hers. Perhaps it was the emotion of recent events, but his touch stirred something in her. Despite their not-so-great first meeting, Lily found herself liking him. Oliver was his own man, that much was obvious. There was something exciting about his self-assuredness, but at the same time she sensed he had a gentler side to him. What harm would a few drinks do? It would do her good to go out.

'Why not?' she replied. 'Yes… I would like that very much.'

Oliver thought her quite stunning. She had a delicate, almost ethereal, quality. Her almond-shaped eyes were hazel, but up close he could see they were flecked with gold, and her dark hair had all but escaped the hastily pushed-in slides, falling in long soft waves over her shoulders.

'Great, how about tonight?' he said. 'I could come back at eight o'clock to collect you? I know a nice traditional pub near the seafront.'

'Tonight?' replied Lily, taken aback.

'Why not?' he grinned. 'No time like the present.'

'It wouldn't be the Black Dog Inn, would it?'

'Ah-ha,' he joked. 'So you haven't been working all the time!'

'Mostly,' she laughed. 'But Timothy's office, my mother's solicitor, is practically next door to it. After our meeting, I confess we did go in there.'

Oliver smiled. 'Look, I'm sorry if I upset you just then. I always seem to be saying the wrong thing to you.'

'It's not your fault…' replied Lily. 'My life has been turned upside down lately and I'm still trying to work out a few things. That's all.'

Oliver spoke gently. 'I lost my mother not long ago. She had been ill for some months with terminal cancer, but it didn't make her death any less easy to bear.'

Lily already knew this, from Dr Morgan, but she didn't want Oliver to think she had somehow been gossiping about him. Right now, this man was sympathising with her and opening up about something personal, even though she had just instantly shut him down at the mere mention of her own family.

'I'm sorry to hear that,' she said kindly.

'It's okay,' Oliver smiled. 'I just meant that I understand this is a difficult time for you. I know we've not long met, but if you need someone to talk to... well, you know where I live.'

Lily met his dark eyes, now filled with concern. 'I do, and thanks. It's nice to know there's a friendly face nearby.'

CHAPTER 14

'How're things? I haven't seen you for a while,' Marcus said, pouring Oliver a pint of Butcombe.

'Good, thanks, just busy with the farm.'

Marcus noticed the attractive lady Oliver had walked in with. She looked familiar, but he couldn't quite place her.

'Where's Horace?' asked Oliver.

'He's fine, asleep upstairs. Saturday nights can be a bit too noisy for him. He prefers lunchtimes,' Marcus smiled wryly.

Oliver nodded, laughing as he carried the drinks to the booth where Lily had just sat down. The pub was low-lit and cosy, with couples stowed away in its various nooks and crannies. The melodic tones of 'Fields of Gold' were playing in the background and there was a low buzz of people chatting and laughing, enjoying their Saturday night, most of them happy in the knowledge that they had no work to get up for tomorrow.

'Thanks,' Lily smiled, taking a sip from a glass of Chardonnay. 'This place looks different at night, more welcoming.'

It was beginning to fill up – mainly couples, but a few crowds of younger people had gathered around the bar, too. Oliver sat opposite.

'So, what's all this about you leaving?' he grinned, unable to help himself. Lily looked more relaxed than earlier that morning and, to him, more radiant than ever. She'd dressed simply in jeans, a plain white cotton shirt, and wore her hair to one side in a long, loose plait. She smelled good too, of Jasmin maybe.

'No pressure then!' she laughed. 'Bristol's my home, or at least it has been for a very long time, and my rental at Kleger Cottage is up at the end of the week.' She knew it would be difficult for them to chat without mentioning Penwyth House; after all, it had been her whole reason for being in Lostmor for the past few weeks. Besides, she found herself wanting to chat… just not about everything.

'How long have you been in Bristol?'

'Twenty-four years.'

'Until now?'

She nodded. And so she talked and Oliver listened. She explained about her mother's illness and the surprise letter from Timothy Walker and, before she knew it, had told him of her unknown inheritance and of Joe Newman, who was still looking after Penwyth Estate.

Oliver was captivated, not only by her incredible story, but by her. She was articulate and engaging; yet, despite the recent upset she had been through, still managed to find humour in the strange circumstances she now found herself in. He knew about the terrible accident that had happened at Penwyth House all those years ago. No more than a teenager himself, he remembered seeing it on the television. A man, whom he presumed was Lily's father, and a little girl, her sister, had fallen from the roof of the mansion and died. A truly horrific tragedy. Returning to her home now must have been very difficult and yet she seemed to be facing it all alone.

'So, you've nearly finished clearing the house?'

'Well, as much as I physically can,' she smiled. 'The rest is due to be collected this week. I'm going to auction it all off.'

'So there is no question of you keeping the place?'

'I don't think so.' Lily sensed he wanted to ask more, but appreciated that he didn't attempt to. He was charming company. Why spoil a lovely evening talking about her family's tragic history or her recurring nightmares?

'I seem to have been talking about me all night,' she said. 'How about you? How are things at Bligh Farm?'

'Well, nothing I have to say could be half as interesting,' replied Oliver. 'But, if you're ready to be bored, how about I get us both another drink?'

She nodded. The wine had taken the edge off and she was enjoying the laid-back atmosphere of the pub. Maybe she had become a bit too set in her ways in Bristol? Too much work, not enough play. She sneaked a peek at Oliver who had his back to her and was laughing amicably with Marcus. A curl of dark hair skimmed the collar of his navy shirt. She liked how he looked. He was a striking man, she guessed over six feet tall. The type of man you couldn't help noticing when he strode into a room.

At that moment, a thick-set muscular-looking guy walked in. Oliver turned to see Douglas Holt standing there. Douglas glowered at him before heading for the pool room at the back. *No love lost there*, Lily thought. Oliver leant over the bar slightly and said something to Marcus, his body language less relaxed. When he returned, he looked thoughtful, his mouth set in a hard line.

'Thanks. Everything okay?' she asked.

'Yes, sorry,' he smiled, as he slid back in the booth. 'No big deal. I just saw someone I wish I hadn't. A young man I hired not so long ago to help on the farm, turned out to be a big mistake.' Oliver took a swig from his pint glass. 'Not only was he lazy and unreliable, but when I told him he had to go, the little hothead took a swing at me!'

'And you just said that you had nothing interesting to tell me,' said Lily, shaking her head. 'I mean, I hope no one was hurt, but as stories go it's definitely not boring. What happened in the end? Did he leave of his own accord?'

'I admit I was tempted to punch him, but I refrained. It wasn't worth it. He's just some low-life who thinks everyone owes him something. I threw him out, he drove off and that was that. I doubt he'd start anything in here. He's sloped off into the pool room at the back. I asked Marcus, the landlord, to keep an eye on him for me, and he won't take any messing. Anyway,' said Oliver, breaking once more into a smile, 'I'd much rather be talking to you than thinking about him, and you are way more attractive.'

Lily laughed and the conversation came easily. Oliver chatted about the farm and how, with his mother's help, he had taken it over while he was still just a teenager. It turned out that his father had collapsed whilst working in the field behind the farmhouse and it had been Oliver, aged only ten, who had found his body. The doctor later said that his father had suffered a massive heart attack and died instantly. Afterwards, Megan had managed to keep the farm going single-handedly for a few years, during which time Oliver had had to grow up fast. He recounted how he had willingly become more and more involved with the farm's upkeep. His mother taught him everything there was to know about arable farming and how to run the business side of things, too. By the age of sixteen, he knew how to maintain and repair the machinery and fences. He learnt to drive tractors and farm vehicles and to harvest and store crops.

'It must have been difficult losing your father so young and awful finding him that way,' said Lily. It seemed that they had both suddenly lost a parent as a child, and in dramatic circumstances.

'Yes, but it was a long time ago now...' replied Oliver. 'Tell me about your art. What do you most like to paint?'

'Landscapes... seascapes. But I do quite a lot of commissioned work, to keep the pennies rolling in. That can be anything from local landmarks to people's pets and sometimes portraits.'

'I confess to knowing little to nothing about art, but they do say the light here is perfect for painting.'

'Do they?' Lily smiled, leaning in towards him. 'I have to get back to Bristol… but I will be back.'

'I'm glad.' His steady gaze met hers. 'Thanks for coming out this evening. I've really enjoyed your company.'

'Me too.'

Oliver seemed at a bit of a loss for words, but his dark eyes were locked on to hers. 'Do you think we could meet up again before you go… if you have time?'

'Yes,' she said, feeling more relaxed than she had in ages. 'I'd like that.'

'Tomorrow?'

She looked away, contemplating. 'I ought to go to Penwyth House tomorrow, there are still things to sort out and I need to track down Joe. Let him know I'm off soon.'

'Well, I have tomorrow free,' said Oliver. 'It's Sunday and things are pretty quiet on the farm. Why don't I come with you?'

'To Penwyth?'

'Why not?'

She looked concerned.

'I might come in handy, you know,' Oliver added. 'If you need any help lugging things around, I'm your man.' He gently squeezed her hand. 'Wouldn't you like a bit of company?' his eyes implored.

Lily studied his face. She had the feeling he was not a man easily dissuaded. Besides, it would be nice to have him along, especially since her hasty exit from the house the day before. *Maybe*, she thought, *it is time to stop trying to deal with everything on my own.*

CHAPTER 15

Tuesday, 8ᵗʰ December 1992

It was no quicker, but it bypassed the busier A-road and Maggie preferred the quiet scenic route. The forest trail wound its way down the hillside; dense woodland eventually giving way to pastureland and West Hill School in the valley below.

Maggie glanced at her granddaughter, who was humming along to tunes on the car cassette player. Disney characters, Ariel and Flounder, benignly smiled up at her from the Little Mermaid backpack resting on her lap.

'Will you be picking me up from school later?' Ellie asked, twisting a strand of long blonde hair around her finger.

'Yes, it'll be me. Your mum will be home a bit later. Macaroni cheese for tea alright?'

Ellie nodded. 'I love macaroni cheese. Can I have ice cream for pudding, too?'

Maggie laughed gently. 'If you promise to draw me your best picture ever at school today, then yes, it's a deal.' She straightened the car, which had strayed a little to the right as they approached another bend in the road. Not that her slight lapse in concentration would have made any difference. The motorbike appeared from nowhere, hurling towards them, its curve way too wide and travelling way too fast.

The biker had no time to react. No time to brake. It smashed headlong into the car, the impact throwing Maggie backward into her seat, bones crunching, before bouncing her forward just shy of the windscreen. The force fractured her spine in two places. Two seconds that guaranteed her chronic back pain for the rest of her life.

Ellie sat stunned. She had banged her head on the dashboard, but was conscious and otherwise unhurt. The bike had buckled on impact. The rear end arced high before dropping onto its side, its engine still turning over refusing to die, the back wheel spinning relentlessly. The force had propelled the biker half on to the bonnet before he slid down to the ground.

Helmet man, as Ellie later named him, struggled to his feet. The effort caused a searing pain to shoot down his left leg, his jeans already soaked through to a deep red beneath his hip bone. Using the car to steady himself, he shuffled along to the front passenger door. He appeared at Ellie's window, his face obscured by a dark visor and looked across at the old woman whose eyes were closed. She was quietly whimpering. He then staggered back past his ruined bike like a drunk man, when he swung around wildly, seeming to look for something.

From inside the car, a dazed Ellie watched. Helmet man slowly looked back in her direction, then upwards. She was distracted by leaves fluttering onto the windscreen. At that moment, the old Sycamore's branches gave up its new weight. The girl who had been riding pillion followed, smashing onto the bonnet with a sickening thud that rocked the car. The bike's impact had catapulted her into the air and headlong into the tree trunk, instantly snapping her neck. She lay prone, splayed booted legs hanging off one end of the bonnet, one hand resting at an impossible angle against the windscreen. Her helmet visor had been partially ripped off, revealing one dead eye that stared blankly. The cheery notes of Flounder singing 'Under the Sea' started up, just as Ellie started to scream.

One of Marcus's biggest regrets was not having seen Rose one last time, of not having the chance to hug her and tell her he loved her. When the phone call came, she was screaming at him – his ex-wife – who was normally so even-tempered and calm. Before he could even make out what she was saying, he knew Rose was dead. He heard the words 'accident' and 'crash', then the phone had slipped out of his hand. Rebecca's wailing faded from his consciousness as he slid into a very dark place.

He couldn't remember much about the funeral or the months that followed. He had tried to help Rebecca with the arrangements. He wanted to be occupied, a desperate attempt to not lose control. But she had Roger now. Roger the reliable. Marcus watched as Rose's coffin was lowered into the earth. Rebecca softly weeping, Rose's friends hugging each other, teary-eyed and disbelieving. He had drifted through the wake like a ghost. When the unbearable had been borne, he caught the first flight back to Croatia where he was stationed.

In 1972, nineteen-year-old Marcus Cole, a rookie of six months, met and fell head over heels for Rebecca. Knowing that he was going to be away with the army for long periods at a time, the fresh-faced lad had wanted to show his commitment to her. Not surprisingly, their parents had disapproved when, four months later, they had announced their plans to marry. It was a small affair at Bristol registry office with a pub reception afterwards. They had little money and their honeymoon had been a week in Devon in Rebecca's aunt's caravan. For them, young and in love, it was perfect and when, a few years later, Rose was born, they could not have been happier.

Rebecca had known from the start that Marcus would be away a lot of the time and she was certain she could handle it. And, for many years, she did. Whilst Rose was very young, she had plenty of help, friends who were themselves army wives, many also with young families. They all supported each other. He tried to think back to when things had begun to change between them, and the truth of it was he wasn't sure. There were no blazing rows. It was more the case that they had just drifted apart. In the end, Rebecca and Rose had grown older without him. Bit by bit, each absence became longer than the last. It seemed to them like he had just faded out of their lives until, eventually, it was almost like he had never existed.

Military life had suited him. From early on, he had wanted to step forward, to lead, and was quickly promoted up through the ranks. He was deployed to Northern Ireland many times. On one occasion, during his fourth tour of duty, there followed a particularly violent shoot-out with an IRA unit that had been holed up in a house in County Antrim. The patrol had cost a fellow soldier and good friend his life. Jack had enlisted at the same time as him. They had known each other as man and boy and previously been assigned to missions abroad on special ops, as well as in Northern Ireland.

On this occasion, the IRA unexpectedly opened fire just as his team approached the front door and Jack was shot in the chest at close range. Marcus somehow managed to drag his friend around the corner before rejoining his unit, who entered the house returning fire and killing the three IRA members. Jack had died almost instantly, the armour-piercing bullets fired from the insurgent's M60 machine gun inflicting fatal wounds. As a result of his actions that day, Marcus was awarded the Military Cross and promoted to Major. As a mark of respect, he had the medal inscribed with the words *Jack Caldwell – for bravery in the field* and presented it to his widow.

In 1982, ten years after he first enlisted and whilst stationed in the Falklands during a particularly long and bloody encounter at Goose Green, he was wounded. The bullet split his right femur. He spent three weeks in a military hospital before being sent home to convalesce. In time, the bones healed, but not perfectly. Marcus's options were a medical discharge with full honours or the offer of another promotion, this time to Colonel in a non-active role as Staff Officer. He chose the latter.

Perhaps that was when things had started to crumble for his family. After his leg injury, he knew they wanted him to stay home, but what else would he do? Could he do? He was still only twenty-nine and not yet ready to leave the army. Rebecca had gently tried to persuade him to resign. Rose had pleaded with him to stay and told him how much she loved her daddy. He hugged her and said he loved her, too, but he knew he couldn't walk away from the military. As soon as he was deemed medically fit he left, promising he would see them both again soon.

He wasn't surprised when Rebecca eventually left him. He was half expecting it. She told him she'd met someone else. Some white-collar guy called Roger – reliable hours, reliable life. He signed the divorce papers without argument. He knew that gradually he had let the army become his whole world, up to the point that life outside of it seemed muddled and pointless. As his trips home became less frequent, his family moved past missing him. They moved on from the upset and frustration of not having their love requited. Or, at least, Rebecca had, as she had gone back to school and qualified as a primary school teacher.

Rose, however, was a different matter. Her mother had watched her once happy little girl grow into an angry and confused teenager. Instead of applying for college or university, she dropped out of school at eighteen, adamant that she needed time off to think and to decide what she wanted to do. Meanwhile, she worked at a local restaurant so she could save up to go 'travelling' – maybe across Europe, she had told her mother.

Rebecca understood that her daughter needed her own space and tried not to pry, even though she was out most nights. She noticed that Rose's friends hardly came around any more, but presumed that now they were older they were out together, frequenting Bristol's many pubs and clubs. She explained to Marcus how secretive Rose had become, barely speaking to her. When he tried to speak to Rose on the phone, she was quiet and sullen. Yes and no answers, as befitted an absent parent who was now divorced by her mother and disconnected from his daughter's life.

For the next decade, he was stationed in operational commands all over the world. He still missed the camaraderie of a tight-knit troop, but not the killing. He had lost too many good men, seen men blown to bits and men whose minds were damaged beyond repair. Somewhere along the line, perhaps after Jack's death, the fighting had become personal. If he hadn't been shot, if they hadn't offered him a promotion and non-active duty, he was certain he would have eventually died in battle.

After Rose's death, for a few months Marcus functioned – as a human being. But, even the Croatian war could not detract from his own personal one. The nights were the worst. With nothing to occupy him, he'd spent his time looking through photos of Rose that Rebecca had sent over the years. Rose as a baby, Rose as a toddler, giggling and looking unsteady on her feet, clutching a teddy bear by one foot. Rose about to start primary school, wearing a stiff over-sized grey pinafore dress, red jumper, and a big cheesy grin. Not nervous about her first day, he had smiled, then stiffened. How could he know? He hadn't been there. Not for her first steps, or school, or any of the other many birthdays and milestone dates he had missed. Guilt and an overwhelming sadness engulfed him. Everywhere he looked he saw Rose and, when he closed his eyes, he could see her even more clearly. Rose, Rose, Rose.

For the first time, army life was no longer enough. He was hiding behind his commission. He had to face life and what had happened, to allow himself to grieve. Six months after his daughter's death, he resigned from the army.

He informed the UK police that he was returning and gave them his new contact details in Bristol. He asked, as he had numerous times, if they had had any new leads on the accident, any news at all, but it was clear that her murderer had vanished into thin air.

Months went by and the grief that he had been running away from finally hit home. Waves of despair came over him so fast and relentlessly that he could hardly breathe. He rarely left his rental apartment, only venturing out when he was forced by days of hunger or to buy more alcohol to help numb the pain. Losing Rose was worse than any physical injuries he had endured and more frightening than any combat situation he had faced. He wanted to lash out, to scream, and shout at anyone he encountered. How could people be casually walking past him, smiling, and laughing as if nothing was wrong in the world? Did they not know how dark a place it was?

In the past, he was always the guy everyone wanted around in an emergency, but not any more. Now he was teetering on the edge of an abyss and contemplating jumping, of bailing out altogether. It was his training that stopped him. To take his own life went against everything he had ever been taught. In the military, you were trained to survive in the direst of circumstances. To take his own life felt cowardly – it felt like failure. But the only way he could cope with living was to drink himself into a constant state of oblivion – and there he stayed, for months. A few times, old army friends tried to reach out, but he ignored their messages and eventually pulled the phone out of the wall. He existed on the couch, either half unconscious from drinking or staring unseeingly at the television, surrounded by empty bottles and half-eaten meals.

One morning, he awoke with a thudding in his head from the effects of the previous night's bottle of whiskey. The television was muted, a stretch of road was being discussed by a newsreader. Marcus stared, blurry-eyed, in disbelief as a picture of Rose appeared in the corner of the screen. He struggled to find the remote buried under the debris on the floor and managed to max the volume, just in time to catch the end of the news item:

'To mark the twelve months since Rose Tindall was killed in a fatal collision, police are appealing for anyone who might have information about the identity or whereabouts of the biker who fled the scene. A reconstruction of the tragic events on the little-used country lane near the village of West Hill on Tuesday, 8th December, will be aired tomorrow evening on Crimewatch...'

He blinked, for a moment doubting his own sanity. Was he dreaming? The shock of seeing Rose's face and of being told by a stranger that it was a year since she had died gave him a massive jolt. He looked around him, at the one-man chaos he had created. Could it really be twelve months to the day and he hadn't even realised? He staggered into the bathroom and dared to look in the mirror. He hardly recognised himself. Usually close-shaven, his face was covered in a dishevelled layer of matted hair and his eyes had dark circles etched beneath them. Sharp, observant eyes that once took in every detail now looked haunted. He splashed cold water on his face, grabbed a razor from the cabinet...

CHAPTER 16

January 1995

Marcus pulled the pump towards him, slowly levelling the glass with a pint of creamy-topped ale for Tom, one of his regulars. The old guy settled at his usual table in the corner, back to the wall so he could see who was coming in and out.

'What's new in Lostmor, then?' he asked, nodding at Tom's local paper.

Tom peered at him over the pages. 'Oh, you know, the usual I suppose. It says 'ere the council are planning roadworks along Beggar Bush Way.'

Marcus smiled and went back to tidying the bar. He liked the simplicity of running the pub, washing glasses, keeping the place clean and tidy. Living where he worked; he was used to that. He handled the weekly deliveries, changed the kegs, and kept the bar stocked with the usual pub fayre. When he had taken over the Black Dog from a retiring couple, he had kept on chefs, Bernie and Debra, who shared kitchen duties. The bar staff came and went – at the moment, a local lad, Andy, and Susie, a university student, helped him run the bar on evenings and at weekends.

Marcus was friendly and welcoming to the clientele and there was rarely any trouble. It wasn't that kind of place, or town for that matter. Lunchtime and early evening saw mainly families coming in for food. Sometimes, local tradesmen or shop workers might stop for a drink after work, but, except for at weekends, this time of year was quiet. More often than not, there were just a few diehards like Tom for company.

The Black Dog Inn was a Tudor-fronted building, squashed between an Italian restaurant and a gift shop that overlooked the harbour. Only a handful of fishermen still operated out of Lostmor, but like other Cornish coastal towns people had learnt to diversify. In the summer, Tresor Bay was lined with motorboats and larger vessels that, in a few months, would be offering various trips and deep-sea fishing experiences. For now, the smaller boats were hunkered down under canvas and the 'For hire' signs stored away. The once-humble fishermen's cottages, crowded together in ancient cobbled streets, had over time become restaurants, cafes and pubs. Marcus had been in Lostmor for a year, but Tom still called him a 'newbie'. He suspected he would call him that even if he stayed for the rest of his life. He liked Lostmor, the way it nestled into the cliffside – its inlet cloaked by dramatic rock formations that almost enveloped the bay, as if to protect everything within. Horace sloped into the bar, wagging his way over to Tom's table.

'Good day to you, Horace,' said Tom, one hand on his pint, the other rubbing behind the dog's velvety ear. 'Didn't you say you were going away this weekend, Marcus?'

Marcus looked up from tidying the bar. 'Yep. I've got cover for the bar, but I'm not sure what to do about Horace.'

'Can't you take him with you?'

'Well, it's difficult,' said Marcus. 'It would mean a long drive for him, probably at least six hours each way. That's why I'm going overnight.'

'Can't he stay here, then?' Tom asked.

'Well, the staff aren't here 24/7.'

'I'd have you, Horace, but there's not much space in my two rooms,' Tom added, 'and the landlord says no pets.' The dog grunted and slumped to a lying position, seemingly resigned to his predicament.

'That's funny,' Tom said a moment later, rustling his paper. 'Look 'ere. There's some sort of fancy kennels opening up on the coastal road, Fern Retreat. Run by Julia Sutton. "Open seven days a week. A home from home for your dog" and such like.'

'Well, maybe I should check it out,' replied Marcus. 'I might even drive by there in the morning.' The bell above the door pinged as a young family shuffled in from the cold. Marcus greeted them with a smile. 'Looks chilly out there. What can I get you?'

The next morning, he set off for Fern Retreat with Horace perched stolidly in the front seat of his truck. Marcus didn't want to leave him behind. He had visions of a long line of cold kennels containing a row of frustrated dogs, all barking in crescendo whenever someone approached, but he didn't have much choice.

'We're just going to take a look today, okay?' Horace gave him a glum sideways look. 'If you do stay here, it will only be for one night, fella.'

Marcus followed the small sign on the road directing him down a lane. A larger, dark green sign with '*Fern Retreat - a home from home for dogs*' painted in swirling yellow letters was swinging in a frame that was mounted on a post. It had the quirky semblance of a pub sign. He clipped Horace on to his lead – not that he would have strayed, but just in case there were other dogs loose. A young springer spaniel came happily bounding towards them.

'Hello!' a lady shouted across from where she was painting a wooden gate that led to a row of what looked like brand-new kennels. They were all empty, so it wasn't noisy after all. Marcus walked over to her and she rose to greet him.

'I won't shake your hand,' she grinned, showing him her paint-spattered hands. 'I'm Julia. How can I help?'

'Marcus, and this is Horace. I'm sorry to just turn up like this. You look busy.'

'Hi, Horace,' she said, dropping momentarily to one knee to stroke the Labrador. 'Is Horace okay with other dogs? If not, I'll put Bella inside.'

'No need, he's fine,' said Marcus. Horace stood wagging while the spaniel, eager to play, danced around him.

'Are you thinking of booking Horace in for a stay?' asked Julia. 'As you can see, things aren't quite up and running yet.'

'Yes, just for one night, this Saturday coming. Sorry, I must have missed that part of the advert. Someone said that your place was opening up and I was in a bit of a spot, so I headed on over.'

'No problem,' said Julia. 'I am planning to officially open in a couple of weeks, but it would be fine for Horace to stay in the house with Bella and me. He seems a friendly enough chap. That's if you don't mind Horace mixing with the staff!'

'No, no that would be perfect!' Marcus sighed with relief. 'He's never been in kennels before, so being in a warm, cosy house is even better.'

'I'm doing my best to make the kennels warm and cosy, too,' she smiled, 'but I know what you mean. I have had heaters fitted in individual bedrooms at the back of each run. I've even fitted piped music. It's meant to have a calming effect!'

'Well, maybe Horace wouldn't have minded that so much,' Marcus laughed. 'We live in a pub so he's used to a bit of background music.'

'Oh, really? Are you in Lostmor?'

'Yes, the Black Dog Inn. Do you know it?'

'Not the pub,' replied Julia, 'but I know Lostmor fairly well because I grew up in West Hill. I moved with my family to South

Devon years ago, but when this place came up, to be honest, I jumped at it. It just looked ideal for kennels and it's such a lovely spot. Don't you think?'

Marcus noticed she also had flecks of white paint on her face. A few long strands of hair had broken loose from her ponytail and her cheeks were flushed red from the cold.

'It's a great spot alright and it looks like you've got a nice lot of space for the dogs.'

Julia beamed. 'Do you want a quick look around whilst you're here?'

'Sure, why not?'

She showed Marcus the large paddock to the rear of the house where he unclipped Horace, who immediately bounded off to play with Bella. There was a large wooden hut adjacent to the house with a front desk inside, presumably for people to pay and to pick up and drop off their dogs. At Julia's invitation, he poked his head around the kitchen door to her home. She explained that Horace would sleep there with Bella. A red brick inglenook housed a big old Aga so he could see they really would be lovely and warm.

'At this rate, he won't want to come home!' Marcus laughed. 'This is a great help, thanks. Would you like me to pay now or on the day?'

'No, when you pick him up is fine. Here, please take one of my leaflets. It's just rates and opening times.'

'Thanks. Do you have many bookings yet?'

'Only two, so far... but I'm hoping word of mouth, you know. I'm expecting a big rush soon,' she grinned.

'If you like, I can leave some of your leaflets in the pub for customers to pick up,' Marcus offered. 'And I can always hand out a few to any local business people that come my way.'

'Would you?' said Julia. 'That would be great.'

Armed with a pile of leaflets, he retrieved a reluctant Horace from the paddock and bade Julia goodbye. At least he knew Horace would be fine. Apart from the long drive to Norfolk ahead of him, he could not take him to meet Maggie King. They were strangers. She was the grandmother badly injured in the accident that had killed his daughter, Rose.

Marcus was tired – tired of waiting for the police to do something. He had to act. If there was the slightest chance that this woman could help him, then he had to speak to her. Last year, the *Crimewatch* programme had uncovered a few leads, all of which turned out to be dead ends. The man responsible for killing Rose was still out there and it was eating away at him like a canker. So he had contacted the old lady, asking if it were possible to meet for a chat. He just wanted to ask her a few questions about the day of her car accident.

At first, she was reluctant, thinking he was some kind of journalist; but when he explained who he was and that he hoped that speaking to her would give him some kind of closure, she softened towards him. All the same, she thought it only fair to tell him that her memory of events was vague. It had all happened so quickly. But he had been gently persuasive. He had no wish to upset her, but the real reason for his visit was that she could somehow help him track down the man that had smashed his daughter to bits. The same man that had then casually walked off, leaving Rose's dead body, an injured old lady, and a little girl alone in the middle of nowhere.

Since losing his daughter, life had taken on a different meaning for him. Now, his only purpose for existing was to find the murdering bastard and make him pay. That – he thought – really would be closure.

CHAPTER 17

Marcus sat patiently waiting in the cramped sitting room overstuffed with furniture. A lifetime of knick-knacks were dotted around the room, family photos smiling cheerily back at him. Maggie was making them all tea in the kitchen of her bungalow, whilst her daughter, Amanda, sat in a mustard-coloured armchair looking uneasy.

'Is that Ellie?' he asked, nodding at a framed school photo of a beaming little girl whose front teeth were missing.

'Yes, that's her, she was eight there. She's nearly ten now.' Amanda's smile was short-lived when she remembered that this man, a stranger to them, had lost his own daughter. She looked away from him, feeling even more uncomfortable with the situation.

'She's very pretty,' he smiled, trying to sound reassuring. Maggie came back with the tea. Amanda helped with the tray whilst her mother slowly sat in a tall, upright chair opposite Marcus.

'Thank you both for agreeing to see me,' he said. 'I appreciate it.'

'What happened that day,' the old lady replied, 'never really leaves me, and I am so, so sorry for your terrible loss.'

She was thin and frail looking. He thought it was probably as a result of the accident, judging by a photo on the windowsill of her with her granddaughter. Ellie looked younger in this one, maybe five or six. They were stood holding hands in front of some palm trees. It was sunny and Maggie looked relaxed and tanned – and probably three stone heavier. The old woman in front of him was stiff and hunched over, with sunken eyes, her complexion grey. He knew that look – the look of someone living in a whole world of pain.

'Thank you, Mrs King.'

'Call me Maggie, please.'

'Maggie, I'm Marcus.'

'What is it that you think my mother can help you with?' Amanda interjected.

'I'm sorry to disturb you both,' replied Marcus. 'I realise you're trying to put this behind you, but I wondered if Maggie could tell me anything more about the man – the biker? I know that you have told everything to the police already, but you must also know he was never caught and it is over a year since Rose died. Please, try to understand, he killed my little girl...' He paused. 'She was only nineteen.' He stared at the red-patterned carpet, trying not to show the sheer wave of grief that had hit him so hard and so unexpectedly. He rarely spoke of Rose to anyone. The last time, apart from the police, had been at her funeral.

'Take your time,' Maggie urged, leaning forward as much as she was able.

'Why are you here, Marcus?' Amanda probed. 'Are you planning on seeking out this man yourself?'

He took a shaky breath. 'Yes,' he admitted. 'I wish there was something I could do to change what has happened – to you, to Rose, to our families. But I can't. What I can do – all I can do – is to try and find the man responsible. Finding him is the only thing keeping me going. I have waited – for days, weeks, months, desperately hoping that the police would find him. As I'm sure you know, the motorbike was stolen and gave them no leads. A few times the police have given me some fresh hope, some snippet of new information, but nothing ever materialised. I don't think they have even come close to finding him. I'm told the investigation is ongoing, but the more time that has passed the less communication I have had with the lead detective. My calls either go unanswered or I'm met with the same old lines.'

As he spoke, he heard the same responses he had received, time and time again... *'We're doing everything we can.' 'If we learn anything new, you'll be the first to know.'* In other words – *'Don't call us we'll call you.'*

'I'm truly sorry for what happened to your daughter, but what makes you think you can find him when the police can't?' Amanda asked. 'Especially after all this time.'

'That is why I am here. To see if there is anything, no matter how small, that you,' he said, addressing Maggie, 'or possibly Ellie, may have remembered since that day.'

'I wish I had,' said Maggie, 'but I honestly couldn't remember anything after the first few moments of impact. The force of the crash threw me backward and forward so hard that I fractured my spine and I was in and out of consciousness. I never even saw him. Ellie described the man as best she could to the police, but he had a helmet on so she never saw his face, either.'

But I remember that poor, broken girl on the car bonnet, thought Maggie. *I hope to God you don't know how she was found.*

'The police told me at the time that Ellie had not seen his face. How is Ellie?' he asked Amanda. 'It must have been a terrible experience for her. Has she managed to put it behind her?'

'I think she is good now,' Amanda added quietly. 'Children can be resilient. At the time, from what Mum remembers, Ellie was actually quite calm. Especially as it was nearly half an hour before someone happened to come along. It's such a little-used road. She was left with this terrifying situation to deal with. Anyone would have been traumatised, let alone a child. Afterwards, I think shock did set in and Ellie found it difficult to settle at night – she had bad dreams for weeks. But we've encouraged her to talk openly about what happened and now I'm glad to say she is much more herself. She's now more interested in how to style her hair like Baby Spice.'

Marcus smiled. 'That's good to hear… I hope you don't mind me asking, Maggie, but were you staying with Amanda and Ellie for a while? Norfolk is such a long way from Cornwall.'

'Yes,' said Maggie. 'Amanda was born here, but moved to West Hill when she got married. Her husband, Peter, is away on business a lot and she invited me to stay for a few weeks. It was supposed to be a change of scenery for me. Plus, as Amanda had just started a part-time job, I could help out with Ellie a bit, too. You probably know I was dropping Ellie off at school that morning. It was just pure bad luck we were on that stretch of road at that moment.' The old woman's voice trembled. 'I don't know what to say to you.' She looked at him with pink-rimmed, rheumy eyes. 'If I could somehow go back and change what has happened, I would. It would have been better had I died than your girl. But that bike came from nowhere, it just flew round the bend and there was nothing I could do to avoid hitting it.'

'Oh, Mum, you mustn't talk like that,' said Amanda. 'None of this is your fault. You and Ellie were victims and could have been killed, too. The only one to blame is that cold-hearted man who cruelly took this man's daughter.'

'I'm sorry,' Marcus added. 'I didn't mean to upset you, Maggie. Perhaps I'd better go.'

'No, really I'm alright.' She straightened in her chair and dabbed at her eyes with a tissue. 'Have you found anything more yourself about this man? I don't think I can tell you anything that will help you find him.' She glanced at her daughter. 'But now you're here, we can at least listen.' Amanda nodded in agreement.

'There's not much to tell,' he replied. 'Only what Rose's best friend, Lisa, told the police at the time. I have spoken to her, too.

Rose had hinted shortly before the accident about having a new boyfriend, but she was quite secretive about it. Lisa got the impression that Rose was pretty smitten with him. The only thing Rose did confide to her was that he was older – by ten years, she had said. Rose had asked her not to tell anyone as people might not approve. Rose also let slip once that he had family in Lostmor, but that was really all she knew. The police looked into it. Went door to door, appealed on the local TV for help, but no one was ever traced.'

'Lostmor? Isn't that where you've come from today?' Amanda asked.

A young girl suddenly appeared in the doorway. 'Mum, I've finished my homework.' She looked shyly at Marcus, then to Amanda, wondering who the stranger was. Granny didn't have many visitors.

'Well done, Ellie,' said Amanda. 'This is Marcus, he's – well, he's come to visit Granny, just like us.'

'Hello, Marcus,' said Ellie, balancing awkwardly on the arm of her mother's chair.

'Hello, Ellie, nice to meet you.' He had hoped that she might be around; but, faced with such a young girl, it didn't seem appropriate to suddenly start quizzing her about the accident.

Amanda sighed, put an arm around Ellie and hugged her. 'Marcus is just trying to find out more about the motorbike accident,' she explained. 'About the man riding the bike.'

'You mean helmet man?' said Ellie. 'Are you the police?'

'No, Ellie, but you could say I'm trying to help the police,' he replied. 'I knew the girl who died that day. I cared for her very much, so if you can tell me anything at all about the biker... helmet man…' Marcus spoke softly, not wanting to upset her. 'Even something really small might be useful.'

'It's up to you, Ellie,' said her mother. 'You don't have to talk about it if you don't want to.'

'I don't mind,' Ellie shrugged, 'but it's the same as what I've told the police.'

'I understand,' said Marcus. 'I only want to try and build a picture of helmet man. I know he never took his helmet off, but did you see him up close?'

'Yes. He came to the car window.' Like her grandmother a few moments ago, Ellie flashed back to the dead girl on the car bonnet. Her twisted body and staring eye. Ellie was perceptive for her age; she wondered if this was the dead girl's daddy. She didn't mention Rose or how she had fallen, seemingly from the sky. 'He had a black helmet and leather jacket. He hurt himself – he was bleeding from his leg, his left one – his jeans were red from the blood.'

'It must have been very scary indeed for you,' Marcus said softly.

'You were so brave that day, you really were,' her grandmother added, 'and you looked after me until help came, too.'

'It was really scary and awful,' said Ellie. 'After the man left, we had to wait a long time before anyone came.'

'I'm so sorry that you and your gran had to go through that,' said Marcus. 'So, the biker just walked off? Did he leave straight away?'

'Yes, he looked at us in the car, then he walked a bit up the road. He was limping. When... when he knew that the girl was dead, he kind of staggered into the woods. I never saw him after that. He wanted to get away.'

Marcus knew from the police that Rose had died instantly. That she had been propelled off the back of the bike and into a tree trunk. For the millionth time, he tried not to visualise it.

'When he was up close, did he say anything to you?' he asked.

'No, he just looked at us.'

'Could you see the colour of his skin? Maybe you saw his hands or his neck? Did he have any tattoos or scars?'

'No, his face was covered and he had black gloves on. I told the police that, too.'

'Thanks for talking to me, Ellie,' said Marcus. 'You have been really helpful.'

He rose to leave. He was disappointed, but not surprised. He hadn't learnt anything new, but he was glad to have met Maggie and Ellie. They were connected for all the wrong reasons, but on some level he had found it comforting; a relief, perhaps, to have finally spoken about Rose to someone, even if briefly. Since the funeral, he and Rebecca had not seen each other, or even spoken on the phone. Rose had looked so much like her mother that he couldn't face her. And, as for Rebecca, he was pretty sure that she blamed him for what had happened. Maybe if he'd been around more Rose wouldn't have rebelled, taken so many risks. It didn't matter any more. They had both moved on and that was that.

'Is your mother okay?' he asked Amanda as she showed him out to the front door.

'Not really, but she's a tough lady,' she replied. 'She's suffered from chronic back pain ever since the crash and I'm afraid it's aged her.'

'Does she live here alone?'

'Yes, Ellie and I are just visiting for a few days. We lost Dad about three years ago now. Before the accident, Mum was just beginning to get her life back on track. That's partly why I invited her to West Hill. She was helping me out. I had just started working in a local jeweller's, but I also thought it would be fun for her, too. That the three of us could go shopping, maybe take Ellie to the zoo...'

'I really am sorry for upsetting your mother,' said Marcus. 'I know it's unlikely, and I don't like to ask any more of you, but just in case Ellie should remember anything else at all, would you mind taking this?' He offered Amanda a business card with the Black Dog Inn printed on it and his contact details.

Amanda considered him for a moment. 'Okay, sure,' she said in lowered tones. 'I can't imagine she will, but I know how I would feel if anyone hurt my daughter. I don't blame you for wanting to find this man, but when you said on the phone that you were looking for closure, we thought you meant that talking to my mum would help you put it behind you. Is it closure you want, Marcus? Or is it revenge? This man is dangerous. Let's suppose you get your wish that you do find him. What then? What would you do?'

He met her concerned eyes squarely. 'If I find out who he is, or where he is, I'll tell the police. Let them deal with him.' The army had taught him to lie well.

As he walked off, Amanda eyed him suspiciously. She noticed he walked with a slight limp, but he looked like he could handle himself. She just hoped he knew what he was doing.

CHAPTER 18

Marcus checked out of the little B&B early Sunday morning. The drive back was quicker, but it still took over five hours. Not that he minded; since moving to Lostmor, it felt as if he had spent more hours driving around Cornwall than he had sleeping. Hours spent learning where all the local farms and smallholdings were, and – thanks to the willingness of people to gossip – learning about who lived in them.

The Black Dog Inn was the perfect place to get folk talking and who were often more than happy to chat about their colleagues, friends, or neighbours in a conspiratorial way, especially after a few drinks. He watched for anyone parking a motorbike in the pub car park and, if someone looked out of place or didn't feel right to him, he made it his business to find out more about them. He figured that the man he was looking for was staying below the radar, maybe as a casual worker.

He'd kept a watch on a few guys from the area. Learnt their daily routines, where they worked, what sports they liked, clubs or pubs they frequented and who their friends and relatives were. It sometimes took a while to establish whether someone had an alibi for over a year ago, but that was one thing he had plenty of – time. He was friendly with the customers and the locals, but never talked at length about himself. If anyone asked where he had lived or worked before, he would keep things vague. His stock answer was that he had managed a bar in Bristol then moved south after his divorce. People generally believed what they were told without questioning too much.

He knew that, if he was ever to seek out helmet man, he needed to stay as anonymous as possible, and he definitely didn't want people to know he was Rose's father. Because he had been abroad and already divorced from Rebecca when Rose was killed, it was Rebecca who had received the most media attention. Marcus had refused to speak to the few reporters who had managed to track him down by phone and, after a few weeks, they had left him alone, moving on to fresh pickings.

Now he was back in the UK and the good thing about coastal towns was how easy it was to go unnoticed. People came and went with the seasons. He liked that he was just the latest manager of the Black Dog Inn and took comfort from being in Lostmor. It made him feel closer to Rose in some small way. That said, he was still no closer to finding her killer. At the time, the police had interviewed scores of men from the area with no real leads. The killer may have moved on, even if he did have family close by. But, what if he hadn't? He could have decided to lay low somewhere else, just about anywhere else, until things had settled down. It would have been easy – no one knew what the man looked like. If that were the case, then sooner or later wouldn't he risk coming home once he thought the police were no longer actively searching for him? In Marcus's experience, most people tended to navigate back to their roots sooner or later; and, if helmet man did, *when* he did, Marcus would be waiting for him. Besides – he had no place else to go.

When he had first arrived at Lostmor, Marcus had spent hours every day walking the coastal paths. The recently acquired Horace, being only two years old and full of energy, had loved every minute. But what started as a necessity – Horace needing a walk became a welcome distraction from the sadness that, at times, he still felt so acutely. Often, he awoke early in the morning with an all-encompassing wave of despair so crushing that it seemed to physically pin him to the bed. So, to shake off this morning fog of grief, he started to walk. The weeks went by and each day Horace nudged him to get up, shaking him out of his despondency. They had walked their way through the winter. Now, when Marcus strode out on the clifftops he felt his head starting to clear and a lightness of heart that he had not felt for a very long time. Some days as they walked he would watch the sea rolling in fast to the rocks below, where spiralling lengths of froth flicked up spray; other days, the water was docile and silvered.

Today, the wind was up and, overhead, scores of gulls pitched and turned weightlessly on the updraught, their yelling almost lost to the sound of the waves grabbing at the shingle. Marcus walked the short length of the bay, then climbed up the steep track leading to the coastal path beyond. He turned his collar up against the cold and walked for a couple of miles before cutting across pastureland that eventually met the road. As he walked through the gate to Fern Retreat, he could hear Horace barking and found him in the paddock, bounding after a ball, hotly pursued by Bella. Julia was wrapped up in a puffer jacket, bobble hat and gloves, hurling the ball over and over at an impressive overarm distance.

'Hi, there!' he called out. Horace immediately dropped the ball and came bounding over to him.

'Hello, I didn't hear your car?' called Julia in return.

'No, I'm on foot today,' he smiled, kneeling to hug Horace. 'Hello, big fella!' Horace stuck his head into Marcus's side. 'I thought Horace would enjoy the walk back.'

'It's a nice day for it,' Julia agreed, 'if a little brisk!' She threw the ball for Bella one last time before they retreated to the warmth of the house.

Inside, Marcus paid for Horace's stay. 'I hope he's behaved himself?'

'He's been no trouble at all,' Julia replied. 'I feel bad taking your money. I've enjoyed having him around.'

'You're going to have to be more businesslike than that if you want to make any money!'

'I know!' she laughed, pulling off her hat and unravelling herself from a long, woolly scarf. 'You're right. I'll try and be more assertive at the open day.'

'Ah, yes, of course. Have you got any more customers?'

'Yes. A few people have dropped by and booked their dogs in there and then, and I've had enquiries over the phone. So, things are looking up, thanks. That may well be down to you displaying my leaflets at the pub.'

'Maybe, or they saw you in the *Lostmor Gazette*,' Marcus said. 'Either way, I'm glad things are working out.'

'Well, if my future clientele are as well behaved as Horace, my job will be easy,' said Julia. 'And as he was my first-ever guest, that means he's welcome to stay in the house if ever you need to drop him off again. He really is very affectionate, isn't he?'

'I think the word is "needy"!' laughed Marcus. 'But thank you, that is a very generous offer.' Horace softly woofed at them both, his tail swishing on the kitchen slabs in agreement. 'To be honest, it was more of a one-off trip. Although… if you need any help around here... To help you get ready for opening. I'm pretty handy?'

Julia thought for a moment. *Why not?* she thought to herself. He seemed nice and she could do with the help, not to mention the company.

'That is an offer I just can't turn down!' she smiled. 'What are you like at fixing fences?'

CHAPTER 19

Flynn sat between Oliver and Lily, tongue lolling, eyes fixed eagerly on the road ahead. The sun was a golden globe hanging low in a cloudless sky, transforming the sea into a vast expanse of tinselled water. Spongy green pasture rolled out to meet the horizon as the coastal road widened and gradually turned inland.

'Just there,' Lily said, pointing at the moss-covered iron gate to their right. They followed the track that wound its way through the estate. As the house came into view, Oliver stared in disbelief at the size of the building and its dramatic façade. The Land Rover slowly crunched to a halt on the drive.

'Wow, I knew the place was big, but this is very imposing,' he said.

Lily silently chastised herself for feeling nervous about returning and put from her mind the image of herself fleeing from the house like a mad banshee.

'Come on,' she grabbed his arm. 'Let's go inside.'

They stood gazing around the vaulted hallway, Oliver in awe. Even in its neglected state, it was extraordinary. Light streamed through the glass dome above the sweeping staircase. She had given copies of the house keys to Mr Carne of Lostmor Antiques and she could see that his team had taken all of the boxes she had left in the main reception area. The place looked lighter, and she realised that someone had pulled the curtains down from the arched leaded windows either side of the front door.

'This place is incredible, Lily,' said Oliver. 'I don't know what I was expecting, but not this.'

'A creepy Gothic mansion, you mean?'

'Well, kind of, but in a good way.' He put his arm reassuringly across Lily's shoulder. 'Ready to show me more?'

Downstairs, they roamed from room to room. Flynn trotted along behind them happily, sniffing every nook and cranny, picking up the many layers of smells. Some of the other boxes that Lily had filled with old lamps, ornaments, and artefacts had also been taken from the various rooms. She felt a little sad that her old home was gradually being stripped of its past, but she knew it was for the best. As they walked, she reminisced about happier days. Days spent with Alice playing hide and seek or building a den in one of the many unused rooms. When they reached the basement kitchen, she was struck by the memory of a large, jolly lady called Margaret. She had been the cook, and she and Alice had sometimes sat for hours at the kitchen table shelling peas that they had collected from the vegetable garden.

What else might I be able to remember?

'Phew! Shall I open some windows? The air in here is really stagnant,' Oliver said.

'I have tried, but they're jammed fast,' Lily replied.

The small sash window frames were rotten and blistered where rain had seeped through for decades and permeated the now damp, peeling walls. Oliver turned to Lily, with a serious but kindly expression.

'I can't quite believe you've been trying to cope with all this on your own. Not that you're not a capable woman,' he quickly added. 'It's just not a one-person job!'

Lily smiled. He was right; she must have been crazy to think that, in a few weeks, she could empty the house single-handedly, then give it a quick tidy before leaving.

Oliver was quiet for a moment. 'Come on,' he smiled, reaching out for her hand. 'It's too nice to be inside. Shall we sit outside on the front lawn for a bit? Did you say you'd brought a flask of tea?'

'Yes, it's in the car.'

They unlocked the small kitchen door, the edges of which were rotten and crumbling, and, with a hard shove, walked out into the sunshine.

'Something on your mind?' she mused.

'Surely you cannot know me that well already!' Oliver flashed a cheesy grin whilst walking backwards away from her across the lawn. They sat on his coat in the meadow, sipping tea and munching on some shortbread that she had also thrown in. Flynn stayed close, lying contentedly in the sun, with his head on his front paws, eyes closed, nose twitching.

'I could stick around for the rest of the week if you like?' said Oliver.

'Are you sure?' Lily asked. 'Don't you need to work on the farm?'

'It's fine for a few days. If I'm honest, I have kind of lost interest since Mum died. Don't get me wrong, I don't want to leave there. Much like painting is your life, farming is mine, but a break from it might do me good.' Oliver paused for a moment, as if reflecting. 'Besides, there really is no competition, if it means spending time with you.'

'Okay,' she smiled. 'I would like that. But we won't be alone. I have people coming from Lostmor Antiques to move the rest of the boxes out. Then there's a surveyor coming to assess what work needs doing. I hate to think how much that will cost. I haven't been up on the roof to look, but the water damage to the bedrooms in the west wing is really bad.'

'You have a lot to think about,' Oliver empathised. He gently touched her cheek, brushing a wisp of hair from her face. His touch made her skin tingle. She rested her head on his shoulder.

'You know,' Lily began, 'since reading my mother's will, it feels like every part of my life has been swept up then scattered to the four corners of the Earth, and right now I'm not sure how to piece things back together.' She looked up into his kind eyes. 'But one thing I do know is that I'm very glad you're here.'

CHAPTER 20

The removals team arrived at Penwyth House en masse. A thin, middle-aged man wearing dark blue overalls, his hair tied back in a lank ponytail, stuck his hand out.

'I'm Richard – this is quite some place!' he said, looking around the vast hallway.

'Hi, I'm Lily,' she replied. 'And yes, I'm afraid you've got your work cut out.'

'We've come prepared,' he grinned, revealing uneven, nicotine-stained teeth. 'Mr Carne did explain it was a big job, but me and my men like a challenge!'

'That's a relief. Shall I give you a quick tour so you know your way around?'

'Yeah, great,' he replied. 'Then I can work out roughly how long we might be here. I've got some men tasked with packing boxes and loading up all the furniture, and others who will be stripping out all the soft furnishings. It is my understanding that all the stuff for auction has gone and everything remaining is for our disposal?'

'Yes, mostly,' said Lily. 'I've got a few things labelled up that I'm keeping. I'll show you as we go around.'

Lily heard another vehicle pulling up outside.

'Oh, that's the skip arriving,' Richard continued. 'Mr Carne ordered it, for all the old carpets and curtains and such like. So there will be a lot going on and a fair amount of noise, just to warn you.'

'No problem. I'm meeting a surveyor here shortly, so Oliver and I will be about if you have any questions.' Oliver smiled and nodded in agreement.

Lily walked off with Richard, while Oliver said he'd keep an eye out for the surveyor. He wandered out onto the drive, where two large trucks were parked at the far end and a flatbed truck with an enormous skip was being guided in by one of Richard's men.

A wiry man with shoulder-length black hair jumped out of the passenger side and watched as the skip was lowered onto the drive, giving the thumbs up to the driver when he had unhooked it on the ground.

'Quite a place,' the man smiled, whilst climbing back into the cab and signalling goodbye. As the truck pulled away, Oliver caught sight of the driver's face, who looked equally surprised to see him. It was Douglas Holt – again.

Later that day, Oliver and Lily prepared to leave.

'You're not going to believe who I saw earlier,' Oliver glanced over at Lily in the passenger seat, where Flynn had taken up residence on her lap. 'Douglas Holt, the man I told you about from the farm, and then again at the Black Dog.'

'Where?'

'At the house. He was one of the men who delivered the skip today.'

'Really? Well, he is a Jack of all trades, isn't he?'

'Hmmm, and master of none I expect.' The man was trouble and Oliver didn't want him anywhere near them or Penwyth Estate.

He dropped Lily off at Kleger Cottage and arranged to pick her up again early in the morning. Richard and his team were due back to finish off, as was the surveyor, who had disappeared for the entire day investigating the house and its grounds. He would be returning with a colleague to assess the structural damage to the roof.

Oliver couldn't quite believe how drawn to Lily he was. Even though she was clearly an independent woman and a successful artist, he sensed she had a more vulnerable side and it made him feel protective of her. He knew she had secrets, things that had happened at Penwyth House that she was not ready to share with him yet, but he also sensed a quiet inner strength. Perhaps it was something she had needed to draw upon in the past – or maybe *because* of her past.

'You like her too, don't you, Flynn?' Flynn, who was sitting in Lily's now-vacated seat, barked once in agreement.

The following day, Lily dropped by at Edhen Cottage to let Joe know she would be back the following weekend. Oliver loaded up his car with most of the stuff from the house that Lily was keeping; there were still some paintings, including the one of her father, stacked in the hallway that needed a bit more care with removing. Richard and his men loaded up the final boxes and furniture for disposal, whilst Oliver watched as the flatbed truck arrived to collect the now overloaded skip. He was relieved to see Douglas wasn't there, just the other guy.

'Why don't you come over to mine for dinner later?' he asked Lily on the drive home.

'That would be lovely,' replied Lily. 'I can tell you all about my chat with Joe. He's agreed to keep some of the surrounding land as well as Edhen Cottage.'

'That's good. Perhaps I could go with you next time? It would be nice to say hello.'

'I would love for you to meet him. How about next weekend?'

'You're on,' Oliver grinned. 'Now then, how about I pick you up at seven this evening?'

'Early is good. I'm starving!'

'Great… I *can* cook, you know.'

'I never doubted you,' Lily laughed.

'Cheese on toast okay?' Oliver teased. She prodded him and he faked pain. 'Ahhh, only joking! I mean, I'm not brilliant, but I can manage a curry or pasta.'

'Either is fine, as long as there's lots of it!'

CHAPTER 21

Bligh Farm was bigger than it looked from the front. The bungalow was L-shaped with a small courtyard and garden that backed on to open farmland. The low-beamed kitchen was warmly lit, and making the most of the warmest spot was Flynn, curled up fast asleep on a rug in front of a huge range that was set back in an inglenook.

'Hmmm, whatever you've made it smells wonderful.' Lily was trying not to sip too much of the large glass of wine in front of her, conscious of her empty rumbling stomach. It was easier said than done, however, when she was feeling both happy and relaxed and enjoying being somewhere other than at Penwyth House or Kleger Cottage.

'It's the least I can do to repay you for all the flasks of tea and shortbread this week,' Oliver smiled at her, taking a bubbling dish of lasagne from the oven and placing it between them on the table.

Lily inhaled the aromas of mild spices and heat. 'Wow, this looks amazing.'

'I'm not just a pretty face, you know,' he smiled again, offering her a large helping of food.

Outside, it was already dark and rain started to lightly patter on the windows. Oblivious to the storm that was building, they ate hungrily, sipping good red wine and chatting about the day's events.

'So, it went well with Joe today?' Oliver asked, leaning back and feeling comfortably full.

'Yes,' said Lily. 'I already knew he wanted to stay on, but now he's agreed to keep a small pocket of land surrounding Edhen Cottage, too. About five acres, I think. I said that I would arrange for the necessary papers to be drawn up and we'll agree where his borders lie, but it's all just formalities. He didn't say, but he must be finding it difficult to maintain the entire estate on his own now that he's getting older. This way, he keeps his home with a bit of land, which includes the glasshouses… and it's also where Alice is buried…' Oliver waited for her to continue. It was the first time she had mentioned her late sister. 'She was laid to rest on a hill overlooking the sea. Joe told me that he has always looked after her grave and is happy to keep doing so.'

'And your father? Is he buried there, too?'

'No,' replied Lily. 'His ashes were scattered at sea. It was what he wanted. He didn't have a will or any surviving family, just Mother and I. She said that he had never liked the idea of being buried and had once told her that, if he should go before her, to scatter his ashes at the cliff's edge. So that is what we did. Just the two of us. I remember it being a very warm, still summer's evening. Afterwards, Mother said a few words. I cried… she didn't. Then we walked home again.'

'Have you been to visit Alice's grave?' Oliver asked warily. 'Since you've been back?'

'No.' Lily rose, taking their empty plates to the kitchen sink. She had wanted to, but at the back of her mind there had always been a creeping, unthinkable question, worming its way into her consciousness. What if she was somehow to blame for her sister's death?

Sensing her unease, Oliver sat forward, speaking softly. 'You don't have to talk about that night, Lily. Not if you don't want to… but maybe it would help.'

'That's kind of the problem,' she said, her eyes glistening in the low light. 'It's difficult for me to talk about it because I can't remember what happened.' She fought to contain the emotions and frustration she had been struggling with for so many years.

'Come on,' he whispered. 'Let's sit by the fire in the lounge and I'll pour us another glass.' The rain was falling harder now, drumming on the windows, and a faint rumble of thunder stirred out at sea. 'I didn't mean to upset you.'

'You haven't,' said Lily. 'Honestly, it's a relief to have someone to talk to about it, but all I have are fragments of memories of that night. For years, I have had flashbacks and nightmares where I see the same images over and over, but I can't make sense of them. I don't remember if I was there when my father and Alice fell from the roof or not, and my mother would never talk to me about it. Not properly. She said that I'd been with her downstairs the whole time, but I remember my father standing amongst the steeples on the roof and a terrible storm… Alice screaming… and me running, running away… And the strangest thing… a crazy mask-like face. I have no idea where it came from or what it means. I can't tell you how many times these images have run through my head, but I don't think they're the imaginings of a traumatised child. I think they're memories still trying to come to the surface…' She stopped and looked at Oliver. 'Sorry, I didn't mean to spoil a perfectly lovely evening talking about this.'

They sat close, gazing into the fire. Oliver smiled at her warmly. 'You couldn't possibly spoil anything. I can't think of anywhere else I'd rather be right now than here with you… Tell me more.'

Blue and orange flames crackled and danced in the hearth, sending flickers of light and dark across their faces.

'After Mother died,' Lily continued, 'and I discovered that Penwyth Estate belonged to me, I was terrified of returning to the house. The first time was so daunting, but gradually I got over my initial fear, to the point that I started to feel strangely connected to the place. After a few more trips, I plucked up the courage to go in

Alice's bedroom. It was a very sad and poignant moment for me, but when I came back out, I was determined to go up on the roof. Up until then, I couldn't face going there, but I hoped it might in some way jog my memory… if I stood where they had stood. But, when I got to the stairs leading up there, I heard my father's voice calling my name, clear as day. Then, as if he was stood right next to me, I heard him whisper in my ear, "Why did you run away, Lily?" I panicked. I was so terrified that I ran straight out of the house and thought I would never go back… You must think I'm completely mad, but it really did feel like he was actually there.'

'Of course I don't,' said Oliver. 'What a scary experience… and yet… you did go back, didn't you?'

'I did, but the next time it was with you.'

Oliver's eyes shone black in the firelight. 'I don't know any more than you what happened in that house, but I do know that you don't have to face whatever this is alone any more. I'm here…' He kissed her gently, holding her close. 'I'm falling in love with you and, whatever lies ahead, I'm right here by your side, for as long as you'll let me.'

In the early hours of the morning, the storm moved closer, while black, static clouds raced across the sky. Thunder boomed and crashed above Bligh Farm that night; but, midst the raging tempest, safe inside its thick stone walls, they made sweet tender love. Rolling together under the sheets, they caressed each other with their hands, lips, and tongues. He wanted her so badly his whole body ached in anticipation. She smoothed her hands down the tensing muscles in his back and drew him slowly into her, stroking his curves, feeling his solid rhythmic thrusting. He whispered something inaudible to her as his grip on her tightened and she heard a soft moan fly from her throat. Aroused even more than he thought possible, together they soared, bound tightly, before suddenly and gloriously falling. Exhausted, they lay silently listening to the storm recede. That night… it felt as if no one else in the universe existed except them.

CHAPTER 22

Lily smiled at her own fickleness. She had been so keen to leave Kleger Cottage and return to her painting, but now she couldn't wait to go back to Lostmor and see Oliver again. All week, a steady stream of people visited *The Blue,* some browsing, quite a few purchasing. Not to mention a handful of enquiries waiting for her on the answerphone. She had just completed one such enquiry – a commission for a painting of the Christmas Steps, a popular historical street in Bristol. From where her easel was set up in the rear of the shop, she smiled back at a well-dressed lady who had come in a few minutes earlier. For once, Lily was glad when the customer headed for the door. It was nearly closing time and she was eager to get home and pack.

She had no sooner let herself into her apartment when her mobile rang.

'Hi, how were things at *The Blue* today?' Oliver asked.

'Busy again. Things are going well. How about you? What have you been up to?'

'Spreading slurry, ready for sowing wheat when the last frosts are over.'

'Wow, and here's me, sitting wafting a paintbrush around.'

He laughed. 'What you do is a talent. Farming is just work, anyone can learn to do it.'

'I'm not so sure about that. You must have to be pretty disciplined, what with all those early mornings.'

'Most of the time I love it,' said Oliver. 'I feel cooped up if I'm inside for too long. Although, I have to admit, it's a bit of a struggle when it's pitch black outside and blowing a gale. Are you still coming tomorrow? I can't wait to see you.'

'Yes, of course…' said Lily. 'I've missed you.'

'It's a damned nuisance, but I have to go into St Oswald's to meet my mother's solicitor,' replied Oliver. 'I'm sorry, but he only rang yesterday. It's just some signatures he needs, to do with ownership of the farm, but it shouldn't take too long. I will be back by six, or six-thirty the latest.'

'Not to worry,' said Lily. 'I was going to open the shop just for the morning, so I probably won't reach you until four, anyway. I'll still leave after lunch in case the traffic is bad. Besides, Flynn will keep me company.'

In the end, her journey had been long with constant stopping and starting due to roadworks. Four hours after leaving Bristol, she finally reached the farm. She used the key Oliver had left under a rock to let herself in and was welcomed by an excited bark. She let Flynn out and they wandered around the yard, Lily just glad to stretch her legs. It was late afternoon and the polar sun was a pale, sinking orb on the horizon. The acrid smell of freshly spread fertiliser lay heavy in the air, carried across open fields by a low wind. She shivered and turned back towards the house.

At 7.00 pm, Lily fed a hungry-looking Flynn with dog food she found in the cupboard. By 8.30 pm she was worried. Oliver should have been back hours ago. She had tried his mobile umpteen times, but it was switched off. What if he had crashed? It was so dark this time of year and the A-roads were mostly unlit. She lit the fire and sat on the couch, picking at a leftover chilli she had found in the fridge.

All she could do was wait and keep trying his phone.

She wasn't sure how many hours she sat, worrying and willing her phone to ring, but in the end she had drifted off to sleep. She awoke just before dawn, shivering from the cold. Flynn, who was curled up beside her, jumped down, tail wagging, head tilted, wondering what this new game of someone sleeping on his couch was all about. Lily squinted in the half-light. There were no missed calls on her phone. She knew she would have heard the landline if he had rung, but checked the machine anyway. She searched in vain through an address book she found on the kitchen dresser, looking for a solicitor's business card or any obvious numbers. At least then she could try and work out what time Oliver had left St Oswald's, or if he had even made his appointment. Visions of him lying unseen in a ditch filled her head. She told herself she was being melodramatic. He probably broke down miles from anywhere, his mobile out of charge, and couldn't reach a phone. Any second now the phone would ring, or he would walk through that door, sweeping her off her feet and all would be well.

Trying not to panic, she checked each room, searching drawers and shelves for any clues as to who his late mother's solicitor might be, but nothing. Eventually, she resorted to calling the hospital in St Oswald's. No one of his name or description had been admitted yesterday or overnight.

Lily stood in the kitchen, sipping a mug of hot tea, trying to think what to do next. His address book; she could go through and ring all of the numbers listed. Just then, she heard a car pull up outside. She rushed to the door and pushed up the latch.

'Oliver!'

CHAPTER 23

Douglas Holt sat in one of two armchairs that sagged and bowed like battle-weary soldiers, the once beige fabric now a greasy, indiscernible colour that reeked of cigarettes. He flicked the pull tab off another beer.

'Do we have to leave? I don't wanna live anywhere else.'

Leaning forward, his older brother, Luke, carefully placed more logs in the hearth. He sighed. He was tired of having little or no money.

'Yes,' he snapped. 'Unless we sell this place, we have a few hundred left, that's it.' That wasn't entirely true, but it was close enough.

There was none of the usual flotsam and jetsam of a family home. The small living room was devoid of furniture, apart from a heavily stained brown rug as threadbare as the armchairs, and an old chest of drawers, the top of which was littered with empty beer cans and dirty plates overspilling with cigarette butts.

'We've always lived here,' said Douglas. 'Where would we even go?'

'Not sure,' replied Luke. 'St Oswald's maybe, or Bristol? Anywhere where's there's more work and that would get us away from this shithole. This place isn't worth much, but it would give us enough to put a deposit down on something else. Then things would be good again, Doug… better, even. It would be a fresh start.'

Douglas stared at the dwindling fire. It was a particularly cold evening for March and an icy chill was rapidly creeping into their small, broken-down bungalow. Exposed to the elements on three sides with a dense copse of conifers behind, the squat building and breeze-block garage overlooked disused fields. The only access was by a narrow, hidden track leading to it from the nearest road over a quarter of a mile away.

'Maybe we don't have to leave...' Douglas leant forward, suddenly animated by an idea that had slowly been forming. 'What if I've found a way to make us both rich?'

Luke regarded him with sharp, suspicious eyes. It wasn't the first time his brother had come up with a get-rich-quick scheme. It seemed to him that all his life he had been bailing Douglas out of some trouble or other. Not that he was any saint himself. He could have done better at school, or so his school reports informed. No one else in the family had any brains and his frustrated father had hoped for more from his eldest son. But Luke had found the whole thing extremely boring. Not just the teachers and the lessons, but the other kids, too. Immature boys mock fighting and bragging about who had scored the most goals or made the best tackle.

The girls weren't much better, giggling and pulling up their skirts whenever some kid they fancied passed by. Except for one girl, he remembered with a wistful smile – she had been special. She had the most amazing poker-straight blonde hair that fell nearly to her waist, and mesmerising blue eyes. They had got chatting in the school library. She was in the year above, but neither of them had cared about that. They had a mutual love of books. Each day after lessons ended they talked for hours in earnest, debating such titles as the *Lord of the Flies* and *The Outsiders*. He had liked the idea of challenging people's perceptions of what constituted 'normal', of what was considered right and wrong. She had listened to his theories and opinions and taken him seriously. Or, at least she had, until that dickhead Josh had come along. With his perfect white teeth and stupid flicked-back hair. Luke refused to talk to her after that, even though she had tried. He had been so mad at her he had wanted to set the whole fucking school alight. In one glorious blaze, he could have sent all those petty conformists to hell. But he didn't. Instead, he started to skip classes. Then he learnt that she had moved away with her family.

By the age of fifteen, he stopped attending school altogether. The school, and eventually the social services, wrote letters to his father, most of which he managed to intersect. Thankfully, there was no phone line at home. Once, social services came to the house – at least, he guessed it was them. The woman looked official and no one else ever called. Fortunately for him, his father had been out, so he and Doug had played a game, hiding in their bedroom until the nosy woman had given up and gone away. It had been their secret, one of many that he had easily coerced his younger brother into.

When Luke turned sixteen, no one bothered him any more. Ever since, he had gone from one casual job to another, both of them had. Since Douglas had blown his job at Bligh Farm and now their contract with Eastgate Skips was ended, they needed to find some more work pronto. All he needed was the chance to get his hands on some real money. Then, he and Doug would never have to worry about anything ever again. He knew that, one day, he was destined to own a big house, drive a flash car and fly to his villa in Spain whenever the hell he felt like it.

Since the bitch had walked out on the family – Luke refused to refer to her as his mother, even in his head – their dad had brought them up as best he could, but it had all gotten too much for him in the end. Now, Luke's enduring memory of his father was of him sitting by the fireplace drinking whiskey and smoking himself to death. A few years back, he couldn't bear to see his dad like that any more, the constant coughing and wheezing. When his old man could no longer get out of the chair without help, Luke took matters into his own hands. He hadn't even given any resistance; as he held the pillow firmly over his father's face, he had passed peacefully away.

It was a blessing, he told Douglas, him slipping away in his sleep like that, but he was surprised how badly his brother took it. His gambling, usually on the horses, and drinking escalated. Eventually, Luke took control of the remaining few thousand pounds that their dad had unimaginatively stashed under his mattress. He taped half to the bottom of a drawer in his bedroom, then buried the rest in the copse behind the house. Doug would never think to look there. He protested for a while, but gave up trying to find it in the end. That had cut his drinking down. It was how things had always been between the Holt brothers. Douglas fucked up, but Luke sorted it out, even when things got really bad.

Luke watched his drunken brother with curiosity. Douglas was shorter than him, heavyset, with slabs of natural chest and shoulder muscle. It didn't seem fair, as Douglas ate and drank whatever he liked and never worked out. Not that Luke tried any harder, but he was more like his mother – jet black hair, and a paler complexion. He hated his noodle arms and envied his brother's bulging biceps. He studied Douglas's broad, square forehead and thick, auburn hair and, not for the first time, suspected that he was the result of one of 'the bitch's' frequent dalliances. Either way, what did it matter? They were still related and now all they had was each other.

'Luke! Are you listening to me?' Douglas slurred. 'That place we went to the other day, the big old house.'

'Penwyth House?' said Luke. 'Sure. What about it?'

'Well, do you think anyone's living there? I mean, those men were clearing out the furniture, but a massive place like that... There could still be valuables in there. It could be stuffed full of antiques for all we know… We should take a look, right?'

'Hmmm, maybe, but how do we find out? It's an estate, with a mile-long drive. It's not the kind of place where you just turn up and say you're lost, is it?'

'We could go at night,' said Douglas. 'Leave the van on the road first off and walk right in. I bet there's no security, and there's not even a gate to get past. The place is wide open.'

Luke pondered the idea. Maybe, for once, his brother had had a good idea. It could be feasible.

'I suppose we could keep a watch on the place,' he replied. 'See who comes in and out. What about that guy, Oliver Bligh, you saw there? I mean, it can't be his house – he has a farm the other side of Lostmor. So what, I wonder, was he doing there? I'll think on it some more tomorrow... and that's enough beer for tonight, okay? If we're going to do this, you need to get sober.'

'It's a good idea, right?' Douglas asked, throwing his empty beer can at the log basket.

'Maybe... maybe.'

Above the tiny bungalow, the last of the day's light drained out of the sky and the woodland sheathed the building in shadow. In the canopy of the tall trees, roosting crows struck up a cacophony of noise, their black avian eyes alert and watchful.

CHAPTER 24

'Thank God you're okay! I was so worried!' Lily went to hug him, but he gently took her arms from around his neck and made his way past her into the kitchen.

'Are you hurt? What happened?'

'No, it's nothing like that.' Oliver sat down heavily, for once ignoring Flynn's excited bids for attention. 'I'm sorry. I should have called you... I had some news... some very bad news. I've been sitting in my car for most of the night just trying to get things straight in my head.'

She looked into troubled eyes. He looked exhausted. 'Why? Whatever's wrong?'

'What I'm about to tell you is going to change things for us forever.'

'I don't understand. Oliver, you're scaring me. Surely, whatever it is we can work it out together?' She looked at him, fearing the worst. 'I'm here for you, just as you said you were here for me.'

'Of course, and I meant it,' replied Oliver. 'But this is different... things are now different. You'd better sit down.'

Lily slowly sat. She'd never seen him look so serious before.

'You know I went to see Mr Reece yesterday?' he continued.

'Your mother's solicitor, yes. When you didn't come back, I tried to find a number for him but I didn't even know his name. Weren't you signing papers?'

'I was… I did, but he also gave me this.' Oliver placed a large envelope on the table. 'Apparently, my mother asked him to wait six months before handing it over. Now I've seen its contents, I think I know why. She was waiting until after the funeral and things had settled down for me.'

Lily stared at the envelope, then at Oliver. He looked lost. 'What does it say that is so awful?'

'I don't think I have the words. Maybe it's just easier if you read it.' From the envelope, he pulled out two smaller ones and passed her the one with his name handwritten on the front. 'This is the letter my mother left.'

My dearest Oliver,

This is not an easy letter to write, but I need to tell you something about yourself that I perhaps should have told you a long time ago.

When I was young, I did something impulsive that the next day I bitterly regretted. I betrayed your father with another man and what happened that night changed everything. You see, I fell pregnant. The man in question never knew about you and I never saw him again.

George, who loved you as his own, couldn't have children. He told me right at the start. When he was a young man, he contracted measles and became very ill. He survived a terrible infection, but it left him sterile. I told him it didn't matter to me and that I loved him all the same. And I meant it, but I was a foolish, young girl impressed by an older man's attentions. It was such a long time ago and I think I must have taken leave of my senses to have risked everything that way. One thing I know to be true is that, from the second you were born, you were George's and mine. You were 'our' son and the most precious and cherished of gifts. We loved you so much and he would have been very proud of the hardworking boy he raised that grew into the honourable man you are.

When you were still very young, we talked about whether we should one day tell you the truth about who your birth father was. Right or wrong, we decided against it. We just wanted to give you the best start in life and I hope that, in your heart, you can find it within you to forgive me. Just as, even though I know I hurt him deeply, George forgave me my betrayal. When he was taken so early from us and you still a boy, I could not find it in me to break your heart a second time. Then, just a few years later I learnt that your birth father had also died prematurely. After that, with them both gone, it seemed easier to say nothing.

Knowing that I will soon die has made me reflect upon my own life and I know I have been blessed. George and I were content together, but when you came along you made us even happier. You completed our family. I am sorry for lying to you son and for not having the courage to tell you who your birth father was. You have the right to know.

Your loving mother

Lily looked perplexed. 'I am truly sorry, Oliver. This must be a terrible, terrible shock for you. But I don't understand what this has to do with us?'

He pulled his birth certificate out from the second envelope, placing it flat on the table.

'Here,' he said, almost in a whisper, pointing to his birth father's name.

For a moment, Lily said nothing, but just stared at her own father's name in disbelief. She looked anxiously at Oliver. 'How can this be? It can't be real?'

'It is. Why wouldn't it be? Mother hid this certificate from me. She lied to me. She told me it was lost a long time ago and I had no reason to doubt her.'

Oliver saw the fear in her eyes. 'Lily, I want more than anything for this to somehow be wrong. I can still hardly believe that Vincent Sanders, your father, is also mine, but I don't see how my mother could be mistaken. She knew George could not have children.'

A chill ran through her. She sat, motionless. 'You're right, this does change everything,' she said sadly. 'God, Oliver, we're half brother and sister.'

'I'm so sorry,' he said, equally distraught. 'I've been running this through my head all night. Mother knew that Vincent had died, it's in her letter, so she must have heard what happened. She also may have known that you and your mother moved away. She had no reason to think that the two of us would ever meet, yet alone... fall in love.'

Lily could only look in dismay at him. Had it not been so heart-breaking she would have laughed out loud at the sheer irony. She had finally found someone special, someone she wanted to be with, only to find out he was her step-brother. Worse than that, they had spent the night together as man and woman. She felt ashamed and devastated.

Oliver looked helplessly on as she gathered up her things. Yesterday morning he couldn't wait to see her again and spend the whole weekend together. Now, because of a single piece of paper, everything was ruined. He had lost her.

'Can't you stay awhile and talk?' he asked. 'I know things can never be the same between us, but that doesn't stop me caring about you. And that night we spent together... God, I don't know... it didn't feel wrong.'

Lily couldn't trust herself to speak. Grabbing up her bag, she smiled weakly but couldn't stop the tears as she walked out the door.

CHAPTER 25

Lily drove towards the motorway, feeling weary and downright miserable. It was hard to take in what had just happened, but one thing was certain. It was over between her and Oliver; there was no going back for them. She had not got the chance to meet Megan, but from what she had learnt of her, she and her own father, Vincent, seemed an unlikely union, even if it had only been for one night. They would have moved in very different circles. She remembered how her father behaved around other women. Always flirting and laughing too loud, leaning in just that bit too close. Once, she had seen him kissing a much younger woman. The pair of them had sneaked away from a group of people milling around downstairs. Lily had been walking by her father's study door when she had heard a noise. She'd pushed the door open very slightly and there he was, fawning all over an attractive brunette. They were kissing and giggling like teenagers. She had quietly backed out and walked away before they saw her. Her father had been no saint. The more she discovered about him, the more disappointed she felt. Not a good father and an even lousier husband.

She approached the slip road and the imminent refuge that was Bristol, the familiar contours of the landscape opening out onto more level plains, when she was struck by something… she didn't want to leave. At the last moment, she changed lane and drove back the way she'd come, this time heading for Penwyth House. She had told Joe she would see him that weekend to talk about what would be happening up at the house over the coming weeks and what to expect. She wished with all her heart it could have been with Oliver by her side, but so be it. It didn't mean she should turn her back on everything else. She was going to have to try very hard not to think about him. To bury what had happened. After all, she was good at that.

A short time later, she was driving slowly through the orchard of her newly acquired estate – another fact that was still hard to fathom. She pulled in for a moment to gather her thoughts before making her way to Joe's cottage. She noticed up close for the first time the recently pruned apple trees standing dark and naked, their trunks glossy with the green of lichen. A movement in the thick branches of one of the trees startled her. A pure white peacock dropped to the ground and ruffled its feathers before strolling in front of her car. She watched in disbelief as it sauntered across the road to the trees on the other side. She smiled, despite herself. It had to be Joe's. He had always loved birds and had enjoyed taking care of her mother's aviary.

A few minutes later, Lily stepped out on to the drive. Even with her coat on, a sharp coastal wind buffered her. In the unseen distance, waves smashed against the rocks like angry, watery fists. She turned away from the house and walked to Edhen Cottage. She knocked, but there was no reply, so she decided to keep walking, the woods protecting her from the sideways wind blowing in from the sea. As she passed under the eaves of the outer trees at the far side of the woods, what took Lily by surprise the most was the noise; the twittering and chirping of what sounded like hundreds of birds.

She had all but forgotten about the small clearing that opened up in front of her. Two massive Victorian glasshouses with arched roofs that, as children, she and Alice had happily dived in and out of all summer long. In one, her mother had grown her beloved orchids, delicate brightly coloured blooms in hues of pink, white, yellow, and blue. The girls had spent many hours sitting amongst the flowers, or in the second glasshouse where produce was grown for use in the kitchen, the air full of the earthy smell of tomatoes and herbs.

Most of the glass panes were gone. Instead, heavy netting had been erected and attached at various points of the framework. She approached open-mouthed, in awe of the spectacle before her. Joe was sitting inside. He was facing away from her and looked to be mending part of the netting. She slid the door open and quietly shut it behind her. Not that he would have heard her above all the commotion. Grass had grown up through its base along with a few young trees. Large pots filled both sides of a narrow walkway containing all manner of evergreens, tall tropical plants, and palms. Dispersed amongst all of this, mounted on small shelves and makeshift tables, were orchids. Dozens of plants laden with exotically shaped petals or elegant tubers that formed a stunning rainbow of colours adorning the green. Above her, she could see small bird tables attached at varying heights to the framework and long, horizontal perches that ran the length of the roof. Finches, canaries, and even parakeets were perched in groups or flitting about, darting and swooping between the trees and flowers. The air around her was alive with birds.

Ever since she had seen the framed photo of her mother at Edhen Cottage, she had known in her heart that it was Joe who had written the notes hidden in her book. On more than one occasion she had wanted to ask him, but could not seem to find the words. Now, being here in this beautiful place, so full of vibrant life and colour, she knew that it was built on love. It was an ode to her mother. She felt overwhelmed that one person could still be so dedicated to someone that they had not seen for over twenty years; overwhelmed, but also sad.

'Lily!' he called, beckoning her to come to him. There was a small crow perched on the table next to him. 'Oh, don't mind Roy, he's harmless. I fixed his wing six months ago but he flies a bit crooked, so most of the time he hangs around here now.'

She chased thoughts of Oliver into a dark corner of her mind and, as Joe stood to greet her, she hugged him tight.

'Well, that's what I call a welcome,' he smiled.

'Joe, this place is unbelievable. It's so beautiful!' she exclaimed. 'How long has it been like this?'

'Well, a long time, but it kind of happened slowly.'

She noticed more netting was hung between the two glasshouses, forming a tall walkway between them.

'May I?' she gestured towards the makeshift tunnel.

'Yes,' he beamed. 'I'll show you.' They walked through to the other glasshouse that was filled with more lush greenery and orchids. In this one, Joe had built a waterfall that trickled down a purpose-built rockery into a large, raised pond. There were fewer birds in here and a bench for sitting placed near to the water.

'Shall we sit?' Joe asked, pulling some plastic padding from underneath a nearby table. 'Here, this is clean,' he grinned as a finch landed briefly on his shoulder before skimming off across the pond. Now she knew why he was sometimes hard to track down. The estate no doubt kept him busy enough, but the rest of the time she imagined he was right here, in this magical place that he had secretly created.

They sat side by side watching the birds on the water. Joe spoke first...

'I cannot begin to imagine what it must have been like for you back then,' he said. 'You so young, losing Alice and your father like that. I grieved for your family... for your loss. When you and Elizabeth suddenly left not long after, there was this gaping hole left behind. I didn't know what to do next. Luckily, as you know, Timothy asked me to stay on cos, to be honest, I had nowhere else to go. I hoped for many years that one day you and your mother might return. In the meantime, I was kept busy with the estate. I enjoyed the work, still do. But, as I've got older, I've had to slow down a bit.

Let some of the less important jobs go. When you first left, the glasshouses were no longer needed to grow produce and, over the years, the panes got damaged in high winds and storms. Your mother's aviary had also seen better days, so I decided to move her birds into here. Over time, the number of birds increased, partly through them breeding, but I also collected a few lame ones along the way and others just flew in! The plants and orchids I nurtured, and they just seemed to have increased along with the birds. Now, as you can see,' he smiled, 'it is something of a passion.'

'What I see – is a little corner of paradise. It truly is lovely here.' Lily watched two yellow finches dozing high up on a perch. 'I'm guessing the white peacock I saw in the orchard is yours, too?'

'Ah, that's Percy. In the orchard, you say? He shouldn't have roamed that far, it's a bit too near the road. I'll try round him up later. He hatched out from a breeding pair I took on years ago. I've others, too, that fly in and out. Injured birds mostly that I've helped, who can't quite seem to cut the apron strings!'

Lily smiled. He was full of surprises. 'The orchids remind me of Mother,' she said. 'I think she loved them nearly as much as her birds.'

'Aye, she did.'

'Joe…' she said softly. 'I found the notes you sent her. They were in Mother's bedroom, hidden in one of my old storybooks.'

He looked stunned. 'Notes? I didn't know she had kept them. I'm sorry, Lily, I never meant to cause you or anyone any upset. It just happened… I loved her very much and I would have done anything for her. Anything.'

Lily squeezed his hand reassuringly. 'It's okay.'

He sighed. 'Elizabeth once told me that when she first met your father they were happy and very much in love. But, as the years went by, his drinking got worse and he spent more and more time away from her and Penwyth House. It was about then that your mother decided to keep birds. It was something, she told me, she had always wanted to do. So, I built her an aviary and we learnt together how to properly care for its residents. We laughed a lot and enjoyed each other's company. I fell in love with her. It's as simple as that and, for a while, she loved me too. I truly believe she did.'

'Go on,' said Lily softly. 'Please.'

Joe paused for a moment and looked at her. 'Do you remember much about your father?'

'I remember his drinking. He would get angry and shout a lot at Mother, and us if we didn't make ourselves scarce. Sometimes he would disappear for days on end. I used to like it when he did, but Mother used to get upset.' Lily fell quiet for a moment, thinking. 'It wasn't always like that. They used to laugh together sometimes, but I think towards the end things were pretty bad between them. In the summer months, it was easier. I would take Alice away from the house and we'd spend whole days playing in the woods or following you around in the gardens.' She looked at Joe and smiled.

'So, it will be no shock to you to know just how much your father's drinking spiralled out of control,' replied Joe. 'One day, Elizabeth came to find me, she was upset. Your father had come home drunk, out of his mind. She said he taunted her, told her he could have any woman he liked. She had screamed at him that she didn't care what he did any more, just so long as he left her alone. He grew angry and struck her across the face. Her eye was bruised for days. In the end, I think that's why she finished things between us. We had been seeing each other for over a year and we were happy – so happy when we were together. But she was afraid of what he might do to me if he found out. I pleaded with her, said that I would tell him we were in love and that she was going to leave him. But she was scared, begged me not to. Anyway...'

He sighed and shook his head slightly before continuing. 'That was that. She broke it off between us and I think she tried hard to make it work with him. He never knew of our affair. Things were okay for a while, she even got him to stop drinking, but it didn't last. By the time Alice came along, he had gone back to his old ways, staying out late and coming home drunk. It broke my heart to see Elizabeth unhappy and to not be able to help her, or be with her, but I stayed here, anyway… in case she needed me.' Joe lowered his head, visibly upset. 'In the end, though, I failed her.'

'What do you mean you failed her?'

'That night, I don't know what happened on the roof, Lily. But maybe if I had been stronger, tried harder to get her to leave him…'

'It's not your fault,' said Lily. 'None of it is. My father broke her heart…' She spoke gently, not wishing to upset Joe further. 'I see now how difficult things must have been for her, and I'm glad that she at least found some fleeting happiness with you.'

They sat quietly watching the birds on the water, both lost in their thoughts. For a short time Lily felt cocooned in Joe's sanctuary, protected from the wind by the aviary's tropical plants and trees…

Lily awoke with a start. Not to the sound of birds calling, as they were mostly roosting now, but by a loud rattling sound. For a moment, she was confused as to where she was. The wind had picked up and was tugging at the netting like a spiteful child. She peered upwards, noticing for the first time lots of holes and tears in the fabric. She was slumped against a cushion that Joe must have fetched. Her neck was stiff from dozing at an awkward angle and a dull pain pulsed in her forehead.

'You okay?' he asked from somewhere behind her.

'Yes…' She twisted round to see him reaching from a ladder to attach some newly patched netting to part of the glasshouse frame. 'Sorry! I can't believe I fell asleep like that!'

'No problem. You must have needed it,' Joe smiled kindly down at her.

'How long was I asleep?'

'About an hour,' he replied. 'I was gonna wake you soon. It looks like there's rain coming. It might be best if we head off.'

Lily shivered. She was tired after her restless night on Oliver's couch. Instead of bringing him along to meet Joe this weekend, her world had been turned upside down. She could have easily high-tailed it back to Bristol. If she had, she would not have discovered Joe's beautiful bird sanctuary, or discovered his true feelings for her mother. She wondered what other secrets were hidden behind Penwyth's solid, unyielding walls.

CHAPTER 26

At first, Julia wasn't sure that anyone would show. The colourful bunting that she and Marcus had spent hours hanging the day before was flapping wildly in a bracing sea breeze. Two recently acquired stone Labradors, affectionately named Bert and Ernie after the *Sesame Street* characters, sat either side of the front gate wearing little red and white scarves she had hastily knitted, and a blue and red 'Welcome!' banner hung above the hut door. Inside, a large tea urn bubbled and churned.

'Don't worry,' Marcus said reassuringly. 'It's only ten-forty.' The leaflets that he had done his best to distribute around Lostmor had stated a 10.30 am start for 'Fern Retreat's Much Anticipated Opening Day!'

Sure enough, five minutes later, several cars crawled up the drive. Families bailed out with their kids wrapped up warmly and dogs bouncing on leads, barking excitedly. The gathering crowd was welcomed with hot drinks or squash and homemade cookies. By lunchtime, a dozen cars were squeezed into the gravelled parking area and the urn was on its second refill. People wandered along the wooden walkway decorated with more bunting that ran the length of the large, currently empty kennels.

Julia explained how each run had a comfy bed, toys, and piped music and that the private sleeping areas at the rear of each kennel were heated and housed a second bed. Only eight kennels were built, she continued, so that she had the time to give each dog lots of attention and lots of exercise. Marcus's job was to show people the paddock and encourage people to let their dogs (where practical and safe!) run and play whilst they were there. Grateful parents let dogs and kids loose to let off steam, while they looked on, sipping steaming hot mugs of tea. By late afternoon, most people had drifted away and Julia was counting the number of provisional bookings she had taken.

'Fifteen! Not bad, eh?' she said to Marcus, who had just returned from his last tour of the exercise area.

'Well done. That's a good result, isn't it?'

'Yes, promising,' she smiled, reaching up to kiss him. 'I think it's mostly down to your marketing skills. You must have posted a lot of leaflets?'

'A fair amount, but I'd put some on the bar too. I enjoyed it today, you know. It was fun watching the kids throwing balls and their dogs tearing around. Horace loved it, too, didn't you boy?' Horace grumbled an acknowledgement of his name, but his eyes remained rooted on the now empty tray of cookies. There was always hope.

'Why don't you come over to the pub tomorrow night?' said Marcus. 'Susie and Andy are both working behind the bar, so I'm sure we can sneak a few drinks in later on? You haven't seen my bachelor pad yet, have you?' he winked.

'Is Bella invited?' Julia asked as they locked up the hut for the day.

'Goes without saying. Come on,' he said, hugging her. 'You may as well come to mine for a change. Once your doggie clientele start rolling in, you may never get the chance to leave again!'

She laughed. 'Who knows? At this rate, I might even need to hire some help.'

Later that evening, a few couples enjoying a quiet drink gradually turned into a livelier affair, as more people took refuge from the cold and the Black Dog Inn filled with younger locals meeting up for a few pints.

'I'll be with you in a minute!' Marcus said, pulling draught beer and trying to keep track of who was next. He nodded and accepted the note being proffered. 'A bit busier than I thought,' he said to Julia, who was perched on a stool at the end of the bar.

'So I see! Don't mind me. I'm just enjoying being out on a Saturday evening,' she said, sipping a pint of bitter.

He returned a few minutes later. 'It's always busier on the weekend, but it should die down soon. The kids usually head off to the trendier bars or "Revellers", the night club on the edge of town.'

Sure enough, by 10.00 pm the room suddenly emptied, and standing room-only reverted to people sitting in booths or alcoves. Marcus and Julia moved to a small table by the window. Julia gazed at the street lights lining the harbour front. There were strings of multicoloured bulbs hanging between the lights and a dazzling full moon illuminated the clear sky, transforming the black water of the bay into sparkling shards of light.

'It's a good place for a pub,' she smiled. 'Atmospheric inside and out.'

'It does the job for me,' Marcus replied, leaning back on a chair that looked way too small for his frame. Sometimes, he worried that he had become involved with Julia too fast. Not that he had changed his mind about her – quite the opposite, but he felt he had taken his eye off the ball by spending so much time with her. After all, he had only moved here because it was near to where Rose died and he had been hell-bent on finding her killer – that hadn't changed. But Julia was a distraction, a very lovely one who had softened his edges. She had made him feel better than he had in a long time and she had given him something else – hope. Hope for the future. Nothing would ever bring Rose back. He had lost her and he still had nights when he was back on the edge of that precipice. Just not as often.

As the weeks passed, his heart felt a little lighter. Walking the coastal path to Fern Retreat, with Horace bouncing alongside him, lifted his spirits. More often than not, Julia would be outside waving enthusiastically when she saw him coming over the brow of the hill. Whenever he could get away from the pub, he was at Fern Retreat and, if he wasn't needed for the evening shift, would stay over. He helped lay gravel to form the new parking area, fixed the front gate and lifted Bert and Ernie into their prime welcoming position. After several years of solitude, he was surprised how easily he and Julia had fallen into step. She was bubbly and easy-going and he loved how her ponytail swished when she walked and the dimples that appeared high up on her cheeks every time she smiled or laughed, which was often. But she wasn't just a distraction. He cared about her.

'Marcus!' Andy shouted across the bar, interrupting Julia who was chatting excitedly about what her first week of running Fern Retreat might be like.

'There's someone on the phone asking for you.'

Marcus couldn't think of a single person. 'Who?'

'Amanda, Maggie's daughter?'

That was the moment the shutters went down. When everything good that had happened to him since coming to Lostmor slipped away and a familiar feeling emerged – retribution.

CHAPTER 27

'Hello, is that Marcus, Marcus Cole?'

'Yes, hello Amanda. Is everything alright?' He could hardly hear her above the noise of 'Sweet Child O' Mine'. 'Can you hold on?' he half-shouted. 'I'm in the bar. I'll go upstairs so I can hear you.' He glanced over at Julia mouthing 'sorry', then asked Andy to put the phone down when he had picked up. He closed the door on the humdrum below and grabbed the phone. 'Thanks, Andy...' There was a clunk, then silence.

'Hi Amanda, are you still there?'

'Yes, can you hear me now?'

'Yes. This is a surprise. How are you and your family?' he asked, squeezing between Horace and Bella on the couch.

'We're all fine, thanks,' replied Amanda. 'Look, I know this is a bit out of the blue, but you did say to call you if Ellie or my mum remembered anything about the day of the accident.'

'Yes, of course. What is it?'

'I've found something in Ellie's room that may be of interest. I was moving the furniture because we are going to redecorate in there. She's getting a bit too old for fairy-themed wallpaper.'

'I see.' He tried to be patient.

'Anyway, I found a little silver trinket, a dragon's head, behind her chest of drawers. I asked her what it was because I hadn't seen it before. At first, she seemed unsure, but then she remembered and looked a bit worried...' Amanda paused. Marcus waited. 'She told me she found it on the road that day... where the accident took place.'

'Please, go on,' he said.

'After the collision, when the biker had gone and she couldn't wake Mum up, she got out of the car. As you know, she ran up and down the road for some time hoping someone would come. She remembers that she tripped and fell, and that was when she saw something shiny among the leaves. So she picked it up and put it in her pocket. By the time someone finally arrived, she was back in the car and found clinging to my unconscious mum. She told me today that, when she got undressed that evening, the dragon's head fell out of her pocket and she thinks she might have put it in a little bowl on top of her chest of drawers. She keeps hair slides and bits of jewellery in it. After that, she forgot all about it. Anyway, she must have knocked the bowl over at some point for the dragon's head to have ended up behind the drawers. There were a few other slides back there, too. I guess I'm not a very good cleaner because I think it's been there ever since... I realise it could have already been on the road, but I thought it would do no harm to take it into work.'

'Work?' Marcus probed.

'I work in a jeweller's.'

'Sorry, I remember now.'

'I wanted to see if anyone had seen anything like it before. It looked like it was part of a bracelet perhaps. I told my manager it was just something I found in the street. It turned out he recognised what it was straight away because he used to work in a kind of antiques and collectables shop that sold accessories for bikers... he says he's pretty sure it's part of a wallet chain.'

'A wallet chain? What's that?'

'That's what I said. Apparently, one end attaches to a person's belt and the other end fastens to a wallet that's maybe kept in a jeans pocket. He said that, more often, the chain is just hooked on to a belt and worn as a fashion accessory. He thinks the rest of it may either be made up of similar heads linked together, or perhaps scales to form a kind of snake body. I know it might not be relevant, or of any help, but you're welcome to have it.'

'I'm not sure, but yes I would like to see it.'

'You can have it. It's of no use to us.'

'Well, I appreciate you thinking of me.' Marcus paused for a moment. 'I take it you haven't mentioned this to the police yet?'

'No...' replied Amanda. 'I was in two minds, but... well, I'm not sure why I've contacted you instead... it just felt like the right thing to do.'

*

Amanda and her family lived on Julyan Close, a cul-de-sac off West Hill high street. Ellie was on a sleepover and Amanda's husband, Peter, was out for the evening. Marcus wondered if she had deliberately waited for Peter to be out before phoning him, perhaps avoiding a debate about who they should hand the dragon's head to – him or the police. Either way, it was her decision.

Marcus thanked Amanda again and stuffed the small trinket inside his jacket pocket. His mind was racing as he drove back towards Lostmor. He also felt bad about leaving Julia like that in the bar. Not surprisingly, she had looked bewildered when he'd dashed for the door, promising to explain as soon as he got back. Maybe he could trace where the wallet chain had been purchased, but it was a long shot. There were a lot of antiques and bric-a-brac shops in Lostmor. That was if it had even been bought locally, plus it must have been bought at least a year ago, or longer.

The road back to Lostmor was incandescent, bathed in moonlight. His thoughts were interrupted by the sight of a large white transit van. It was pulled up in a lay-by. Its lights were off, but he glimpsed the face of the man in the driver's seat as he drove past. He looked heavyset, with short thick hair. A couple of things struck Marcus. Firstly, he recognised the man and, secondly, why was he sitting in a van late at night, in the middle of nowhere, right next to Oliver Bligh's farm?

'Fuck it,' Douglas muttered under his breath. He hadn't noticed the truck's headlights in his rear mirror, or heard it approaching until it was almost upon him. Luke was down by the side of the van, screened from the road and busy watching the farm through a gap in the hedge.

'Luke! Get back in here.'

'What's up? He's gone by, hasn't he?'

'Yes, but he was staring at me.'

Luke got back into the van, sliding the side door quietly shut. 'Who was it? Do you know him?'

'I only saw him for a second, but I think it was the guy who runs the Black Dog.'

'It doesn't matter. We're not breaking any laws, are we? Anyway, it doesn't look like Bligh is going anywhere. We may as well get going.'

Luke had also been watching Penwyth House. He had only once seen anyone leaving the estate – last weekend, some hottie in a little red car. Whoever she was, he hadn't seen her since and she had a face you would remember. After she had driven off, he had waited a good hour before approaching on foot. It had been dark, so he had kept to the drive for as long as he dared, then crept closer, making his way along the edge of woodland until he could see the ominous outline of the mansion house. There were no lights on inside or cars parked out front. The place looked dead.

He had since been back three times, always in the dark and each time he became more convinced that no one was living there. Last time, he had even walked right up to the front door. He had peered through the leaded window, but even with the small torch he had brought, it was difficult to see in. Luke was tempted to smash the window there and then, but then what? His van was out on the road. He needed it to be closer and he needed Doug with him for that. If the place was uninhabited, he realised it was unlikely they were going to find expensive jewellery or mounds of cash lying around. No, he was thinking more along the lines of brassware, antiques, even paintings. He didn't know the value of things, but if they got lucky in there, he would take what looked valuable and what they could carry.

Having walked around the side of the house and discovered steps down to a basement door, Luke had made his way back to the road. He was beginning to feel more optimistic about his brother's plan. He still didn't know Oliver Bligh's connection to the place, but every time he'd driven by the farm Bligh had been home and not once did he come out when Luke had been watching. He'd decided that, when he had seen Bligh that day at Penwyth, he was probably just there on business. Being local, he was bound to know everyone. Maybe he was doing some work for them, fixing machinery or working on the estate? Whatever it was, he wasn't going there regularly. When Luke had first seen the woman drive out, he had wondered whether she and Bligh were an item. Luckily, it wasn't looking so likely now. It could have complicated things, having him sniffing around.

Douglas started the engine and pulled out, only flicking his lights on when they had passed the farm. He had talked Luke into letting him come because he was getting bored at home. He liked the idea of spying on people. Luke hadn't wanted him there because, the truth was, he was too noisy and too unpredictable. Luke had convinced him he was needed more at home. To tidy up the garage and make some space. The place was a mess and who knew if they might need room to stash things after 'the job'?

A lot of their old man's belongings were still in the garage, including his old Triumph motorbike. Douglas had mentioned before about rebuilding it. He was good with mechanical stuff. Luke had suggested that, once they had made room, Douglas could strip the bike down in one corner, and wouldn't it be great to try to get it going? So, for most of the week, Douglas had been preoccupied with dismantling and cleaning its parts, which was fine by Luke. It had not only kept him sober, but out of his hair, too. But, yesterday, Douglas had reached a hiatus. He was waiting for a new battery and spark plugs he'd ordered at Tasker's garage. When Luke had said he was going to drive by Bligh Farm one last time, Douglas had wanted to tag along, so he had relented. Hell, he had even let him drive.

Not too far ahead of them, Marcus was driving back towards the Black Dog when, on impulse, he pulled in on the left of the high street. It was the only main road into Lostmor, so unless the van had turned around or disappeared up a side street, it might pass by. Sure enough, a few minutes later, it passed him. Marcus pulled back out, making sure he kept some distance behind. The van drove through and then out of town.

Once on the coastal road again, Marcus slowed a little in case Douglas Holt caught sight of his headlights. When the van finally turned left into a hidden lane, Marcus pulled in just before and turned off his lights. He decided not to follow, just in case he gave himself away. He could see the rear lights of the van growing smaller, then disappearing from view. He was pretty sure there was a house hidden away down there, but he swung the truck around and headed back to town. He didn't know what Douglas was up to, but he intended to find out. And now, he knew where he lived.

CHAPTER 28

Julia sat waiting for Marcus to return. It was gone midnight by the time Susie and Andy had locked up and headed off. She had let Horace and Bella out and was now staring at an old Hitchcock black and white movie with the volume turned down. She was worried about him. Was it all too good to be true? When he had strolled into her life she had been instantly drawn to him. Marcus was forty-two, ten years older than her; he was not handsome in the traditional sense, but attractive in a rugged kind of way. She liked how his eyes creased at the corners when he smiled and his voice was strong and pleasantly deep. The first morning when she had woken up with him by her side, she had looked in awe at the manly body in her bed. Listening to the sound of his slow, rhythmic breathing, she lightly ran one hand down the solid, hard contour of his back, more for reassurance that he was actually there than to wake him.

It was the first time she had been with anyone since splitting from her long-term partner, Clive, three years earlier. Leaving him had been a lightbulb moment – a moment of clarity, when she realised that, if she didn't follow her dream, it would never happen. So that was it. She left her office job in recruitment and started looking for suitable premises to open up a boarding kennels. Now, she had made that dream come true and opened the doors of Fern Retreat. And she had gradually stopped worrying that she and Marcus were moving too fast. True, they had not been together long, but he was one of the good guys. She was certain of it. She chose not to dwell on the feeling that he was holding something back from her and that he was guarded when she had asked about his family.

There was not much to tell, he had shrugged. He had enlisted in the army at a very young age and, not long after, he had married Rebecca. The army had become a huge part of his life, which had meant he was away from home much of the time. They had never had children and, after ten years of waiting and hoping that he would finally leave the army, his wife had met someone else. They separated and she filed for divorce.

Marcus had been distant with Julia after telling her that. However, it was not for long and not in a standoffish way. More like he was reliving something. He seemed… temporarily not present and it was unnerving. She had asked him what was wrong. He had smiled and said it was nothing, but there had been a glint of something else behind those steely grey eyes. Something hard to read and she had seen that look again… tonight, when he had headed for the door. What, she wondered, was so urgent that he had to rush off late at night to see this woman, Amanda? And now here she was, sitting in his apartment waiting and wondering if she had been wrong to trust her instincts.

'Hi,' he said, suddenly appearing in the doorway. He threw his keys down and sat heavily in the adjacent armchair.

'You okay?' she asked.

'Yep, I'm fine. And I'm sorry.' Marcus leant forward and cupped her hands in his own. 'I'm sorry for running out on you like that.'

'What is going on, Marcus?'

He looked at her anxiously. 'Do you fancy a nightcap? There are some things I need to tell you.'

'Okay.'

Marcus poured them both a whiskey and sat beside Julia on the sofa. 'I haven't been completely honest with you... I guess it was partly my way of dealing with what happened.' He paused, trying to find the words. 'My marriage to Rebecca and my time in the army is all true. But I didn't tell you about our daughter... Rose.'

'Rose?' said Julia in surprise. 'You have a child? Why would you not tell me that?'

He took a large swig of his drink before replying. 'I did have a child. She died in an accident... she was on the back of a motorbike that collided with a car head-on... over a year ago now.' He spoke quietly, his voice faltering.

'I'm so sorry, Marcus...' said Julia. No wonder he'd seemed distant, she realised. He was still grieving for his daughter. 'Why didn't you tell me?' she asked gently.

'I should have, I know that now...' replied Marcus. 'It wasn't intentional... not telling you. I guess I'm used to keeping things to myself, more so since I lost Rose. When I first moved here, I didn't want people to know who I was. Partly because it was easier, I didn't want sympathetic eyes following me wherever I went or hearing whispers of "that's Rose Cole's father". I should say Rose Tindall, as that's the name she was referred to by the papers. I always hated the fact that Rose took Roger's surname when he married Rebecca. Ironically, though, when I moved here, it meant no one would link my surname to her... now, I expect most people won't remember.'

He paused for a moment, taking another sip of his whiskey. 'I hadn't seen Rose for over six months when she died. I was out of the country... stationed in Croatia. The man she was with had been driving recklessly and the bike had been stolen. He was solely responsible for her death and for seriously injuring an elderly lady driving her granddaughter to school. For a few weeks after it happened, Rebecca's face became synonymous with the accident. Photos of her were shown in the papers and on TV in appeals to the public to come forward if anyone knew anything or suspected anyone, but the bike rider was never caught.'

'How awful,' said Julia softly. 'I cannot begin to understand what you have been through... are still going through...' She took his hand. 'Is that why you moved here? For a fresh start?'

'Not exactly,' he paused.

Julia studied his face, looking for answers. 'Tell me, please don't shut me out.'

'I promise... I won't, ever again,' Marcus said, putting his arm around her.

'Then tell me... tell me everything... starting with Amanda.'

So he did. He told her about the day he lost Rose, of how he had hoped and waited for the police to track her killer down. He told her how he had discharged himself from the army after twenty-two years' service because he could not cope with losing his daughter. And, he confessed that the only reason he had moved to Lostmor was because it was close to where the collision had taken place. It was as good a place as any to start hunting Rose's killer down. Finally, Marcus told her about his visit to see Maggie, Amanda, and Ellie.

Julia looked bewildered. 'So, why did Amanda call you this evening?'

'Because of this,' he said, pulling out the silver dragon's head and placing it on the coffee table. 'When I met her, I asked if she would contact me if Maggie or Ellie ever remembered anything that could help me find the biker. I didn't honestly expect to hear anything. But tonight, out of the blue, she rang. That is why I left in such a hurry.' Marcus then explained how Ellie had found the trinket, then how Amanda had later discovered it and told him what it might be.

'I am sorry,' he added, 'but the chance to finally get my hands on this... something tangible, however small. You never know, it may help in some way...'

'It's okay,' said Julia, squeezing his hand. She still had questions, but they could wait.

Marcus continued. 'I drove to Norfolk to meet Maggie King – that's how I came to be at Fern Retreat. I didn't want to drag Horace along, it was too far and I couldn't take him to Maggie's house.' His eyes shone darkly in the low lamplight. 'It's because of you, Julia, that I feel like life is worth living again. For a while, I thought that was impossible... I admit there were times when I had thought of taking my own life.'

'But you didn't,' she empathised.

'No, I didn't,' Marcus replied. 'And even though I miss Rose every single day, and will do for the rest of my life, I promise you those darkest of days are behind me.' He stiffened. 'But I know what I have to do and please don't try and talk me out of it. I'm going to find the man who took my little girl's life. And, when I do, I'm going to kill him.'

CHAPTER 29

It was late afternoon under a blackening sky, heavy with rain, that Lily drove out of Penwyth Estate, her thoughts reeling after her conversation with Joe in the aviary. Her plans for the house no longer seemed so pressing. She had learnt so much more about him, dear sweet Joe. He was the only person she still knew from her childhood, and he had not only shown Alice and herself kindness all those years ago but had clearly been in love with their mother. And theirs had not been a hasty affair quickly forgotten, a joyless escape for a woman feeling trapped in a loveless marriage. No, they had risked everything for over a year. Her mother had loved Joe, too, but had been afraid of what her husband might do to him. In the end, Joe couldn't have the woman he loved, so instead he had created the most beautiful aviary — as homage to the woman he adored. He had lost her... *Just as I have lost Oliver*, she thought sadly.

Without her even noticing, a low fog had crept up over the cliff tops, flowing like volcanic lava across the landscape, smothering everything in its path. Lily flicked her fog lights on and tried to focus on the road ahead. A hotel or B&B for the night would do. She couldn't face the long drive back to Bristol now. Then, just as the first twinkling lights of Lostmor came into view, her car began to lose power. She checked the petrol gauge. The tank was still half full. Try as she might to accelerate, the car slowed to a stop.

'No, no, no! Not now, please…' Lily thumped the steering wheel in exasperation. She turned the key several times, but the engine was completely dead.

She peered through the mizzled windscreen. The dwindling light and eerie mist created a strange, barren wilderness. She would normally have enjoyed such a dramatic scene, but in these circumstances she felt uneasy. She would either have to call someone, although she wasn't sure who, or make her way on foot to Lostmor. Then, unbelievably and to her relief, she saw headlights in the rear mirror intensifying as the vehicle drew closer. It struck her how vulnerable she was parked on a deserted road alone. Then she considered the alternatives and she was already exhausted.

'Sod it,' she said angrily, flicking her hazard lights on.

Lily jumped out and waved at the vague human outline peering at her through the station wagon's windscreen. The big, square car pulled slowly behind hers. The woman driver twisted as if checking something on the back seat before climbing out.

'Oh hello, I know you, don't I?' she said, peering at Lily. 'The lady who brought Flynn in… yes, it's Lily, isn't it?'

'Good memory!' Lily smiled, relieved to see a friendly face. 'And you're Dr Morgan.'

'Please, call me Janet, everybody does.'

'Well, I am so glad to see you, Janet. My car seems to have completely given up the ghost. Would there be any chance you could drop me off in Lostmor?'

'Of course. This weather is awful and it's nearly dark.'

Luckily, the stretch of road was fairly wide and straight and Lily had managed to steer her car to the side before losing power altogether. 'I hope it's okay to leave it like this,' she said. 'It would be easy to see if not for the fog.'

'Don't worry,' replied Janet. 'It's unlikely anyone will be along now. Even if they do, they'll see it in their fog lights.'

Lily grabbed her overnight bag and gratefully climbed into Janet's car. 'Thank you so much. I've no idea what the problem is. It just died on me. Tomorrow I'll call a garage, but I doubt anywhere will be willing to come out now, and on a Sunday.'

'You're right, not around these parts,' Janet sympathised. 'So, where in Lostmor were you heading?'

'It's a bit of a long story,' said Lily. 'I was meant to leave for Bristol hours ago, but a few things happened unexpectedly and time just got away from me. Before I broke down, the plan was to stay at a hotel or B&B tonight and drive home in the morning, but now I guess I'll have to find out what's wrong with my car first! Perhaps if you could drop me along the front... there has to be something vacant this time of year.'

'Oh, my goodness, it does sound as if you've had a bit of a day of it!' Janet glanced sideways, noticing how pale Lily looked. 'Look,' she added, 'if you haven't actually booked anywhere, why don't you stay at my place tonight? I'm not far from here. It's only me and a few scrawny cats. Oh, and Snowy!' She nodded at the back seat.

Lily turned to see Percy sitting quietly on the back seat pruning his feathers. He looked as if it was the most natural thing in the world for a peacock to be hitching a lift in a station wagon.

'Percy!'

'Percy, huh?' said Janet. 'Ah well, that is a better name than Snowy. It suits him!'

'How come he's in your car?'

'The damned silly thing was in the middle of the road. He was barely visible in the fog, I nearly hit him,' Janet said exasperated. 'He's really quite tame, though. He sauntered up to me and, as you can see, he's not at all phased by any of this. How bizarre! Firstly coming across Percy here, and now your good self... and how do you two know each other, by the way?'

'He must have roamed from Penwyth House,' said Lily. 'It's a few miles back the way you came. He belongs to a friend of mine, Joe. Joe Newman.'

Janet looked across at Lily for a second. 'Well, that's a bit of luck, because now I know where to return him to,' she smiled. 'Ah! Here we are then.' She slowly turned into a lane that wound off to their right. The headlights swung around as Janet parked in front of a small cottage, illuminating a large front garden with an iron rose trellis over the gate.

'Oh, um… are you sure that this is not too much of an inconvenience?' asked Lily.

'No trouble at all,' replied Janet, patting Lily's knee. 'You know, some would say this is the outskirts of Lostmor. But, being a romantic at heart, I like to think that I am living on the edge of the wilderness here on the moors and quite separate from the town itself.' She grinned. 'Come on, let's go in and get warm. I'll come back out for Percy in a moment. He'll be alright in the woodshed for tonight.'

Lily could see that the decision had been made for her. Not that she was ungrateful for being rescued or for the hospitality offered her, but all she wanted now was to sleep – or, at least, try and rest. She didn't feel up to polite conversation or expanding on why her plans had changed.

'Here, why don't you dump your stuff in there?' Janet shoved open a heavy, wooden-latched, low door to a quaint bedroom at the end of the downstairs hallway. 'It has its own en suite. My room's upstairs so it will be nice and quiet for you.'

'Thank you. This really is very kind.'

'Nonsense,' Janet smiled. 'I hope you don't mind me saying, but you do look quite pale. If you would rather just retire for the evening I won't disturb you, but if you are hungry and want to eat first, I do have plenty of leftover chicken and some pasta in the fridge.'

Lily felt guilty. Janet wasn't trying to pry, she was just trying to help, and the mere mention of food unexpectedly caused Lily's stomach to rumble.

'You're right,' she laughed, embarrassed by the sudden, loud growling. 'I am tired, but I've hardly eaten today, so something to eat would be great.'

'Marvellous. Well, I'd better bed down our feathered friend for the night. Come on through to the kitchen whenever you want.'

Lily looked around the cosy bedroom. Janet's home was a bit like Kleger Cottage. Traditional Cornish stone with slate-tiled floors and low-beamed ceilings. There was a watercolour of bluebells in a woodland copse above the bed and another above the dresser of a fox and its cubs curled up in a burrow. She threw a few clothes from her bag on the armchair and washed and changed. She felt a bit better and glad of the distraction. She didn't want to try and process everything that had happened in the short space of one long day.

'I've warmed it through,' Janet smiled, nodding at the stove. 'Help yourself.'

Lily joined her at the table. Two shaggy, tortoiseshells cats were lying flat out on the slabs in front of a wood-burning stove that Janet had just lit.

'That's Fatface,' she said fondly, pointing to the one on the right. Lily supposed his face was quite large, but it was hard to tell through all the long fur. 'And that's Healey, after Denis.'

'Now that I can see!' Lily replied. The slumbering tom obligingly lifted his head; above sleepy eyes were two long, sweeping wisps of dark brown fur.

'Well, that's my family introduced and Percy has been fed,' said Janet. 'He's happily perched on a shelf in the shed.'

'I'm glad he's okay,' said Lily. 'When I get my car fixed I don't mind taking him back home, if you like? It's the least I can do.' She paused, savouring the creamy pasta and chicken. 'Hmm, this is really good, thanks.'

'Thank you… You do have a bit more colour now. Tea, coffee… or something stronger, perhaps?'

'Do you have wine?' Lily asked coyly.

'Yes, splendid,' replied Janet. 'I have an unopened bottle of Chardonnay in the fridge. If you like, I can ring Tasker's in the morning before I head off to the surgery?' she offered. 'It's the nearest garage. I could arrange for them to pick up your car?'

'You've been so kind, Janet. I don't like to impose any more than I already have.'

'Nonsense, they know me so they might react a bit quicker. It's just a phone call. How long it will take to repair it, of course, is anyone's bet. Do you have to get back to Bristol tomorrow?'

'Well, I definitely won't be back to open my shop in the morning,' replied Lily. 'But if I could make it for Tuesday, that would be good.'

'What kind of shop do you have?'

'It's an art gallery, called *The Blue*.'

'You're an artist?'

Lily nodded, polishing off the last of the chicken.

'How interesting,' said Janet. 'I've always wished I could draw, but I'm utterly useless! What sort of thing do you like to paint?' She sat forward, resting her chin in her hands.

'Seascapes or landscapes,' replied Lily. 'Give me a tranquil pink and orange sunrise or a wild, raging storm at sea and I'm at my happiest…' She laughed. 'Sorry, I can be a bit of a bore when it comes to my work!'

'Not at all. It makes a pleasant change to have someone to talk to who is not of feline origin. By the way, did you say Percy comes from Penwyth House? I don't think I know it.'

'Yes, it's a big old place about three miles back up the road.'

'I'm surprised I haven't heard of it. I've been called out to so many farms and smallholdings around here over the years.'

'Well, this is more of an estate,' said Lily, 'but no one has lived there for a very long time. Not for decades. Joe, the man I mentioned earlier, he's a groundsman and stays in a cottage on the estate. He keeps birds. Hundreds of birds, most of them in a giant aviary which I only discovered today. Over the years, he's kind of collected other birds that roam in. I met Percy perched in an apple tree just this afternoon.'

'Goodness!' said Janet. 'So your friend Joe is an aviculturist.'

'Apparently so,' Lily smiled.

The welcome heat from the stove, together with the good food and wine, started to take their effect. Lily's eyes grew heavy and her second wind quickly diminished. If she hadn't felt so tired she would have liked to chat with Janet more; she was kind, funny, and engaging. As it was, she took herself off to bed, where thankfully she fell into a deep, dreamless sleep.

CHAPTER 30

Thanks to Janet, Lily's car was towed away late the next morning. Percy was still ensconced in the woodshed, having polished off a huge amount of grain for breakfast, and the cats were fast asleep. She was glad of the time alone. She needed to think. She longed to phone Oliver, but what would she say? Tasker's rang her a few hours later with the news. They'd got the car running. It was just a faulty alternator that had drained the battery. Relieved, she agreed to pick it up later. She would have to cadge another lift but, as often happened, Janet was waylaid by an emergency. This meant her afternoon rounds were bumped and, by the time they had both returned from Tasker's with Lily's car newly fixed, it was past six o'clock.

'Why don't you stay another night?' said Janet. 'Make a fresh start in the morning?'

'Oh dear, haven't you had enough of me?' Lily replied, laughing.

'Nonsense. It means I will have your company for another evening.'

'If I did, I could return Percy to Penwyth in the morning,' said Lily. 'I admit, I don't much relish driving back to Bristol in the dark, just in case something else goes wrong with the car. It is pretty old.'

'Excellent, excellent!'

'Well then, why don't you let me cook something for tea by means of a thank you for your hospitality?' Lily suggested.

'Okay,' said Janet. 'It would be nice not to have to cook for a change. I'll go feed Percy and then clean up. I hadn't planned what to eat, but I'm not fussy. There's some cod or frozen mince, I think. You're welcome to have a rummage.'

Over a very decent fish pie, Janet chatted merrily away about her busy day and the emergency callout that had delayed her. A local farmer had rung the surgery about a labouring mare. Only one of the foal's legs had emerged. He heeded her advice and managed to get the mare back on her feet instead of trying to forcibly pull the foal out. Janet explained that the change of position had, as she'd hoped, caused the foal to fall back into the uterus. By the time she had driven to the farm, the mare had delivered her foal, none the worse for wear.

Lily was feeling a bit in awe of Janet and how she seemed to take everything so much in her stride. After supper, they plonked themselves on the comfy burgundy sofas in the lounge armed with the rest of the previous evening's wine.

'That was truly delicious, Lily. Feel free to come back and stay anytime,' offered Janet, gently sliding a sleeping Fatface and Healey along the couch.

'You're very generous, considering... well, you don't really know me,' said Lily.

Janet seemed pensive. 'I like to think I'm a good judge of character,' she said, pouring them both a glass of wine. 'How are things going selling your mother's place? Isn't that why you said you were in Lostmor?'

'Yes, it is,' replied Lily. 'But I haven't got that far yet. I've realised now how much work the place needs before I put it on the market. You know the estate I mentioned to you yesterday... Penwyth House? Well, actually that is, or rather was, my family home.'

'The place with Percy and the aviculturist?'

'Yes.'

'Goodness, is that why you were staying at Kleger Cottage?

Because your mother's place is not liveable?'

'Actually, no! Originally, my stay at the cottage was just for the weekend because I thought I was here just to sign some papers for my mother's solicitor… That was before I discovered I even owned the property.'

Janet looked puzzled. 'I'm intrigued. Do tell.'

So, tucked up on the couches with the slumbering cats, Lily shared the past few weeks' unbelievable events, starting with Timothy's revelations about her inheritance and bequeathment of Penwyth Estate, to her meeting with Joe for the first time since she was a child. Janet was a good listener. As the winter's evening drew in, Lily spoke of the notes she had discovered in her childhood book. She explained how amazed she was at discovering Joe's stunning aviary. Finally, and this certainly raised Janet's eyebrow, Lily told her about Joe's confession to having written the notes and of his affair with her mother over thirty years ago.

Janet, had no knowledge of the Sanders' family or their history. Lily had wrongly presumed she was from Lostmor, but it turned out that Janet was born in Dorset having moved sixteen years prior.

'I don't know what to say,' said Janet. 'No wonder you were tired yesterday. You have been on such an emotional roller coaster these past few weeks. And you've been dealing with all this on your own? I mean, returning to your home after what you went through there as a child must have been daunting.'

'It's true,' replied Lily, 'there have been times when I nearly high-tailed it back to Bristol. I could have left things in the capable hands of Timothy to deal with. Funnily enough, though, after the first few visits home – when I was, to say the least, a bit shaky – I started to enjoy going there. I rediscovered childhood places and memories. And meeting Joe again was, of course, very emotional and… revealing.'

She didn't mention Oliver. Her breakup with him was still too raw. And, if she did, she would either have to lie about what followed or tell Janet the shocking truth, and she couldn't betray his confidence over something so deeply personal.

'Well, if you are driving back and forth… to oversee things,' said Janet. 'I meant what I said. You are welcome to stay here.' She smiled, topping their glasses up with the remaining wine. 'Especially if you cook!'

'Thanks, I'd like that. I really would.'

Lily awoke in the early hours of the morning. For a moment, she was unsure of where she was. She had been dreaming again and, despite the cold night, was drenched in sweat. She sat bolt upright trying to recall the details. Once more, she saw herself as a young, frightened child standing in the open doorway to the roof. She hesitated, not knowing what to do. Her father was holding his arms out to Alice, who was running towards him through the rain. As Alice reached their father, her mother shouted at Lily to come down. Then she was running back down the steep stairs as fast as she could, but as her foot reached the bottom step she could go no further. It felt like an invisible force was holding her there. Then, she was once more confronted by the strange, pinched face and hateful eyes.

She awoke with arms flailing, trying to protect herself… but from what, she did not know.

CHAPTER 31

Lily folded down the back seats of her car and, somehow, with help, managed to gently manoeuvre Percy into the back. Janet watched in amusement at the bird's tiny head staring passively out of the rear window as Lily drove off. She pulled up on the estate, near to the woods and bailed out Percy with a gentle shove, who sauntered off none the worse for his little adventure. She had intended to turn around on the drive and head straight back to Bristol, but instead found herself drawn to the house. She took a step back, hands on hips, staring up at the roof. Chimney stacks and spires of varying heights protruded upwards like a giant pumpkin mouth of jagged teeth. *Now is as good a time as any*, she thought.

On impulse, she grabbed the house keys from the glove compartment and, a few moments later, was standing inside gazing at the resplendent staircase. Luckily, the formidable hallway had not been as exposed to the elements as some other parts of the building. Thanks to her previous cleaning attempts, the large dearth of cobwebs and filth – at least, those she could reach – were gone and the newly polished stairs shone majestically in the light streaming in from the dome above.

Lily walked slowly up the stairs, turning left where it divided in the middle. She lightly trailed a now trembling hand along the cool bannister as she made her way up. The house was silent. Today, there was no familiar wind whistling through its chimneys or rattling the windows. She felt at that moment as if the house had been waiting for decades in trepidation of her return. A familiar feeling of dread and foreboding came over her and she felt her heart quicken. She heard voices below – raised voices.

Thursday, 7th June 1971

Lily looked down and saw her father standing in the hallway. He had slammed the door a little too hard behind him. Her mother called out in a raised whisper, 'Ssshh, Vincent, you'll wake the girls.' Her father sloped off into the large parlour room on the right. Lily silently crept down the stairs and hid behind the open door.

'Did you even remember it was Alice's birthday today?' Her mother was seated on one of two claret-coloured, velvet couches placed either side of a large, heavily ornate marble fireplace.

'Of course I did. I got waylaid, that's all,' he slurred.

'Oh please, spare me the thinly veiled excuses.'

Vincent made his way unsteadily to the mahogany dresser and poured himself a whiskey. Elizabeth looked at him with disdain. Once she had been afraid of him, but not any more. Now, she hated him. For all the disappointment and hurt he had caused her and the girls for years. She would have liked nothing better than if, one day, he just didn't come home at all. But life was never that simple.

She was also worried about Lily. She had seen how her daughter looked at Vincent. She had grown wary of him, afraid even. And what about Alice? She was too young to realise yet that her father was a drunk, but she would learn soon enough. Today, Alice had repeatedly asked when Daddy would be home. In the end, her sixth and final birthday had come and gone. School friends had waved goodbye as, one by one, their parents had arrived to pick them up. Laughing and chatting excitedly, clutching balloons and soggy pieces of cake wrapped in paper serviettes.

Elizabeth had tried to console Alice when, at bedtime, she had burst into tears, pleading with her to go and find her Daddy. 'Why didn't he come home, Mummy? He promised he would.'

Elizabeth had read to Alice from a book of fairy tales until she had fallen into a fitful sleep. She had then checked on Lily, who was lying on her bed reading. She would normally have retired for the evening as well, but tonight her emotions were running high. She was angry, angry with herself for not being stronger. If she had been brave enough to leave Vincent years ago, she would not now find herself in this situation. Things could have been different. But she was even angrier with her lazy, drunk, bullying husband and the weak, cowardly man that he had become.

She was on her second glass of wine, but her thoughts were crystal clear. Tonight, she was going to tell him that she wanted a divorce. She knew he would be difficult about it, but she had to tell him, needed to tell him... to make it real. In the morning, she would go see Timothy Walker. She could trust him; he would help her. Vincent could shout and scream at her all he wanted. She wanted out... or, rather, she wanted him out.

'Did Alice enjoy her party?'

'Yes, I think so, no thanks to you. She kept asking when you would be back. At bedtime, she cried because you had promised to be there.'

'Look, I told you I was waylaid. It was business.'

'Don't make me laugh, Vincent. When have you ever done a day's work in your life?'

'Don't push me, Elizabeth, or you'll regret it.'

'Regret? Regret is a word I understand... aren't you wondering why I'm still up? Why I've waited for you?'

'Do tell.' Vincent gave an exasperated sigh.

'I want a divorce,' Elizabeth said quickly. Vincent paused a moment, then swung unsteadily round to face her. She could see a vein in his temple pulsing.

'Don't be ridiculous. Have you gone mad?'

'I can assure you I'm perfectly sane. In fact, I have never been more serious. I will be seeing my solicitor in the morning. I was hoping, for the sake of the *children, that we could be grown up about this. But, either way, I'm leaving you. Or, more accurately, you'll be the one who's leaving. After all, I do own Penwyth Estate, not you.'*

Lily, hiding unseen outside the room, gasped and shrunk back against the wall. She couldn't quite believe what she was hearing. Her mother wanted a divorce and she wanted father to leave them, to leave their home.

'Listen here, you little bitch,' Vincent snarled. 'You are not throwing me out of my own home.' Sitting opposite Elizabeth now, he leant forwards, drunken eyes bulging. He grabbed her roughly by the arms and hissed at her. 'I am your husband. If you insist on doing this, I will fight for my share of everything. I'm entitled to half.'

'No court in the land would hand my inheritance over to you,' replied Elizabeth. 'What have you ever contributed? And what about all your infidelities? Most of the town probably knows. I imagine it would be fairly easy to prove.' Vincent's eyes narrowed.

'I'll take the children.'

Elizabeth was genuinely shocked. She had expected him to fly into a rage. Attack her even, but not this. This was worse.

'Why? What interest have you ever shown in either of them?'

'They're my flesh and blood.'

'You can't just take them, Vincent. I won't allow it. The law won't allow it!'

'The law!' he mocked, pulling her closer still. Elizabeth tried to push him away, but he was good and angry now. He studied her face, then suddenly let go of her, pushing her back against the couch.

'Go ahead! Divorce me, then. See what happens if you do.' Vincent spat the words at her. 'Lily and Alice are mine. If I have to leave this house, you can be sure that, one day, I'll be back for them. You won't know when. Maybe at night when you're sleeping, or I might turn up outside school one afternoon. You can't be with them all the time.' His lip curled in an ugly grin as he rose to refill his glass.

The colour had drained from Elizabeth's face. Vincent knew he had her worried. He was beginning to enjoy himself. 'Maybe I'll take them abroad… a nice new start somewhere… somewhere far from here, where you'll never find them. You think it's just talk? Try me.' He smirked, raising his glass to her.

Elizabeth composed herself and sat up straight. 'Actually, Vincent, they're not strictly speaking yours… at least, not both of them.'

'What do you mean?' He swayed, regarding her suspiciously.

'You're not the only one who strayed from this joke of a marriage.'

'You're lying. I would have known,' he retaliated.

Elizabeth laughed loudly. 'How would you? You weren't around most of the time, and when you were you were drunk… you didn't know what was going on right under your nose.'

He paused, trying to think his way out of the chemical fog shrouding his brain. 'You're telling me what? Alice is not mine? That you slept with someone? That you're a dirty little whore!'

Lily gasped again and this time her hand went to her mouth. She felt sure they would hear her and seek her out at any moment.

'Not Alice… Lily,' said Elizabeth, unphased by his insult. 'It's true, Vincent. But, unlike you, I didn't sleep with just anybody.' She spoke perfectly calmly. 'I had an affair… he made me happy and I loved him.'

'I should have known…' Vincent's face turned red with fury. 'You're nothing but a slut… Who is he?'

'It doesn't matter.' Elizabeth hadn't intended to tell him about Lily. But, now that she had, she was glad. 'He is a good man. He wanted me to leave you so that we could be together. How I wish I'd been brave enough… but I was young. When I realised I was pregnant by him… I was so happy, but I was also scared. Scared of what you might do. So, foolishly, I finished it between us and made out she was yours. I shared your bed for the first time in months, then lied to you about my dates. Everyone thought she'd come a little early. As it turned out, she was a small baby and you never seemed to suspect. There were so many times when you lost whole days through drinking, your memory was fuzzy.' Elizabeth gave a small humourless laugh. 'I even convinced myself for a while. But I always knew.'

'But her birth certificate…'

'I lied.'

Vincent drained his glass and threw it at the fireplace. The sound of the glass smashing propelled Lily into running. She streaked up the stairs as fast as she could and stood breathless behind her bedroom door, her heart pounding out of her chest. She heard her father's angry raised voice and then heavy footsteps coming along the landing. She held her breath.

CHAPTER 32

'Lily, is that you?' Joe shouted through the open doorway. He could just make her out through the shafts of light pouring in through the ceiling dome. She was sitting on the staircase, clinging to the baluster. She was ashen white.

'I saw your car and the door was open… what's happened? You look scared to death!' He quickly went to her, oblivious to the fact that it was the first time in decades he had stepped foot in the house.

'Joe,' she whispered, visibly shaken.

'Are you okay?' he asked, helping her to her feet.

'I'm okay, really, I just felt a bit dizzy. Would you mind if I came back to Edhen for a few minutes?'

'Of course,' said Joe. 'Here, take my arm.'

They made their way slowly to the cottage. Once there, Lily sat on the couch with a blanket wrapped around her, whilst Joe made her a large mug of hot, sweet tea.

'Are you sick? Should I take you to the doctors?' he looked at her anxiously.

'No, I'll be fine, honestly. I was just unnerved…'

Joe passed her the mug. She looked somehow diminished. 'Unnerved by what?'

'Sometimes I have flashbacks...' she began, 'of the night that Father and Alice died... but I can never quite piece things together. And that's what just happened to me. But this time, it was different. It was so vivid. It felt... much more real.'

Joe looked puzzled. 'What did you see?'

'Usually, I see me as a little girl. I see my father standing on the roof in a storm, Alice so little, running to him, my mother calling my name... and something else, too... A face, mask-like and mean looking. I can't explain what it all means, but I always see the same images.'

Joe was bewildered. They had not discussed that night and he was saddened to think that, all this time, she had been suffering frightening images... flashbacks or whatever they were.

'Lily,' he spoke quietly, calmly. 'It was just a terrible, terrible accident and you being just a girl. It's understandable you've had nightmares.' He looked at her and smiled. 'Maybe it's time for you to try and let go... to stop trying to remember?'

'I don't know... I don't think so. Since I came back here, I've learnt so much that I never knew about my family and my past... and about you.' She smiled at him affectionately. 'I want to know the rest. I need to. In the house just then, I remembered something, but it wasn't how I usually recall things, waking up in a cold sweat with echoes of voices chasing around my head. This time, I saw things play out... so clearly... like I was watching a film. It wasn't me on the roof or running this time. I saw a fight between my parents. It just all came flooding back. It was real, Joe. It was the same evening as the accident and I know, without a doubt, that it happened. Don't you see? My subconscious has blocked out what happened, but being back here at Penwyth House... it is finally helping me to remember.'

Joe slowly nodded. 'What were your parents fighting about?'

'Before I tell you... can I ask you one more thing?'

'Yes,' he agreed. 'I will always be truthful with you, Lily. I have nothing to hide... not any more.'

She gazed into his soft, green eyes. They were the same shade of green that the ocean turned in a storm.

'Are you my father?'

Joe felt humbled by her question. 'I mean what I say about being honest,' he replied. 'But the truth is… I'm sorry, but I don't know the answer. Elizabeth told me you weren't mine. It wasn't until she was showing, some months after we had split up, that I realised she was pregnant. By this time we were hardly speaking. She avoided me. Except for one time when we found ourselves alone together… I asked her if the baby was mine. She said no, that you were Vincent's, even though I knew they had not shared a bedroom for a long time. Because of his drinking, she used to lock her door at night.' Joe looked troubled. 'It feels wrong to be speaking this way about your family.'

'It was a long time ago,' said Lily. 'Please, tell me what you know.'

He sighed and sat back in the armchair. 'I remember Vincent had been home more than usual, so your mother and I had not been able to meet for some weeks. She said that, during this time, one night in a drunken rage he had kicked in her bedroom door and forced himself upon her. She tried to fight him off, but he was too strong… Afterwards, she was afraid of what I might do, so she decided not to tell me. She said that's how she knew you were his child, not mine, because we had not been able to see each other for weeks. I am sorry, Lily, this is not an easy thing to try and explain.'

'It's okay… go on.'

'Well… at the time, I believed her. But, years later, after Vincent and Alice were gone…' Joe's mouth twitched slightly. 'And when you and your mother had left, I had a lot of time on my own. A lot of time to think.' He swallowed. 'I always wondered about you.'

'I don't quite know what to say,' said Lily, looking sadly at him through a sheen of tears. 'I'm beginning to understand how terrible this must have been for you, too. You lost everything, and all these years I had hardly given you a thought.'

'You didn't know. How could you?'

Lily wiped her eyes and tried to gather her thoughts. 'Let me tell you what I have remembered,' she spoke softly. 'On the night of the accident, I was downstairs behind the drawing-room door listening to my parents the whole time. My father had come home drunk. He had missed Alice's birthday and Mother was angry with him. I was shocked when I heard her tell him she wanted a divorce and that she wanted him to leave Penwyth House straight away. Things got out of hand. He said that if she made him leave, if he had to give up his home, he would come back and take us girls. Steal us away in the night or when she wasn't around. He taunted her, saying he'd take us abroad and start a new life without her.'

She paused for a moment, recalling the words she'd heard. 'That was when she told him... told him that I was not his child. She told him about her affair and how she had fallen in love with someone, but she wouldn't say who. She told my father that she had only slept with him so he would think I was his child and that, later, she had lied about her dates. She said that, either way, he was so drunk most of the time, she knew he probably wouldn't remember when they'd last been together. The last thing I heard was a glass shattering. He must have thrown it in a fit of rage. I was terrified he would find me listening, so that was when I ran as fast as I could back up the stairs.'

Lily reached for Joe's hand. 'I hope I haven't upset you with all these revelations... But you were right, she did lie to you, but only because she was trying to protect herself and her unborn baby... and, in the end, she told him the truth. Who knows, if events hadn't taken such a terrible turn that night... maybe things would have been different between you both after that.'

'Thank you...' Joe said, his bottom lip quivering. 'Thank you for sharing that with me...' His eyes filled with tears. 'I never forgot about any of you. I always wondered where you were and what you and Elizabeth were doing. And I want you to know that, whatever else you find out, just having you home again has made me a happy man. And… if I really am your father… well, then that is more than I ever dared dream of.'

CHAPTER 33

Back at her apartment, Lily pressed the play button on her answerphone. None of the messages were from Oliver. What had she expected? There was a call from the surveyor, letting her know he was still working on his report for Penwyth Estate. It was a big undertaking, but he would forward it on as soon as he could, along with the invoice. Lily cringed. She imagined the report to be the size of a book and shuddered to think how much it would cost. A few more bleeps from clients enquiring after submissions, another wondering why *The Blue* was closed. Finally, one from Janet.

'Hello, Lily! Just checking you got back safely. Oh, and I hope everything went okay dropping Percy off. Give me a call when you have time. Byeeee.'

She smiled to herself. It was good to hear a friendly voice. She'd also missed three calls on her mobile from a slightly worried Timothy while she'd been with Joe. She had completely forgotten her appointment with him at the weekend. He had attained copies of the deeds for Penwyth House, including plans of the estate showing the layout and its borders. They were supposed to draw up new plans outlining the parcel of land Joe would soon legally own, including Edhen Cottage. He was happy to reschedule, but was just checking she was okay.

The next morning, Lily returned calls and apologised to Timothy for forgetting their appointment. They rescheduled for the following Saturday and he cheerfully agreed to her offer of buying him a drink at the Black Dog afterwards to make amends. That evening, she managed to catch Janet at home. Fatface had killed a mouse and left it in the kitchen as a present. Lily found it hard to believe that as she had not yet seen him upright! She promised to drop by next weekend after her appointment, but Janet was having none of it.

'Why don't you stay over Friday night, then go see Timothy in the morning?'

Lily gratefully agreed. She was look forward to seeing Janet again. Plus, she needed some advice.

Over the coming week, Lily worked long hours either at *The Blue* or in her apartment studio. She welcomed the distraction after her tumultuous last visit to Lostmor. She was still trying to process the fact that her relationship with Oliver had been snatched away from her. She loved him, she knew it in her heart and she knew he felt the same way about her. What a waste. Then there was her last visit to Penwyth, where she'd learnt that the man she had tragically lost all those years ago may well not have been her father, and that her real father was very likely Joe – Joe the groundsman, her mother's lover, the aviculturist extraordinaire. She hoped it was true.

At *The Blue,* she worked on a large rectangular canvas. She blended thick, bold strokes of green and gold to add rolling sun-drenched hills to her late-summer landscape. At the forefront, she used her palette knife to edge in autumnal trees and build up their leafy texture. The scene was taken from a holiday photograph. A cherished memory, shortly to become a piece of art and a wedding anniversary present for her client's wife. She knew it would take most of the week to complete and was enjoying the size of the task and the rustic subject matter. As always happened when she was painting, the hours flew quickly by; but, try as she might, her thoughts kept coming back to Oliver.

Lights flickered on in the shopfronts opposite. Outside, a steady queue of cars crawled towards the brow of the hill, whilst people scurried by, eager to get home. It was early March so the evenings were a little lighter, but tall buildings blocked large segments of the natural light out and the street looked grey and dreary. By six o'clock, Lily finally closed up and made the short walk back to her apartment. The answer machine was stubbornly dormant. No flickering light or repeating bleep.

She felt deflated. Something had shifted – her perception of what mattered. Things that had been important to her just a few, short months ago she found she no longer cared about. Looking around the place she had called home for the past four years, it no longer felt like it. It housed her much-loved studio, of course; but, like the gallery, she didn't own it. It was just bricks and mortar for rent. Why was she here? There was nobody to share this life with. She had pushed people away in the past, kept them at a comfortable arm's length... until Oliver. And Penwyth House. Even though she planned to one day sell it, she liked the feeling of owning her own place, even an insanely huge one. Admittedly, her last visit there had shaken her, but she had got what she wanted, hadn't she? She had hoped returning there would help her to remember – and she had, at least partially.

She sighed and stared out at the same imposing Georgian buildings on the other side of the leafy street. She wished she was snuggled up on the couch at Janet's quaint little cottage, chatting and stroking Fatface and Healey. All she wanted to do was go back to Lostmor as soon as she could. Yes, there were legal things she had to sort out with Timothy, but it was more than that. Lostmor and Penwyth House were beginning to feel more like home than Bristol.

Whenever Lily stopped working for any length of time, her thoughts returned to the events of the past few months and their consequences. She had not had time to fully accept that Oliver was her step-brother, if ever... when she had suddenly been hit by another, equally large, curveball. Bizarrely, if Joe *was* her father as a result of his affair with her mother, and Megan had conceived Oliver as a result of sleeping with Vincent... That would mean they weren't actually related... they *could* be together.

She wanted to see him, to tell him everything she now knew, but what if somehow she was wrong? It seemed pretty certain that Megan was telling the truth and that Vincent was, indeed, Oliver's father. Otherwise, why would she have written such a letter or falsify his birth certificate? Megan had no reason to make such a thing up. And Lily's own mother had not been a vindictive woman, quite the opposite. It seemed more likely that she had lied to Joe to protect herself and her unborn baby, than simply trying to spite her husband in the heat of an argument...

Lily's head throbbed. She no longer felt anything for Vincent. She had tried many times in the past. But who he was as a person had gradually drifted away from her. Or, perhaps he had never been there? She was no longer sure. All she had were vague memories of him either drunk or angry, or both. She wanted to believe Joe was her father so badly, not just because of Oliver but because she had grown close to him.

She sighed, drawing the floor-length velvet curtains on the now amber-lit street. What she needed was proof.

CHAPTER 34

'Hello! Come in, come in!' Janet said, hugging Lily enthusiastically. The welcoming wave of warmth from the kitchen made her feel like she had just touched down in Spain mid-July.

'Hmm... something smells good!'

'Lamb casserole,' Janet beamed, 'but it's not quite ready. Cup of tea?'

'Yes, please, I'm parched. It's taken an age to get here. Traffic jams everywhere.'

'Never mind, you're here now,' Janet sympathised, taking Lily's coat and scarf. 'Why don't you plonk yourself in there?' She nodded towards the living room. 'I'll be right with you.'

Lily flopped down on the squashy couch and instantly felt herself relax. She looked quizzically at the recumbent mass of fluffy limbs lying opposite. Fatface and Healey were indiscernible. Janet placed a wooden tea tray on the coffee table, complete with bone china teapot, cups and saucers.

'Believe it or not,' she said, shoving the furry bundle up a bit with her bottom, 'they do usually venture out during the day. But by night, this is their spot!'

Lily laughed, gratefully accepting the tea. 'Have you always lived in this house? Since you moved from Dorset, I mean?'

'Pretty much, yes,' said Janet. 'I love it here. I'm close enough to Lostmor for my clinic, but when I come home it still feels like I'm living out in the wilds. When my springer, Bailey, was alive, we used to walk on the moors every day. But it wouldn't be fair to get another dog now. I spend too much time at the clinic or on my rounds.'

'Hence these two?'

'Yes, bless 'em,' Janet smiled, rubbing Healey's head. 'Most of the time they're pretty low maintenance. How about you? Do you have any pets back in Bristol?'

'Not any more. My mother and I used to have a pure white cat. She got him for me not long after we moved to Bristol. She let me choose him and he was such a minute ball of fluff that I named him Tiny. Little did we know he would grow into the most enormous tom!'

They laughed and chatted and drank tea. Janet had not long left Willow Farm, where she had trimmed Gloria's trotters, a big old lop-eared pig. Lily relayed her busy week at *The Blue* and how she had just managed to finish the large landscape painting for her client's wedding anniversary in time.

'Oh, and I bumped into Oliver earlier,' said Janet. 'Oliver Bligh.'

'Oh?' Lily paused. 'Is he well?'

'I'm not sure,' said Janet. 'It was funny because I thought of you, seeing as I was coming out of the Co-op with some wine for tonight. Anyway, I asked if he had seen you again. I admit that, last time I saw him, I had hinted he should apologise to you for being a bit curt. He looked at me… well, oddly, especially when I mentioned you were staying with me tonight. He just rushed off without another word. Something was definitely… off with him.' She leant forward, her elbows resting on her knees. 'You can tell me to sod off if you like, but did you two have further words or something?'

'Well, kind of… yes,' said Lily. 'Actually, I wanted to ask your advice about something. It's to do with Oliver and me.'

Janet raised an eyebrow. Over supper, Lily tried to explain as best she could. She shared how she and Oliver had gone from their rocky start to becoming friends. Janet's face had lit up at the prospect. Lily explained how Oliver had visited her at Kleger Cottage and indeed apologised. How she had then agreed to meet for drinks and found herself warming to him. And that they had even made a couple of trips to Penwyth House together. Lily hoped that Oliver would understand her need to speak to Janet about them. She had good reason and there was a lot he didn't yet know – like the fact that Joe might be her real father.

'After my rental was up at Kleger Cottage,' Lily continued, 'and I'd finished for now at Penwyth House, I returned to Bristol for the week, but we chatted on the phone most days. I was really looking forward to seeing him again and I know he was, too.' She felt herself blush a little. 'Last week, he rang me the evening before I was driving back down to see him. He said he would be a bit late, as he had to go and see his mother's solicitor in St Oswald's at short notice. He said to make myself at home, at Bligh Farm I mean, and he would see me early evening. So I waited and waited. At some point, I fell asleep on the couch and when I awoke it was nearly dawn. I couldn't find a contact number for his solicitor. I didn't even know his name. So, in the end, I rang St Oswald's Hospital in case he'd had an accident of some kind, and I was just about to call the police when he turned up… that was when everything just fell apart.'

'Goodness… what on Earth happened?'

'Megan had bequeathed him a letter. She had instructed her solicitor, Mr Reece, not to pass it to Oliver for six months. He presumes that, because the contents were upsetting, she'd thought it best to wait until her funeral was over and things had settled down a bit.'

'Oh, my dear, whatever is it?' Janet asked with a look of concern and bewilderment on her face.

'Janet, can I ask that this remains between us?'

'Of course. You can trust me, Lily.'

'Sorry to ask, but this is deeply personal for us both,' said Lily. 'Oliver doesn't know I'm telling you this yet. The letter his mother left for him was really a confession. In it, she said that George – who, as you know, brought him up until he died prematurely – was not his real father.'

Janet gasped. 'What? Are you sure?'

'Yes. I've seen the letter and Oliver's birth certificate that backs it up. Apparently, she had told him years ago that his certificate was lost and he had no reason to think otherwise. But she left it for him with the letter. Both confirm that his real father was Vincent Sanders.'

'Sanders? Your surname?' Janet looked at her for a moment. 'Oh, my God! You mean… your father, Lily?'

Lily nodded. 'Yes. I know how improbable this all sounds, but I'm afraid it's true. It seems Oliver and I have different mothers, but the same father.'

'Gosh, I'm so sorry…' said Janet. 'I don't know what to say… so Megan had an affair?'

'We don't know the exact circumstances, but her letter said it was just the one time. She fell pregnant by him and she knew it couldn't be George's. He had contracted measles as a young man, which led to a serious infection that almost killed him… and, at the same time, left him sterile. I take it she never told you anything?'

Janet was astounded. 'No, no she didn't. I mean, we were friends, but she never confided in me about any of this. So there's no chance that Megan could have got this wrong?'

'It seems unlikely and she certainly had no reason to lie. I think she'd carried the secret for so long that, when she knew she was going to die, she wanted to come clean. Get it off her chest.'

'And, I suppose… what were the chances that you and Oliver would ever even meet?'

Lily met Janet's eyes. 'I know and I have been trying to come to terms with it. I was so upset when he told me, we both were. I just walked out on him... But there's something else,' she confided.

'I can hardly believe what else there could be,' Janet said. 'I don't know about you, but I think I need something a little stronger.' With that, she went into the kitchen and a few minutes later came back with a chilled bottle of wine and two glasses.

Lily sipped the cool, crisp wine and did her best to describe what had happened next. First, she told Janet about her nightmares and flashbacks and how she had never been able to fully remember the night Vincent and Alice had died. Then how, when last alone at Penwyth House, she had experienced a shocking and vivid recollection of that fateful evening, her parents arguing, the threats. She then repeated her mother's confession to an affair and, the final straw, telling Vincent he was not Lily's father. She could see Janet trying to get her head around her latest exposé.

'So...' said Janet slowly, 'are you saying that Joe may be your father?'

'Yes.'

'Have you asked him?'

'Actually, yes. He found me at the house just after I had this flashback. I was still a bit shaken, but we talked about what I'd just remembered and, not forgetting he had already admitted to having an affair with my mother, when I asked him if he was my father he became quite emotional, as was I. The truth is, he doesn't know. He had suspected as much, but she had denied it. He thinks that's why she broke it off between them. She was frightened of Vincent, of what he might do if he found out about them, let alone if he discovered that the baby, me, wasn't his.'

'So, if Joe really is your father, and Megan and Vincent are Oliver's birth parents...' Janet paused. 'Then you and Oliver would not, after all, be related?'

'Yes!' Lily exclaimed. 'Exactly that, and that's why I need your help. Do you know if there's a way to prove who my real father is by their blood group? This will probably sound cold-hearted to you, but it has always been hard for me to feel a connection to Vincent, the man who brought me up until I was nine years old. If he isn't, it not only means a second chance for Oliver and me, but for Joe, too. Even though I had not seen him since I was a child, the moment we met I felt a bond between us... and that was before I knew any of this. And he wants to know the truth too, Janet, as much as I do. He wants his daughter back... if, indeed, I am.'

Janet looked thoughtfully at her newfound friend. 'You are not cold, Lily. You are a young woman, who had just found someone special only to have your hopes dashed. From what you've told me, Vincent was never there for you growing up and, when he was, treated you badly. Treated your whole family badly... I'm trying to think... as far as blood groups go, I am not one hundred per cent sure it is possible to prove who your father is, but you may be able to prove who isn't. Do you know your blood group?'

'Yes, I'm A negative, quite rare. I've donated blood a few times because of it.'

'Well, your blood group being rare may help. What about your parents? Do you know theirs?'

'I know Mother's... after speaking with Joe, I checked through some old paperwork of hers and, by luck, she kept all her medical info together. I found a very old letter from her GP about testing for rhesus D when she was pregnant. She was blood type O positive. That's pretty common, isn't it?'

'Yes, most people are blood group O,' said Janet. 'I'm going to have to check, but as you are A negative, I think your birth father would have to be either A or AB. I'm a bit rusty on people. Blood group types are different in animals – they can be numerous. In dogs, for instance, there are more than twelve! I think I still have a few textbooks around here somewhere that may help us. At uni, I studied biology for a while before switching to veterinary science. I can check what blood types are – or, more importantly, are not – compatible. It would be a start.'

'Thanks so much,' said Lily. 'I've even brought my donor card and my mother's letter with me in case it helped. But I don't know what my father's blood type is – I mean, Vincent's... or Joe's, for that matter. Do you think Vincent's GP would still hold his medical records? There can't be that many doctors in Lostmor, can there?'

'There are only two practices. There may have been others back then, of course, but medical records are not kept that long. Ten years maybe, but not for over twenty... What about hospital records?'

'Okay, it's worth a try.'

'I was thinking along the lines of post-mortem records,' Janet imparted. 'They should be held by the coroner's office and, as his death happened in Lostmor, the closest hospital would be St Oswald's.'

CHAPTER 35

'Sorry to put you on hold for so long. I have found records for a Mr Vincent Thomas Sanders, deceased 1971. Did you say that he was your father?'

'Yes, that's right. I'm Lily Sanders.'

'I have no wish to pry,' the receptionist continued, 'but I should warn you that the report will contain quite graphic details about your late father. Is there a particular piece of information that you need?'

'I understand,' said Lily. 'I'm trying to establish what his blood group was.'

'Okay, well, that will be in his medical history. It is usually only one page, which I can easily forward on separately if you prefer?'

'Please, yes that would be most helpful.'

'We usually send reports via the deceased's GP,' said the receptionist. 'However, because of the length of time, I'd better check first that the practice still exists. Do you want me to get back to you?'

'I see. Well, would it save time if I pick it up in person?'

There was a pause whilst a muffled conversation took place in the background. 'Yes, okay, that should be fine, as long as you bring proof of ID.'

Later that day, Lily and Timothy entered the Black Dog Inn,

bringing with them a sharp gust of wind. Marcus looked up from his paper. He suddenly realised that was where he knew her from – a few weeks back, she had been in the pub with Oliver and she had been in with Timothy before, too. That reminded him – he must speak to Oliver, let him know that he had seen Douglas Holt parked outside his place late at night. Something didn't sit right with the man, and Marcus had learnt a long time ago to trust his hunches. Horace wagged his way over to the woman and Timothy. He had picked up the rustle of crisp packets. Lily smoothed the Labrador's head and smiled in Marcus's direction.

'He's lovely.'

'Don't be fooled by those doe eyes,' he replied. 'The second you finish those crisps he'll be off to pastures new.'

She laughed as the dog moved to Timothy's side, nudging his hand hopefully. 'We don't mind that you're shallow, Horace,' he sympathised, sliding a cheese and onion crisp to him. 'It's just your survival instinct, isn't it?'

'Hah! You've got to be joking,' laughed Marcus. 'He's just a greedy hound!' He grinned, before disappearing to serve a customer at the other end of the bar.

Being back in the Black Dog reminded Lily of her evening spent there with Oliver. Not that he was likely to be there during the day – at least, she hoped not. She knew he was much more likely to be working on the farm. Her prior meeting with Timothy had been lengthy. She had signed the deeds giving Joe ownership of his beloved Edhen Cottage and the agreed surrounding land. Timothy was keeping them safe until Joe signed, too. Then, they had waded through the surveyor's report and the many issues it had brought to light. Now she had it in black and white. Not surprisingly, the entire roof needed replacing, the west wing was structurally much worse than the east wing, and the house interior needed major restoration work. Having read endless pages of the finite details, the pub was a welcome interlude. But she was itching to get away. She wanted to pick up Vincent's medical record from St Oswald's as soon as possible.

'Thanks for the beer,' Timothy said, raising his glass slightly. She touched it back with her soda and lime. She needed a clear head today.

'Now I understand just how much repair work is needed, I can see I'm going to have to organise builders and tradesmen on quite a large scale.' She laughed at her own naivety. 'When I first got here, I thought I could just get in a few local builders. What an idiot! It's clearly a massive undertaking.'

'You weren't to know,' said Timothy. 'I imagine all of this has been a very steep learning curve... Have you thought of perhaps getting the roof repaired? That way, it would be structurally safe and will stop it deteriorating any further. Then, just sell it on as it is? Presumably, it's worth a lot less in its current state, but God knows how much it will cost to completely renovate it, or how long it would take.'

'You're right,' Lily smiled. 'It would be easier to fix the roof and then cut my losses. That was my initial thinking, too. I'll think on it some more… I appreciate your help with deciphering the report – and with everything else, for that matter. If I do decide to renovate, I'll find someone who can project manage it all, someone who can be on site most days.'

'I'll happily look into finding someone, if that's what you want?' said Timothy. 'I know both the local estate agents and they will have contacts in the building industry, I'm sure.'

'Okay, thanks.' Lily smiled gratefully. 'I really don't know what I would do without you.'

'I am just doing my job,' he beamed. 'But how about you? I hope you don't mind me asking, but it must have been difficult for you to come back here. When we first met, you were understandably shaken by the news that the estate was never sold. Who wouldn't have been?

I just hope that returning here, to Lostmor, has not been too daunting?'

'Well, it's been a bit of an emotional roller coaster!' Lily laughed for a moment. 'I've learnt a lot about my family and made new friends, which I was not expecting. But it's also true that returning to Penwyth House has stirred up some demons. But I'm okay, thanks… And yes, I really am glad to be here.'

An hour later, she had left Timothy to his second ale, promising to be in touch soon, and was on her way to St Oswald's. Janet had offered to drive, as her surgery was closed on Saturdays and nearby West Hill was on-call for emergencies. Lily felt her stomach tightening as they drew closer to the hospital. Whatever the outcome of the post-mortem report, she would talk to Oliver. She didn't want to leave things hanging so… unfinished. No matter how much it hurt, she would try to clear the air with him.

The girl on main reception at the hospital directed them to the coroner's office – a no-nonsense squat, grey building hidden away in a corner of the hospital grounds. Having gone through the formalities with the same receptionist Lily had spoken to on the phone – and whether or not she had familiarised herself with the report details, her expression certainly did not give her away – she was handed the envelope with polite courtesy.

'Good luck, Miss Sanders,' the receptionist intimated, peering at her over heavy-rimmed oval glasses.

'Well, aren't you going to open it? You've been staring at it for the past ten minutes!' Janet asked, one eye on the road.

'I want to, but I don't!' said Lily. 'What if it's not enough? It's possible it still won't prove anything, right?'

'But it just might,' replied Janet. 'If not, it doesn't mean you have to give up. We'll just have to think of something else, that's all.'

Lily tried to be calm as she lifted out the flimsy bit of paper. General details, Vincent's name, age address… and clearly stated, near the bottom, was his blood group type.

'He was O, the same as my mother.'

'Are you sure?'

'Yes, blood type O, that's what it says. Didn't you say last night that he would have to be type A or AB to be my birth father?'

Janet smiled kindly at her friend. 'Yes… I did a bit of research this morning whilst you were with your solicitor. Two blood group O parents can definitely not produce a type A child. Vincent is not your father, Lily. It is impossible. And what's more, if Joe is type A, or AB – and knowing what we know, I think it is safe to assume that he is – then he has to be your father.'

Tears filled Lily's eyes as she stared at the paper in front of her. 'I don't know whether to laugh or cry! I know I should feel upset that the man I thought was my father all these years is not, but honestly, right now, I just feel relieved. Thank you for your help. This means a lot to me.'

'I am sure you would have got there on your own, but I am happy to be of service!' replied Janet. 'Seriously, I'm glad for you. Don't feel bad about Vincent. Remember, that what happened all those years ago at Penwyth was not of your doing. You are just trying to make sense of it all – not just your family's past, but your feelings for Oliver, too.'

Later that evening, the glow of the fireplace from the tiny front window cast a little light on the narrow path in front of her. Lily stood underneath the small wooden gabled porch. She paused, trying to calm herself before knocking, but before she had the chance the door swung open.

'Jesus, Lily!'

'I was just about to knock!' Straight away, she felt foolish. Maybe she should have phoned first.

'I thought I heard a car,' Oliver half-smiled. 'Come in… sorry, come in.' Flynn wove excitedly around them both, anticipating a grand reunion. 'You took me by surprise then,' he admitted, pulling out a kitchen chair for her.

'I'm sorry, I didn't mean to,' she said. 'I thought about phoning, but I just really needed to see you in person.'

'I'm glad you're here…' Oliver softened. 'I've missed you.' He looked at her curiously. Damn it, even with a heavy winter coat and thick woolly scarf concealing half her face, she looked beautiful. He pulled out another chair and sat facing her.

'I knew you were here this weekend. I bumped into Janet in town. Did she tell you?' he said, trying to sound casual.

'Yes, I'm staying with her. Last time I was here my car broke down and, by some miracle, she came along and rescued me. She has been great, offering to put me up and helping me get my car fixed.'

'She's a good egg, alright…' said Oliver. 'It sounds as if you're still busy with the house as you're back in Lostmor… but I'm guessing that's not why you're here tonight?' Concerned dark eyes regarded her carefully. 'We might not be able to be together, but that hasn't stopped me thinking about you.'

Lily smiled and looked at him fondly. 'I've found out something… something about my family's past, and it is going to sound just as unbelievable as the contents of your mother's letter.'

Oliver leant in close. Her eyes looked multi-faceted in the firelight, like shimmering hazel and gold mosaics. He wanted to sweep her up and hold her; instead, he touched her arm reassuringly…

'Go on.'

CHAPTER 36

Douglas was busy in the garage again, fixing up the Triumph, while Luke emptied the amassed junk from the back of the van, adding it to the considerable pile of scrap that once functioned as a front lawn. Afterwards, he slipped two sets of gloves into the glove compartment of the van, along with a torch, and shoved a crowbar in the side pocket of the driver's door. As he did most winter evenings, he carried a basket of wood from a makeshift shed, illegally felled from the copse behind the house, and rekindled the burnt-out fire. The internal walls of the living room were paper thin, fashioned from wood panelling, so any warmth quickly leached away.

'When you're done in the garage we need to chat, okay?' said Luke.

'Alright, bro,' replied Douglas. 'What's for tea?'

'It's on the side.'

Once he had finished tinkering about with the motorbike, Douglas reheated the pie and chips Luke had picked up for them earlier and ate hurriedly. He always devoured his food as if it were his last meal. Luke, on the other hand, ate slowly and deliberately, savouring each mouthful. For once, he resisted the urge to comment on his younger brother's eating habits.

'How are you getting on out there?' asked Luke.

'Good. The carburettor needed a clean, but I can't do much more now till I get those parts.'

'Do you think you can get it back on the road, then?'

'Probably,' Douglas mumbled, shovelling a large chunk of pie into his mouth.

'We could sell it if you get it going. You know how strapped we are.'

'Yeah, I know, but I wanna have a go on it first. Take it out a few times. What about Penwyth House? When are we gonna go there?'

'How about tonight?' Luke smiled.

'Really?'

'Yeah, why not?'

'How close did you get? Did you see inside the place?'

'Not properly. I don't know what stuff might be inside, if anything, but there's no one living there, I'm sure of it.'

Later that night, the brothers, both dressed in dark clothes, jumped in the van and headed for Penwyth Estate.

'So you haven't seen anyone at the house?' asked Douglas.

'Nope. Well, only once,' Luke replied. 'I saw a woman in a red car drive out of the place about a week ago, but nobody since. I've managed to get close up to the house three times now and it's been dead. No lights on, no noise, no cars.'

'Who do you think the woman was?'

Luke shrugged. 'No way of knowing. She was pretty hot, though,' he sneered.

Douglas snorted and play punched his brother in the arm, which really hurt, but Luke stayed silent. 'Well, I wouldn't mind if she was there, then!'

As they wound their way through the estate's orchard, Luke switched to sidelights, then pulled over before reaching a large bend in the road. Any further and they would be visible from the house.

'Okay, grab the gloves and the torch,' Luke whispered earnestly, pulling the crowbar out of the side door pocket. 'And don't slam the door.' They stayed under the cover of the trees, picking their way along the edge of the road. Ahead, the house looked to be in total darkness. 'Think we're in luck,' Luke said as they drew closer. 'There's no one here. Once we're inside, if there's stuff worth taking, I'll run back and get the van.'

Douglas was staring up at the jagged rooftop, its various appendages vaguely silhouetted in the pale moonlight. 'Christ, this place is creepy.'

'Never mind that,' hissed Luke. 'Come on, there's a smaller door round the side that leads to the basement.'

They found the steps leading down to the kitchen. Using the crowbar and his considerable strength, Douglas easily jimmied the door. He threw the crowbar noisily aside and ran his hands through his hair, his thick lips stretched into a broad grin.

'Now what?' he said.

Luke could see he was pumped. 'Don't make so much noise. I know the place looks empty, but we should still try to be as quiet as possible.'

They made their way through the house, checking the rooms for anything worth taking, but there was nothing. Floorboards creaked and strange shadows cast by the torch rose and fell across the walls like an eerie, moving landscape. When the corridor opened up into the main entrance hallway, Luke flashed the torch upwards.

'Woah!' he half-whispered, catching sight of the giant French crystal chandelier hanging centrepiece. 'This place must have been really something once.' Their footsteps echoed in the vast reception as they looked for anything of value. But, again, there was nothing. The place was stripped bare.

'Over there!' Douglas exclaimed, a little louder than Luke would have liked. Sure enough, there was something stacked against the wall with canvas material covering it.

'Who are you?' a voice suddenly called out from the darkness of the corridor behind them. Luke jumped. He swung round and shone his torch in the direction of the voice. Joe moved closer and into the beam of light. He pointed the shotgun at waist level towards the two men, eyeing them defiantly. 'I said, who are you? You shouldn't be 'ere, you're trespassing.' He moved closer again. Fifteen feet away now.

Luke was standing close to his brother. He whispered in his ear. 'We've gotta do something.'

'Hey, sorry, please don't shoot!' he said to Joe, raising his hands, and nudging Douglas to do the same. There was no way he was going to be intimidated by this old man. The gun probably wasn't even loaded.

Without warning, Luke lobbed the torch hard, its light spiralling in an arc, throwing the room into darkness. As Joe ducked, Douglas took his cue. He lunged at the old man, bringing him down in a violent rugby tackle, forcing the barrel of the gun upwards just as Joe pulled the trigger. Two rounds of pellets shattered the arched window to the left of the door, sending shards of glass flying, the deafening noise reverberating in the vaulted space.

Douglas used his bulk to easily pin Joe down. Sitting astride him, he punched him hard in the face. For Joe, it felt like he'd been hit with a shovel; he tried to grab at his assailant's throat, but the younger man was too strong. Douglas raised one meaty fist to hit him again, but instead Luke beat him to it, hitting Joe with the butt of the shotgun.

Joe felt an explosion of pain spread across his face. He clawed at Douglas's clothing and struggled not to lose consciousness, but... he slid into blackness. Douglas stepped off of Joe's limp body as casually as if he'd just got out of bed and walked towards the covered-up paintings.

'Look!' he said, grabbing the discarded torch and throwing the canvas cover to one side. 'Told you! Paintings! There must be five or six. They've got to be worth something.'

Luke casually walked over to where he stood. The artwork didn't look like anything much to him.

'Surely if these were worth anything, they wouldn't just leave them lying around?'

'I suppose so,' said Douglas, deflated. 'Maybe we should check upstairs?'

'Hmmm, we probably should go now.' Luke took the torch and walked back to where Joe lay. He shone it in the old man's face, curious to see what damage they had inflicted. He knelt down and slowly pressed his finger into Joe's right eye, causing more blood to pool in the socket. A slow smile appeared on Luke's face as he studied his handiwork, as if were a doting parent gazing down at his child.

Douglas reluctantly left the paintings and picked up the discarded shotgun. He reached over Joe's body, fumbling in his jacket pockets, revealing a handful of unspent cartridges.

'Well done, Douglas, it seems we now have a gun.' Luke jumped up. 'Come on. Time to go.'

CHAPTER 37

Marcus walked quickly up the track. Five minutes previously, he had watched the rear lights of Douglas Holt's van recede as it turned left out of the lane heading away from town. If he heard the van coming back, he figured he could scramble into the neighbouring field and make his way back to where his truck was concealed, just inside the open cow gate.

The house, he could see, was little more than a shack and in darkness. He thought about breaking in – it wouldn't have taken much effort, but instead tried the garage first. It had an up and over heavy metal door. When he tugged on the handle, it creaked open. He pulled it up a bit more, just enough to slide inside and used a small torch to look around. Going by the amount of stuff dumped in the front garden, including a TV and two fridges, he had expected to see piles more junk strewn around in the garage. Instead, one wall was lined with shelves filled with neatly arranged boxes and tins. The floor space was partly taken up by large cardboard boxes that were stacked against the shelved wall. To his left was an old Triumph motorbike with some of its parts laid out on old newspapers and what looked like an old chest.

His stomach turned over... Douglas owned a bike... of sorts. That, on its own, didn't count for much – lots of men owned bikes and this one had clearly been sitting there for a long time. He turned his attention to the chest. Inside was a large stack of neatly folded clothes that looked like they belonged to an older man. The contents of the garage did not seem to fit with what he'd seen of Douglas. Maybe this was once his old man's place and the bike, too?

Marcus was beginning to doubt his hunch. He was about to take a quick look at the house, see if he could get in and out without leaving a trace, when a dome shape caught his eye. In one of the neatly stacked boxes against the far wall, his torch illuminated the top of a helmet sticking up. He pulled the box out. Inside was a biker's helmet, together with gloves and boots. They weren't that old, except the helmet was a bit scratched up. There were some other loose items in the bottom. He tipped them out on the floor and shone the torch on them. There was a large buckle belt in the shape of a skull, and a strap of some kind, possibly off the helmet.

Then he stared, unblinking, in disbelief. On the ground was a silver linked chain of dragon heads glinting in the torchlight. The same as the one Amanda had given him only a few days earlier. Before he had time to think about his next move, he heard a vehicle approaching. He shoved the wallet chain in his pocket and hastily stuffed the rest back in the box. He switched off the torch and peered through the side of the door. The headlights dimmed and he heard the van door slam shut and then – a second one. Douglas wasn't alone.

With his back pressed against the wall, Marcus listened to the murmur of low voices followed by the sound of keys jangling. Then another door slammed as they went inside the house. He wanted to confront Douglas, right there and then. To rip his heart out for what he'd done to Rose, but he couldn't. Not with someone else there. No. He had to keep his cool. He could wait a few more days. Plan it right. He had no intention of going to prison.

Now he knew he had his man, Marcus needed to think. Think of a way to make his death look like an accident. And, Douglas had no idea who Marcus was or that he was coming for him. He had him; he'd got the bastard.

When there was no further noise from inside the house, he pushed the metal door open a fraction. It groaned a bit, but he slid silently through the gap and quickly pushed the door back down. He waited a moment. There were still no signs of life from inside. He slipped behind the garage, then ran to the line of tall trees behind and, from there, to his truck.

Back at the Black Dog, he made his excuses to the bar staff and went upstairs. All thoughts of Julia were gone. Horace eyed him warily. He knew that look.

CHAPTER 38

After turning up unexpectedly on Oliver's doorstep, Lily recounted everything that had happened since they'd last met. She told him about the notes she had found at Penwyth House, of discovering Joe's beautiful aviary and of his admission to having had an affair with her mother. Finally, she spoke of her impulsive visit to Penwyth House on the day they had parted and how, whilst there, she had experienced a sudden vivid memory of herself as a child. She thought he might think her crazy when she told him about the argument between her mother and Vincent that had come back to her, like a bolt from the blue, but Oliver had listened, enthralled by what she had to say. She explained how, later, Janet had helped her track down medical records for Vincent that gave details of his blood type, and she repeated her explanation of how, without a doubt, he could not be her father.

'So, you think that Joe is your father?'

'Yes, I do. Apparently, it's harder to prove that someone *is* your parent than is not, if that makes sense. So, even if Joe's blood type is A or AB, it only means that he *could* be. Except that, knowing Mother's circumstances, about their affair, and how much they loved each other... He has to be, there was no one else.'

Oliver looked at her incredulously. Her story was unbelievable, as she had said when she had walked back into his life. But, at the same time, it was plausible.

'So, we're not related?' he said. 'Different mothers, different fathers!'

Lily smiled at him warmly. 'Yes, because it wasn't just your mother who had an affair. So did mine.'

'So, wait a minute...' said Oliver, shaking his head. 'That means that Alice was your half-sister and, even though we never met each other, she was mine, too. We had the same father.'

Lily nodded. 'Yes, that is true too.'

'I am at a loss for words,' said Oliver. 'I can't believe that you've found out all of this...' He gently touched her neck with his hand. 'I wish things had been different for you, Lily – I wish things had been easier. It seems we have both lost a sister, but sadly I never even knew she existed. Whereas, you have had to deal with her loss ever since, and Vincent's too.'

Lily looked into his eyes. She no longer had to try and put him out of her mind. She had missed him so much and now here he was, within her reach.

'I can't change the past,' she said, 'but what I do know is that a second twist of fate has brought you back to me... if you still want me.'

Then, without another word, they had fallen into each other's arms as naturally and completely as before. Only, this time, it was not just desire they felt, but a deeper sense of affection and appreciation of each other. He took her to his bed and kissed her slender neck, running his hands over every curve and hollow of her body. And, when her fingers lightly stroked his aching, work-weary muscles, every nerve ending in his body had suddenly become alive. Finally, when their exhausted bodies had collapsed onto the sheets, they had held each other close in the darkness, neither wanting to let go.

It was barely first light when Lily stirred. Sensing she was awake, Oliver rolled over to face her.

'Good morning,' he smiled sleepily and gently brushed a wisp of long hair from her face. He kissed her slowly on the lips before slipping out from underneath the sheets and drawing back the heavy chintz curtains.

'Do you fancy a stroll?' he said.

Lily stretched and sat up in bed. 'Now?' she eyed him curiously.

'Come on, it's a surprise!' he said, cheekily tugging at the bedsheet.

'Luckily for you, I'm a morning person,' she quipped, not minding in the least.

Right now, she couldn't have felt happier. They walked across the fields behind the farm that led to the sea. She could taste the brine that lay heavy in the cool sea air.

'Here,' Oliver smiled, gesturing towards a wooden bench. He laid a small blanket he'd slung over his shoulder for them to sit on. 'We can watch the sunrise together. It's going to be beautiful today. I just know it.'

'What a lovely idea,' she said, gazing out at the horizon. 'The views are breathtaking.'

After a few moments, Lily looked down at the bench. 'How did this get here?' she asked, running her fingers over the smooth, thick slab of oak.

'I made it,' said Oliver. 'About a million years ago… when I was a teenager. It was a surprise birthday present for my mother. I thought she might like to come here and read, or just look out to sea.'

'And did she?'

'Yes. I think she enjoyed the peace and quiet away from the farm, just sitting listening to the waves breaking below. She never said, but I think she used to come here to feel closer to George. He loved the sea. He always dreamt of buying a small boat – nothing fancy, just something with an outboard motor so he could go fishing. But he was always too busy with the farm. He never did get around to it.'

Lily squeezed Oliver's hand. 'It must have been a terrible time for your both, him dying so suddenly.'

'It was at first,' he replied. 'I was just a boy and I missed him a lot. We were a close family. I remember there was always a lot of laughter in our home.' He sighed. 'When he died, I think Mum and I probably kept each other going and it made us closer. She was a strong woman. She threw herself into keeping the farm afloat and I helped as much as I could. When I was about fourteen, she sat me down and asked me what I wanted to do when I left school. I was baffled, because it never occurred to me to do anything else but work on the farm. She wanted me to have the choice, but it was an easy decision for me.'

They sat huddled together on the bench that he had lovingly crafted all those years ago, for a time both lost in their thoughts as an emerging pink and golden canopy gently nudged the stars back into an unseen darkness.

She nestled into him. 'I wish you and I could stay in this moment forever.'

Oliver turned from the glowing sun's ascent and gazed into her hazel eyes, glimmering gold in the changing light. 'Me too, my love,' he whispered, and they watched in contented silence as the first pale rays of light cascaded into calm waters.

*

Back inside the cottage, Lily perched on a kitchen stool, sipping tea. 'I can see why you chose that particular spot to put a bench. That was the most beautiful sunrise I've ever seen.'

'Well, consider the bench officially yours now. I know Mum would approve,' he smiled, passing her a slice of freshly buttered toast.

'I was a bit worried, you know…'

'About what?'

'Well… coming here and telling you what I'd discovered.'

'What, you mean the fact that somehow you'd worked out that we aren't related and are free to be together after all!'

She laughed. 'Well, when you put it like that... It is the best news ever, but so much has happened in such a short space of time. It's a lot for anyone to get their head around. And I was not sure how you would feel about me confiding in Janet over your mother's letter. I just hoped you would understand why. I thought she might be able to help and... well, she did.'

'Of course I don't mind,' said Oliver. 'I trust her, she's a good friend... If it hadn't been for Joe's honesty about his affair, and you and Janet looking into your family's blood groups, you might not be here with me now. If anything, I owe her a debt.'

'I was so upset that day you showed me your mother's letter,' Lily replied. 'I'm sorry, but I didn't even think about what a shock it must have been for you finding out that Vincent, not George, was your real father.'

'Admittedly at first, yes, it was,' said Oliver, 'and I guess I will never understand exactly why it happened, but I'm okay with it. She was young and she made a mistake. And, even though my parents chose to keep it from me, they thought they were doing the right thing.'

'And do you think they did the right thing?'

Oliver considered. 'Maybe, now I have had time to think about it. It certainly would have been too much for me to have coped with after losing George, and as far as I'm concerned he will always be my real father, anyway. But, perhaps when I was a bit older, it would have been healing for my mother at least if she had told me the truth. But I can see how, as the years went by, it became easier to say nothing... And then, of course, she had a much bigger problem when she fell ill.' He paused and looked at Lily. 'What about you? How do you feel discovering Vincent wasn't your father?'

'Honestly?' she said. 'Ours was a very different relationship to yours and George's. I don't remember ever being close to him. I remember being scared of him when he had been drinking. He would lose his temper and shout at Mother a lot. I learnt to make myself scarce when he was like that, and take Alice with me. Much later on, when we had moved away, Mother told me he had not always been that way. When she had first met him, he had been charming and fun to be with, but in the short time he was my father, I have no memory of him being that way.' She reached out and held Oliver's hand. 'What I do know is that being with you has made me happier than I have ever been with anyone. So, finding that piece of paper proving he wasn't my father, when I thought I'd lost you for good... I cried tears of relief.'

The irony of how events had played out was not lost on either of them.

'It feels a bit like we are pawns being moved in some bizarre, indulgent, gods' game of chess, doesn't it?' Lily added.

Oliver couldn't help but laugh at her analogy. 'Like in *Jason and the Argonauts*, you mean?'

'Yes, that's it! With monsters and all,' she said ruefully.

Oliver sat down beside her. 'These past few weeks I couldn't stop thinking about you. I tried to distract myself with work, and God knows farming is an easy job to lose yourself in. But even working from sunrise to sundown, the time seemed to drag endlessly by. Now, whether it be by God's hand or otherwise, we've been given another chance...' He kissed her tenderly on the lips. 'And I'm not going to let you go a second time.'

CHAPTER 39

Lily read the note stuck to Janet's fridge.

Hi. Hope you're ok.

Have been called out to an injured swan!

Help yourself to anything you need.

Maybe catch up later?!

J x

Lily left a sticky note replying that she was fine and would see her later. A quick shower and change and she left, this time heading for Penwyth House. She hummed along to a song playing on the car radio, feeling buoyed. She was looking forward to telling Joe what she had discovered – that she knew for certain that he was her true father. As the house came into view, she felt a little nervous, but in a good kind of way. She knew he would be pleased, but it might still be something of a shock to learn that, after all these years, he had a daughter.

As usual, she'd planned to park on the drive then walk through the woods to Edhen Cottage. However, as she approached Penwyth House she saw that one of the windows either side of the front door was broken. Now she felt even more nervous, but this time in a very bad way.

Broken glass crunched underfoot as she gingerly made her way to the front door. Her hands trembled as she unlocked it. Inside, she gasped when she saw a pool of blood on the floor.

'Hello! Joe! Are you here?' Lily's voice echoed around her. She walked back out, calling his name. Nothing.

She started to run, slowly at first, then as fast as she could towards the cottage. Then she stopped dead as she came around the bend in the lane and saw Joe lying on the ground at the edge of the woods. Next to his crumpled, motionless body was a large seagull, which bizarrely appeared to be standing sentry. The bird gave an agitated, guttural sound as Lily walked closer.

She was desperate to get past it, to reach Joe. She shouted and waved her arms at it, but the loyal seagull held fast. Swallowing nervously, Lily slowly knelt in front of the huge bird. *This is crazy,* she thought. *Gulls just don't behave this way.* Then she remembered – her very first morning at Kleger Cottage – the gull. Cold, beady eyes regarded her with disdain and she knew it was the same creature. Suddenly, it dipped its head as if bowing and outstretched its enormous wings, before jumping a few feet away. It seemed she had been allowed access. Bizarre as the scene was, she knew she had no time to waste.

'Joe?' she leant over him and gently shook his arm. His face was a bloody mess and his blackened eyes so swollen she doubted he could have opened them, even if he had been conscious. She pulled off her scarf and gently placed it under his head, then unbuttoned her coat and laid it on top of him. He was icy cold to touch.

Lily felt panic rising up inside her. She desperately looked around, crying out for help, but there was no one to hear her – except the gull, which was parading up and down on ridiculous pink webbed feet. She looked down at poor Joe's ruined face. She had no idea how long he'd lain there, or what other injuries he might have. She pulled out her phone and dialled 999.

Later that day, Oliver found Lily sitting in St Oswald's Hospital waiting room. She had phoned Janet earlier to explain where she was and left a message on Oliver's answerphone. She rose to greet him and hugged him tightly.

'Are you okay?' he asked with concern in his eyes. Lily looked pale and drawn. The polar opposite to the smiling face he had left that morning as she had driven off, waving and promising to ring him later.

'I'm fine, honestly.' Lily was relieved to see him. She had been waiting for hours and still the doctors wouldn't let her see Joe. A woman who introduced herself as Dr Lake had spoken to her earlier and asked if she knew what had happened. Lily had explained as best she could. She told how she had found the blood and that she presumed that Joe had apprehended someone trying to break into the house. The intruder, or intruders, must have attacked him and then fled. Judging from where she had found him, Lily presumed he had been desperately trying to get home, or perhaps to his car, and he had nearly made it, too. That was all she knew.

'Is he going to be okay?' Oliver asked.

'I think so,' said Lily. 'When I found him, he was unconscious. He looked like he had been lying there a long time, and his face... his face was so bloody and swollen.' She wiped tired eyes that were brimming with tears.

Oliver placed one arm reassuringly around her. 'What happened? Where did you find him?'

'Collapsed, near the woods, but I think he had come from the main house. He must have disturbed someone. One of the arched windows at the front was broken, but it is too small for a person to have got in through and the front door was locked. Whoever did this must have got in and out somewhere else.'

'Do you know how bad it is? Joe, I mean.'

'A doctor told me he had regained consciousness,' said Lily. 'She said he was concussed, with a broken nose and possibly a fractured jaw and broken ribs. I don't know how long he'd been lying there, but he's dehydrated and suffering from hypothermia.'

'Well, thank God you went looking for him today, or he could have been lying there much longer. And he's awake. That's good news, isn't it?'

'Yes…' said Lily. 'Yes, you're right. It is just such a nasty business. Who would do such a thing to an old man?' She began to cry.

Oliver hugged her tight. 'I wish I knew.'

Just then, Dr Lake walked back into the waiting room. She spoke calmly, explaining that Joe's scan had, as they'd suspected, shown a fractured right cheekbone. He had also suffered four fractured ribs and, worst of all, may lose the sight in his right eye.

'It must have been a shock for you finding him like that, Miss Sanders,' said the doctor. 'He's taken quite a beating from someone. At the moment, it's too soon to say how much of his sight he will regain, but, given time and a lot of rest, there's no reason why he shouldn't make a good recovery from his other injuries. He seems a pretty tough character.' She smiled reassuringly.

A nurse finally came out to see them and said that Lily could see Joe for a short time. She was shocked when she first saw him. Joe was unrecognisable. His head was covered in bandages, wires and tubes were attached to his chest and arms, and he was surrounded by bleeping monitors. He could neither see nor speak, but when she softly spoke his name, he raised his hand looking for contact. Lily whispered to him that everything would be fine and that he mustn't worry about anything.

Before she was politely ushered out, Lily promised Joe that she would look after his aviary for as long as it was needed. He squeezed her hand and she was surprised at his grip. She felt reassured. Dr Lake was right – Joe, her father, was pretty damned tough.

CHAPTER 40

The police turned up at Bligh Farm the next morning. The hospital had notified them of the break-in at Penwyth House and the subsequent attack on Joe Newman. Sergeant Weeks was forty-something, tall, with a large head, protruding belly and a small, down-turned mouth, like a tiny, half-crescent moon.

Lily confirmed she was the owner of Penwyth House. The sergeant nodded amicably and scribbled away on his pad whilst she explained that she had recently inherited the property, that it was not currently habitable, and that Joe was the groundsman living on the estate. Yes, he was normally the only person there, certainly at night. No, she didn't think anything was taken. She explained that she hadn't been back to check yet, but that, apart from a few paintings which were family heirlooms and not really of value to anyone else, the place was empty. If the sergeant had made the connection with her and the Sanders family's tragic history, he deemed it not necessary to mention. He explained that he had not been able to obtain a statement from Joe due to his injuries, but was keen to carry out further investigations.

Later that morning, Lily met him again at the house along with another constable and a forensics officer. Unfortunately, they were unable to find any tyre tracks or decent footprints. Fingerprints were taken from the basement door and a couple of the internal doors downstairs. However, the sergeant explained that, unless there was a clear match with someone already on their records, it would be an impossible task to eliminate the prints of everyone who had been in and out of the house lately. Blood samples were taken from the entrance hall, and the shotgun pellets found lodged on the inside of the front door and on the drive were also taken as forensic evidence.

Lily had not noticed the pellets the first time. Clearly, a shotgun round had been fired inside the house, but thankfully Joe had not been hit. It looked as if the pool of blood was a result of his injuries, but tests would show if there was more than one person's blood present. Initial investigations seemed to point to Joe disturbing his assailant or assailants, who had entered via the basement and made their way to the entrance hall. Lily checked upstairs with the sergeant and confirmed that nothing seemed to have been disturbed. A search of the gardens turned up nothing, but the constable did find half a box of shotgun cartridges at Edhen Cottage and Joe's shotgun appeared to be missing.

Sergeant Weeks said that, when they caught whoever was responsible, the police would be charging them with burglary and causing grievous bodily harm. He hoped to gain a clearer picture from Joe when he was well enough to be interviewed. Despite his reassurances, it seemed to Lily that, so far, they didn't have very much to go on.

Two days later, Lily, Oliver and Janet all met together at Penwyth House for the first time. As they walked from under the canopy of trees and into the glade which housed the aviary, they were greeted by a cacophony of noise. Even though Lily had described it to them, they stared in disbelief.

'My God, these glasshouses must be twenty feet high and, what, fifty feet in length!' Oliver exclaimed.

Oliver and Janet were overwhelmed, just as Lily had been, by the sheer spectacle of it. An array of palms, shrubs, and trees – some potted, others rooted in the ground – many of which were evergreen, created a lush, exotic-looking birdhouse, intertwined with a stunning array of orchids. And then, of course, there were the birds. Strolling through, investigating the various nooks and crannies, Janet noted some of the birds' species. She could see mainly parakeets, finches and canaries, and was pretty sure she spotted a couple of quails weaving between the bowed branches of a small apple tree at the far end. But there were also many common or garden birds – sparrows, blackbirds, tits and chaffinches – that had found a way in and out through the gaps in the netting. Meanwhile, at the centre of everything, Roy, the crow, observed all from his residential bird table.

'Have you seen Percy?' Janet asked, as later the three of them sat watching birds skim across Joe's in-house waterfall and pond.

Lily smiled. 'That sounds like a catchphrase. You know. Like, "Where's Wally?"'

'Who's Percy?' asked Oliver. Both ladies laughed.

'I can't believe I haven't told you about the peacock!' Lily exclaimed. 'Oh, and that's not all. I don't think I've told either of you about the seagull!' This time, Oliver and Janet exchanged glances.

'You know, as in the book, *Johnathon Livingston*? This bird is definitely not your run-of-the-mill gull. He must be Joe's. I've seen him twice now. The first was at Kleger Cottage, not long after I first arrived. The second time was when I found Joe injured. It was almost like it was guarding him until help came.' Lily noted their bemused faces. 'Honestly, I am not kidding! The bird stayed with him right up until the ambulance arrived.'

'Okaaay...' said Janet. 'I can see how Joe may have rescued an injured gull and perhaps, like Roy, it likes to stick around or visit now and then. Some birds can get very used to being around humans. But how can you possibly know that it's the same gull you saw at Kleger

Cottage? I mean, surely it could have been any gull?'

'I know it sounds crazy, but I'm certain it was the same bird,' said Lily. 'Both times it came right up to me and it just looked me straight in the eye. Have you ever known any wild bird behave like that?'

'And Percy the peacock, is he another of Joe's rescues?' Oliver asked.

'He is Joe's, but not a rescue,' replied Lily. 'He hatched out from a breeding pair that Joe owned. I first saw him in the apple orchard. I mentioned it to Joe and he was concerned that the bird was roaming too much. Then, unbelievably, Janet found him sitting on the same stretch of road that she found me on when my car broke down, and on the same night! So, basically, she rescued us both!'

Oliver looked incredulously from Janet to Lily. 'Life certainly isn't dull with you two around, is it!'

Janet grinned. 'I think Joe's the really interesting one! I hope one day soon I get to meet this extraordinary man.'

Oliver squeezed Lily's hand. 'That makes two of us. When he's well enough, of course. Now then, Janet, in the meantime, how on Earth do we look after this little lot?'

He nodded at two cute little green parakeets huddled on a perch on the other side of the pond. Lily had fed the birds as best she could for a few days using bags of pellets left in the glasshouses, but wasn't sure what else they needed. So Janet went through what and roughly how much food she thought they should leave out daily. Between them, she said, volunteering to help, they also needed to regularly clean all the perches and various tables they could get to, to prevent disease.

It was evident that the aviary itself needed repairing, but that and the plant life could take care of itself for a week or two. After which time, Lily guessed she might have to spend more time watering and maintaining Joe's little patch of paradise. She had no idea how he had managed to take care of the aviary and still tend to the estate's garden and grounds all this time. She hoped he would still be able to look after his beloved aviary when he came home. Perhaps, with a lot less land to soon take care of, and with her help, they could manage it together.

CHAPTER 41

The police finally got to speak to Joe, the day after he had facial surgery. He explained as best he could, sometimes with the use of a notebook and pen, given to him by the nurse, when it was too painful to talk. He explained about his daily evening round of the house and gardens. A habit he had got into decades ago when the house had residents and something he had just never stopped doing. He heard a noise to the side of the house and found that the door to the basement had been forced open. There were two men, youngish, maybe early thirties. When he had confronted them, one had jumped him, accidentally setting his shotgun off. He hadn't hurt them, although he bloody well wished he had… and no, he had not seen a vehicle.

The sergeant told him there was no gun found where he was attacked. Joe remembered the unspent shells in his jacket. The nurse confirmed there were none in his clothing when he had arrived. So, the gun and ammo were missing, presumably taken by his assailants. When asked, he said he wasn't sure he would recognise the men again. One had longish hair, but he only saw him briefly from a distance, while the one who had punched him 'was strong all right, one of those stocky types whose head and neck are the same width. I don't know what colour hair, it was too dark, but it was short.'

When Lily visited Joe a few hours later, his first question to her was, 'How are my birds?'

She assured him they were being fed and watered daily and that she had friends helping, one of whom was a vet. Getting hold of fruit was easy enough, but the pellets they had were running low. Joe explained that he had loads more stored in the old stables.

Talking was still very painful and laborious for him, but his eyes looked a little less raw and he reassured Lily that he could see, albeit his vision was still blurred. One of the nurses said that he was regularly offered painkillers, although he didn't always want them. They were also constantly chiding him for trying to get out of bed and sit out unassisted. Lily sympathised, whilst secretly taking heart from his determination to get better. He was a fighter.

It seemed odd to be back in a daily routine of driving to the estate; but, this time, rather than going straight to the house, Lily was tending to the aviary. There were other jobs to do, too. She arranged for a carpenter to fix the basement door, and met with a glazier who had boarded up the broken front window until he could come back and fix it. Most afternoons she drove to the hospital to visit Joe, while Oliver helped with feeding the birds as much as he could in between working on the farm. Janet had dropped by at the farm and reassured Lily that all the birds she could lay eyes on looked healthy enough. Lily hoped that they were, she felt like such an amateur. Feeding them and cleaning out was straightforward enough, but if one of them became injured she wouldn't have a clue what to do.

'Well, that's what I'm here for!' Janet had said. 'And when are you going to show me the actual house? You know that I'm dying to see it!'

In truth, apart from when she had met up with the police and various tradesmen, Lily had hardly been in the house lately. And, since getting back together with Oliver, visiting Joe in hospital and caring for his aviary, it had been easier to put thoughts of Alice and

Vincent out of her mind.

Like Oliver, Janet's jaw had dropped when she first entered the vast reception and gazed up at the grandiose staircase and the breathtaking glass dome above it. They were wandering through the downstairs rooms when Janet's mobile rang. She had to go. An elderly dog had collapsed at its owner's home and they were heading for Lostmor surgery. Lily felt for the poor dog and its owners, but was secretly relieved that Janet's tour was cut short. She locked up and, as she pulled away in her little Ford Fiesta, watched the spires and chimneys recede in her rear-view mirror. What an odd love-hate relationship she had with the place!

CHAPTER 42

They sat on his squashy leather couch with Flynn half lying across Lily.

'I've been thinking about something and, now with Joe in hospital, it's kind of decided me,' Lily smiled warmly at Oliver. 'I think I'm going to cancel my lease at *The Blue*.'

'Really?'

'Yes, that is if you can put up with me being around here a bit more?'

'Of course, you know I would love it.'

Lily smiled. 'That's a relief! It just seems that everything I care about is here now – you, of course, Joe and Janet, too, is a good friend… and, dare I say it… Penwyth House. I'm having second thoughts about selling it… or, at least, not yet.'

Oliver turned to face her. 'I can see you've been doing a lot of thinking. You know it broke my heart when I thought I'd lost you. Now, I'm just happy to have you back in my life. For you to be moving to Lostmor… well, that is just the cherry on the cake.' He gently touched her face. 'It's the best news ever. How long do you think you will stay?'

'I'm not sure yet, but I'm hoping to lease a similar place to *The Blue* in Tresor Bay, perhaps with some living space included, too. I wouldn't want you to feel bamboozled by me moving in here lock, stock, and barrel.'

'You can bamboozle me whenever you like,' Oliver grinned, 'but however you want to do this is fine. The past few months have been crazy for you, to say the least... but you know you're welcome here anytime.' He looked fondly at her. 'What about your apartment in Bristol? Will you give that up, too?'

'I've got nearly six months left on the lease, but that's probably just as well. It gives me time to organise myself... if I do move here for good.'

'And Penwyth House? You're not going to sell?'

'I have been thinking for a while about renovating it,' Lily replied. 'You'll probably think I'm crazy, and the surveyor's recommendations are about a mile long. But, while Timothy and I were trying to decipher the report, I mentioned wanting to do more than just fix the roof and cut my losses and he suggested a few contacts. He thinks the local estate agents can put him on to some contacts in the building trade for me. If I do this, I'll need a really good project manager to oversee the day-to-day running of the restoration and help me organise a reliable workforce. I don't plan on being that hands-on. Hopefully, I'll be running a new art gallery and I'm happy to leave it to the professionals, but I will be in Lostmor for any decisions that have to be made on site.' She looked at Oliver quizzically. 'Well, what do you think? Do you think I am mad?'

'No, of course not,' he replied. 'I think it would be an incredible achievement to restore the old place. It's such a unique property, but it is a massive undertaking. If you do this, you'll probably spend a lot of time on the phone and in person talking to people, making decisions and ordering materials. But, if you're happy to be "on-call" and you've got the right people on board, then why not! I'm curious as to what changed your mind, though. I thought you wanted to sell it fairly quickly?'

Lily sighed deeply before replying. 'To tell you the truth, I'm not sure myself. A feeling that I need to set things right. I'm probably not making any sense… I'm trying to move on from the past and, perhaps by breathing new life into the place, it will give me some sort of closure.'

Oliver hugged her. 'Lily Sanders, you never fail to surprise me!'

Flynn jumped down and barked once in agreement. Oliver gave Flynn's head a rub. 'I think someone wants to go out. Do you fancy a walk? It's a nice evening.'

'Good idea, and maybe we can watch the sunset from your mother's bench on the way back?'

'*Your* bench now, remember? Come on,' Oliver smiled, taking her hand. 'We can walk through the fields, then take the coastal path back.'

They walked along the edge of the fields that Oliver had recently ploughed ready for sowing, and then back along the strip of grassland running along the cliff edge. Flynn darted this way and that, excitedly chasing every fresh scent.

'I've got a month to vacate *The Blue*,' said Lily, 'so I think I'd better go to Bristol in a few days. Get things in motion. I could probably clear the place in two or three trips and, in the meantime, I'll speak to Adam at *Seaward Lets*. See if he has any shop premises to rent on his books. I'm sorry to keep asking, but is there any chance you could help feed the birds at the aviary until I'm back? I've roped Janet in, too.'

'Luckily for you,' Oliver grinned, 'I'm quiet for a week or two now until I start sowing crops. I've got repair jobs and machinery to sort out, but I can fit both in.'

'Thanks,' she smiled, gratefully.

'And I'll keep an eye on the house while I'm at it,' added Oliver. 'Maybe you should think about getting some better security in place?'

'You're right,' Lily replied. 'I need to get the entrance gate replaced, for starters. Then I'd better get a security firm in to look at installing an alarm system.'

'Have you heard any more from Sergeant Weeks?' asked Oliver.

'Not yet, but Joe spoke to him earlier today before I got to the hospital.'

'How is he?'

'A bit better,' said Lily. 'He's able to speak a little and, according to the nurse, trying to do too much too soon. He said there were two of them… in the house. He confronted them, there was a struggle. He remembers being punched, but then nothing after that. He passed out. Oh, and he remembered having some cartridges in his coat, which are also gone, along with his gun. '

'Does he remember what they look like?'

'Not that much, it was too dark.'

'Let's hope the police catch the bastards.'

'At least he's going to be okay,' she said. 'But he's got a way to go yet before he's back scaling ladders and fixing fences.'

They reached the bench just as orange sunlight filtered through striated clouds that hung low over a shimmering sea. A small flock of guillemots skimmed the frothy crests of the waves below. They sat watching the day's end and the silhouettes of a few birds flying home, swooping across a fiery sky.

CHAPTER 43

Lily hung a large 'Closed for business' sign in the window of *The Blue* and packed and stacked as much of the artwork as she could into crates ready to go into temporary storage. She supposed she could have flogged off some of the more commercial art in a 'closing down' sale, but she had made her decision and now she just wanted to get it done. She also carefully packed a few of her favourite paintings into her car and, along with her art materials, took them back to the apartment. She really did need a bigger car.

The following afternoon, once the man with a van she'd hired had taken one load of paintings and various office equipment off to a warehouse, she packed some of her clothes and headed back to Lostmor. She felt a little sad to be leaving her life in Bristol behind, but at the same time she was excited about what lay ahead. Whatever the future held, she knew she couldn't go back to living as she once had – hiding away in her apartment, always working and never reaching out to anyone. For the first time, she had opened up her heart to another person and, by doing so, was beginning to see herself in a whole new light.

She understood now how truly fortunate she was to have inherited Penwyth Estate and the money left in trust by her mother. She could start again, open another art gallery. And she couldn't wait to spend time exploring Lostmor. To capture on canvas the raw beauty of the rolling moors, of tumultuous seas and chameleonic skies. But, best of all — she had Oliver.

'Hi, there! Where are you?' Oliver asked on the phone.

'I'm very close.'

'How close?'

'On your doorstep... surprise!!' She hung up her mobile. Oliver opened the door and welcomed her with open arms. Flynn darted out, weaving excitedly between her legs and her suitcases.

'I missed you,' Oliver said, gently kissing her.

'It's only been two days.'

'I know, I'm a hopelessly besotted fool,' he joked, helping Lily in with her luggage. 'So, how's the packing going at *The Blue?*'

'Fine. There's quite a bit still to do and a big clean-up job needed before I return the keys, but I've made a good start.' Lily plopped down on a chair. 'Is it okay to shove these cases somewhere? Hopefully, I'll find somewhere soon. I'm meeting Adam at his office tomorrow and he thinks he already has a couple of possible places for me to look at.'

'You don't need to worry. Here,' said Oliver, passing her a key. 'I got this cut for you anyway, so just feel free to come and go as you please. I want you to treat it as your home for as long as you want to stay.'

'Thanks,' Lily smiled, 'for being so understanding.'

She showered, changed, and unpacked a few things, whilst Oliver lit a fire for later and cooked them lamb for dinner.

'That was delicious!' Lily said, having polished off two cutlets, mash, and peas.

'I aim to please,' Oliver smiled. They huddled together on the couch and watched the flames dance.

'How are things at the aviary?' she asked.

'Good. Joe's eclectic bunch of birds seem to be thriving. Janet fed them yesterday and I went earlier today.'

'Great,' said Lily. 'I'll give her a ring in the morning to say thanks. Any news from Sergeant Weeks? Do you know if he has been back to the estate?'

'Not when I was there,' replied Oliver. 'He may have gone back to visit Joe.'

'I was going to head over to St Oswald's tonight, but I don't think I can face any more driving.'

'It's getting late. Why don't you go tomorrow? Maybe we could go together? If you think he wouldn't mind another visitor.'

Lily smiled. 'I think he'd like the company and I would love for you to finally meet him. When I spoke to the ward nurse earlier, she said he was sitting out in a chair and could walk around slowly with help, so he must be feeling better. His right eye is still blurry, but he can see clearly in the left one. He is still in pain from his facial surgery and fractured ribs, but the nurses said it's to be expected. They've said he won't be discharged until they're sure he can manage at home. I didn't like to mention that his house may be the least place for concern…' She paused briefly. 'I'm more worried about him climbing up ladders or chopping firewood.'

'I'm sure he'll be okay,' said Oliver. 'After all, he doesn't need to take care of the whole estate any more, does he?'

'No, he doesn't,' agreed Lily. 'I've got the papers drawn up ready for him to sign. In the meantime, I can always arrange for a local landscaping company to manage things.'

'And once his ribs are healed… there's no reason he can't climb ladders and do much of what he was doing before, is there? So long as he's careful.'

'I hope so…' Lily's phone vibrated on the dining table. Leaning forward, she picked it up. 'Oh, hi Timothy! How are you?'

'I'm fine, my dear,' replied Timothy, her solicitor. 'I was really just checking on you. I've just learnt of the attempted break-in at Penwyth and that Joe is in hospital. There's a piece in the *Lostmor Gazette* about it.'

'Oh, I didn't know it was in the paper,' said Lily. 'I'm sorry. I should have called and let you know.'

'No problem, I'm sure you've had enough else to deal with. Is he going to be okay?'

'Yes, I think so, but he has taken a nasty beating.'

Lily explained how she had found him and what had followed since. 'Umm, the article in the paper... does it mention my family history... the accident?'

Oliver looked up with concern and could tell from her face that Timothy's reply was not what she had wanted to hear.

'Yes...' replied Timothy. 'The police have given the paper a quote about the break-in, but some overzealous reporter has linked the two incidents together, suggesting that the house is cursed.'

Lily's heart sank. Was she ever going to get past all this?

*

The next day, Joe gave a slightly wonky smile when Lily and Oliver entered the hospital room. He was free of tubes and monitors and sat in a tall chair by his bed.

'You look so much better!' said Lily, leaning in and kissing him very lightly so as not to hurt his face. 'I hope you don't mind, but I have brought a friend to meet you. Joe, this is Oliver. He's been helping me look after your aviary.'

'Pull up some seats,' said Joe, indeed looking pleased to have company. 'Nice to meet you, Oliver, and I guess I should thank you.'

'It's been my pleasure,' said Oliver. 'Your aviary is a remarkable place.'

Joe's face was still severely bruised, but the swelling had gone down. He looked from Lily to Oliver and back again, a twinkle in his eye.

'A handsome couple you two make!'

Lily felt herself blush like an awkward teenager. Oliver laughed, not knowing quite how to answer.

'I'm very fond of Lily,' he replied, taking Lily's hand in his own and smiling at Joe.

As they walked across the hospital grounds a short time later, Oliver turned to her. 'You haven't told him, have you?'

'No, not yet,' Lily replied. 'I wanted to, but… well, when I first came to see him he looked so bloody awful and must have been in so much pain. It didn't seem the right time.'

Oliver placed his hands on her shoulders. 'Lily, he's going to be over the moon. You're his daughter and he's going to love you, just as much as I do.'

Lily looked at him. 'Do you… love me?'

'Yes,' said Oliver, smiling. 'I love you, Lily Sanders. Every time I see you, you leave me breathless. I know it's only been a few months since we met, but I have never felt this way about anyone… Admittedly, I hadn't planned on saying that in a hospital car park.'

Lily laughed and gave him a playful hug. She looked into his deep mahogany eyes that radiated warmth and humour.

'I love you too, Oliver Bligh.'

CHAPTER 44

Seaward Lets was one of three shops fronting a characterless concrete building hidden in one of Tresor Bay's less attractive back streets. In the salon window next door was a pink and white poster of a lady's recently coiffed hair that had to be from the 1970s.

'How nice to see you again, Miss Sanders,' Adam rose and shook her hand. 'Please take a seat.'

Since they had last spoken, one of the two properties he'd mentioned had been withdrawn. The owners had decided to modernise it first. No problem, she didn't need any more decorating! He showed her some photos of the remaining shop and Lily was thrilled to see that it looked perfect.

Hidden Treasures, its previous trading name, had harbour views at the busier end of the bay where, as Adam had once mentioned, more tourists tended to congregate. The shop was an end of terrace, with a separate entrance at the side leading to the living space above.

In the shop front, he pulled up the blinds allowing the light to pour in. The room wasn't particularly wide, but was three times as deep – perfect for her needs. The whole of the downstairs had recently been painted white giving it a fresh, clean feel and there was a small cash desk set off to the side. At the rear was a door leading into what used to be a storage room and makeshift kitchen and Lily could see it would be great to use as a small studio.

While the ground floor was perfectly adequate and functional for her needs, upstairs was completely different and a little unexpected. She had seen a few photos back at the agency, but was still pleasantly surprised. The floors throughout were varnished oak, with funky, multicoloured knotted rugs. At the far end was a small kitchen with chunky oak units and worktops, while a rectangular island with stools created a division between the dining area and the lounge, with more warm-coloured oak furniture and an inviting turquoise couch and armchairs. Three further doors led off the landing. One, a small white bathroom, tiled floor to ceiling, and spotlessly clean, followed by two more bedrooms. The first was no more than a box room, but the second was much larger with double aspect windows overlooking quaint, cobbled streets below. Whoever had furnished the apartment was obviously a fan of oak. A king-sized oak bed dominated. Both sets of windows had floor-to-ceiling, deep purple velvet curtains that matched a two-seater couch.

'Oh, and there's central heating throughout,' Adam continued as part of his running narration. 'Well, do you think you might be interested, Miss Sanders?'

If he had by now worked out who she was as a result of the news story in the local press, he certainly didn't show it. Or, perhaps she was overestimating the level of interest people had in her affairs. She hoped so.

'Yes, I think I am,' she smiled.

Back at his office, Lily signed a six-month contract, paid a deposit, and arranged to pick up the keys in a few days' time. She was about to drive straight on to Penwyth House to meet Oliver at the aviary when her phone rang.

'Miss Sanders, this is Mr Carne, Lostmor Antiques. I'm sorry I missed your call.'

'No problem, I think we keep missing each other. I got your

message about the auction. So, it went well, then?'

'Very well. Very well, indeed. I think you'll be pleased with the final amount raised. Perhaps you could drop by at our premises sometime soon so we can transfer the monies raised for your chosen charities?'

'Yes, of course. I'm in Lostmor right now, if that's convenient?'

'Perfect. Also, one of my men has recovered an album. A family photo album from a desk that was taken, we think from one of the spare bedrooms at Penwyth House.'

'Goodness,' said Lily. 'I thought I checked every conceivable place for anything belonging to the family.'

Mr Carne laughed. 'It is unlikely you would have found this. It was hidden in a concealed compartment. Unless you had looked behind the draw itself, you wouldn't have known it was there. We only came across it because we routinely inspect things for auction very closely for damage.'

'Well, I don't have many photos of my family, so this is very exciting. Thank you.'

The door chimed as Lily walked into Lostmor Antiques, having texted Oliver and arranged to meet him an hour later than planned. Mr Carne's office was at the rear of the ground floor and barely visible behind a row of large wardrobes. A set of angular stairs led up to a labyrinth of smaller rooms spread across two upper levels jam-packed with antiques, books, and ornaments ranging from common or garden bric-a-brac to expensive objet d'art.

Lily circumnavigated several aisles of chairs before spotting him pressing buttons on a calculator at his desk. She was warmly welcomed and gratefully accepted tea whilst they arranged for the impressive sum of just over £28,000 to be divided equally between Lostmor Community Centre, which ran lots of social events and was always in need of funds, and the local hospice, which her mother had vehemently supported and, as Lily had recently discovered from

Timothy, had continued to donate to even after they had moved to Bristol. Free entry, reasonable reserve prices, and Mr Carne's suggestion to provide the excited locals with a buffet after the event, paid off. The auction had been packed to breaking point.

'Oh, and here is the album we found,' Mr Carne said, passing her a flat, rectangular box. 'As it is quite old and I am sure of sentimental value, I took the liberty of packing it in this for you. So it doesn't get damaged in transit.'

Lily thanked him for everything, then drove to Penwyth Estate and parked on the drive. Oliver was yet to arrive. With trembling hands, she carefully unwrapped the album. Enclosed, potentially, were lots of photos of her family. All she'd ever had was the framed photo from her mother's bedroom. At the same time, she was about to be reintroduced to Alice's face, which she could barely remember.

The edge of a large black and white photo was sticking out of the inside cover sleeve. It was her grandparents on her mother's side, Alfred and Jeanie. Lilly imagined they were dressed up for a special occasion, they looked so dapper. Her grandmother sported a shorter hairstyle as was popular in the 1920s, arranged in tidy, smooth, sculpted waves. She wore a simple string of pearls and a light-coloured sleeveless flapper dress. Lily's grandfather was tall, clean-shaven with slicked-back hair and wore a tweed suit. She smiled and slipped the photo back in.

Each page held two photos with white paper corner mounts. Some of the older photos were in black and white, the more recent ones, from the 1960s and 1970s, were in colour. The first pages were of her mother with Vincent, standing smiling outside many world-famous landmarks including the Eiffel Tower, the Taj Mahal, and the Giza pyramid. There were other photos behind the ones mounted that Lily carefully prised out, showing more faraway places. One showed them sitting in a bar overlooking a tropical beach with palms lining the bay, her mother holding a cocktail, looking happy and carefree, another of them sitting at what looked like a captain's table, presumably on board a luxury liner. Lily smiled. At least they had been happy together once upon a time, as her mother had said.

Holiday snaps gave way to photos of Penwyth House. There were no dates on the backs, but Lily presumed her mother had taken them not long after she had moved in. The building looked even more ominous as a black and white image. There was no drive and the gardens were unkempt and overgrown. She guessed her mother must have had her work cut out, a bit like she had now. There were photos of her mother's wedding day, the ceremony having taken place at Penwyth House. She had vague memories of seeing a wedding album as a child. Perhaps her mother had disposed of it after Vincent's death? Lily was glad that at least she had these.

There was a photo of the happy couple standing in front of the oak door that was adorned with hundreds of roses. Her mother looked stunning in a long white gown, slim-fitting with a long trail and a delicate lace bodice that revealed her shoulders. Her hair was loosely pinned in a soft bun entwined with gypsophila and tiny white roses. Other images followed, of them taking their vows under a wooden arch that was smothered with more roses, in front of a gathering of people sitting in rows of tastefully embellished chairs on an immaculate lawn. Lily wondered if Joe had been their gardener from the start and had been the one to tame and landscape the gardens.

She only recognised a couple of faces from the group shots. Margaret, the house cook, was wearing a light-coloured suit that was a bit tight across her bosom, and a large floppy hat that sat a bit low – and Timothy, her solicitor. She had to look twice. He was so slim and clean-shaven, but with the same unmistakable beaming smile. Next, were photos of herself as a baby, a tiny bundle lying in a cot; another of her mother cradling her, looking down fondly. Others of her as a toddler, on a blanket in the garden, crawling after a ball, her short hair fastened in little bunches. Then a colour photo with white borders that she presumed to be her first school photo. That was followed by family shots of her, Vincent and her mother – some of the locations she recognised as Tresor Bay and some were of sandy beaches, probably nearby. In one photo, Lily stood in a hole in the sand up to her knees wielding a spade in one hand and an ice lolly in the other.

By now, her earlier nerves were forgotten, taken over by a fascination in seeing her family's lives played out. More school photos and some of her with friends at a birthday party, a few years on. Then Alice's arrival. More family photos, much like her own – baby shots, the two of them together, Lily hugging her toddler sister on a settee. She touched a finger lightly to Alice's smiling, chubby baby face, hardly aware of the tears streaming down her own face. There was a school photo of the two of them together and a few family ones of the four of them, including the same picture she had found framed in her parents' room. Then nothing but blank pages – a life cut short – a family story abruptly ended.

Oliver appeared at the car window, making her jump. She had been so absorbed by the photos she hadn't heard him pull up.

'Whatever's wrong?' he asked.

'Oh! I'm okay,' replied Lily. 'Come and sit in here for a minute and I'll explain.'

She showed him the album and explained how she had come across it.

'I'm alright, really I am. I can't believe how lucky I am to get this back. God bless Mr Carne. Just think, if I'd have kept the desk I may well have never found it.'

Oliver put an arm around her. 'I wonder why your mother hid it so well? After all, it's only a family album.'

'I have no idea,' she sighed. 'It seems my mother had quite a lot of secrets.'

'Do you still want to go to the aviary?' said Oliver. 'I don't mind going if you'd rather sit here for a bit, or I can just see you back at the farm if you want to go home?'

'No, let's go feed the birds. I want to,' Lily smiled, wiping her eyes.

The bright blue sky above them made it feel more like a summer's day than early spring and the aviary looked dazzling in the sunshine.

'Did you find the pellet supply in the stables, by the way?' Lily asked.

'Yes, there are masses over there and the tubs in the aviary need topping up,' said Oliver. 'We could go over in my car and fill them all up at once. I've already picked up some apples.' He nodded at a hessian sack. 'We can chop these up when we get back.'

'I had completely forgotten about the stables,' said Lily. 'I keep meaning to go there. So we're not going to run out of pellets anytime soon?'

'Pretty much, come see for yourself,' he smiled.

Oliver parked at the end of the narrow lane. 'We'll have to grab the tubs and walk from here, but it's not far. Do you remember the way?'

'Kind of, but I don't remember it looking like this.'

The lane was overgrown with brambles, but wide enough to get through on foot. On their left was what remained of the kennels. It was a harsh concrete building that, with time, had collapsed in on itself completely. They walked into a large, sunlit clearing. To their left, a tumbledown dry stone wall stretched the length of the stables behind it. Betwixt the two was what once must have been an impressive courtyard, its cobblestones now tufted with grass and covered with tree debris.

'Gosh!' said Lily in surprise. 'I mean, it's totally neglected, but what a place!'

Oliver grinned, putting the tubs down and grabbing her hand. 'Come and see!'

The low, wooden building had been partially reclaimed by the encroaching woods behind. Ivy and green-leafed climbers had twisted and strained their way in through broken roof tiles and the stable openings. Each stable had a small gabled wooden front, giving the impression of a row of tiny attached houses. Lily leant over the first stable door and peered into the gloom. Stacked in neat piles were at least twenty large plastic containers of pellets.

'You weren't kidding! There has to be a ton of the stuff.'

The next door was hanging ajar. Its hinges creaked as Lily pushed it inwards and they were hit by a pungent, damp smell. An empty plastic bucket and long-abandoned broom lay in a puddle of stagnant rainwater and the long tendrils of a climber laced the walls and ceiling. She ran her hand over the split, rotten planks of the doors as they wandered the length of the building. Small birds darted in and out of the stables and the fretwork of ivy that covered them.

Lily stood back and looked around the clearing. The stables were in shade, nestled into the trees behind, but the courtyard and overgrown meadow in front were bathed in sunshine.

'I don't know if it's the promise of spring in the air today, but this place feels... almost enchanted.'

'I thought the same when I first saw it, and it wasn't sunny then,' said Oliver grinning. 'Penwyth is certainly full of surprises.'

'I don't remember us coming here that much as kids... me and Alice. We were either in the gardens, woods, or in the glasshouses. The kennels were out of bounds and the stables were never used by the family, so I guess this has stood empty for maybe forty years or more.'

Back at the farm, Oliver looked through the album with interest. Lily's mother was attractive, but in a different way to Lily. Elizabeth had big blue eyes, long straight blonde hair, and rosebud lips, and even though Alice was very young in the photos, she looked like her mother. Lily's darker hair was wavy and almost auburn in the sunlight. Her features were more delicate and her hazel eyes strangely mesmerising. To Oliver, she had an ethereal beauty that seemed to glow from within.

'Vincent looks happy,' he said, leafing through some of the earlier photos of him and Elizabeth abroad. 'Very different to the stern image in his painting. What's this?'

Lily watched with interest as he pulled out another black and white photo, this time hidden in the sleeve at the back of the album. The photo was of Joe and her mother. He was dressed in work clothes and a flat cap, her mother in a simple summer dress. They were arm in arm, looking relaxed and smiling fondly at each other. In the photo, the stone wall behind them was solid, not neglected and crumbling like the one at the stables, and the cobblestones clean and shiny.

Lily looked at Oliver. 'That's why she hid the album.'

'Do you think that's where they used to meet? At the stables?' asked Oliver.

'It could be...' replied Lily. 'He could have left notes for her there, like the ones I found in my old book, knowing no one ever went there. They had a secret love tryst... it must have been exciting... for a while, at least.'

Oliver smiled and looked at the photo again. 'They look at ease together, don't they... like they belong.'

CHAPTER 45

Douglas passed the *Lostmor Gazette* to Luke, who had been sitting waiting for him in the van while he picked up his bike parts from Tasker's garage.

'Look! This was in their waiting room. We're famous, bro,' Douglas grinned, revealing small, widely spaced teeth.

Luke read the article on the front page of the newspaper.

Is Penwyth House cursed?

Not all of our readers will remember the shocking family tragedy that occurred at Penwyth House in June 1971. Witness to that fateful evening was 9-year-old Lily Sanders whose father Vincent and sister, 6-year-old Alice, plunged to their deaths from the spired roof of their Gothic mansion home. A verdict of accidental death was later recorded by the coroner and the house has remained uninhabited ever since.

Elizabeth Sanders, who is recently deceased following a prolonged illness, leaves her daughter, Lily Sanders, now 33, the sole beneficiary of Penwyth Estate. After a recent break-in at the house, Sergeant Weeks of the Devon & Cornwall Police gave the following statement:

'On Sunday 19th February at approx. 7.15 pm an attempted burglary at Penwyth House resulted in a brutal attack on the resident groundsman, Joe Newman. The 74-year-old man is thought to have been on his daily evening round of the house and gardens, as he has done so for over 30 years, when he

disturbed the burglars. He was severely beaten by his assailants and sustained serious injuries. This was a particularly violent crime where the outcome could have been much worse. Fortunately, he is expected to make a full recovery and is currently recuperating at St Oswald's Hospital. Mr Newman showed great courage in trying to defend the property and continues to assist the police with their ongoing enquiry. I would also like to reassure the public that this kind of aggravated burglary is rare, especially in Lostmor, and that Devon & Cornwall Police are doing everything within their power to apprehend the men responsible.'

As Douglas drove, Luke reread the news item with interest; he hadn't known the history of the place. There was a picture of Lily Sanders as a young girl, which looked like a hastily acquired school photo. Could it be the same woman he had seen leaving the estate? Maybe. He was angry with himself for not having known about the groundsman, but it was too late now. He smirked at the fact that Sergeant Weeks hadn't mentioned the gun theft. So as not to alert the public, he guessed. He was pretty sure the police didn't have a clue who they were, and the old man didn't have much of a chance to see their faces, especially in the dark.

As far as Luke was concerned, it hadn't been a total waste of time. Now, they were armed. He hadn't decided what their next target would be yet – maybe a post office or a small jeweller's, or a retail outlet of some kind, somewhere where there would be a guaranteed payout. And, next time, he would research their chosen target more carefully. He would check its quiet times, CCTV, the number of employees, as well as the times they came and went. If they were going to be armed, they could not afford to be caught – or they'd both be doing serious time.

Once they were back home, Douglas returned to working on the Triumph. Luke was glad of the peace. He needed to think. He tore off and scrunched up the first few pages of the *Lostmor Gazette* and placed them in the hearth, ready to add some kindle, when he noticed a familiar name on the next page. Julia… Julia Sutton. He instantly recalled her pretty face, her long blonde hair, and big blue eyes… He could picture her as clearly as if he had seen her yesterday. It had to be the same Julia, didn't it? How many Julia Suttons could there be in Lostmor? She'd moved away with her family a long time ago, but maybe she'd moved back? Luke smiled — she was not married, either. Just the thought of seeing her again after all this time was arousing him.

He read the two-line advertisement in the Jobs column. She had recently opened a kennels called Fern Retreat and was looking for a part-time kennel hand. The ad included her name and number. He tore off the page and folded it neatly into his pocket, grinning cheerfully to himself. *Dogs, eh?* He had always figured her for a doctor or maybe a lawyer. She had been a straight-A student. Luke didn't like animals, especially dogs, but how hard could it be to look after a few mutts? His future and soon-to-be prosperous life of crime could wait a bit longer – first things first.

The address for Fern Retreat wasn't listed in the Yellow Pages – too new, he presumed, but a quick visit to Lostmor's veterinary practice came up trumps. Luke cruised past Fern Retreat, hoping for a glimpse, but she was nowhere to be seen. He didn't want to be spotted, he wanted to surprise her. He pulled in a bit further up the road and dialled the number on the advert.

'Oh, hello, is this Julia Sutton? I'm ringing about the kennel hand position.'

After a brief conversation, he hung up. In a few days, he would finally get to see his Julia again.

CHAPTER 46

'Cheers, and thanks for helping out at the aviary,' said Lily, raising her glass to Janet.

'No problem,' said Janet. 'I didn't do that much, just dished out food, and had a bit of a wander to check on the birds. Anyway, I enjoy going there. It's such a magical place and, as for the house... Our visit the other day just left me speechless. I half expected to see Morticia Addams come wafting down the staircase!'

Lily laughed out loud. 'You are incorrigible!'

'Ooh, I do hope so!' Janet grinned.

'What happened to the dog you were called away for?' asked Lily.

'Stanley? He's doing okay. I had to keep him at the surgery overnight. He's a lovely old Boxer who is partial to drinking out of the toilet bowl. The couple who owned him always kept the seat down for that reason, but their cleaner had squirted a load of bleach and then forgotten to close the lid. Needless to say, he was sick a couple of times. By the time I saw him, he was very weak and unable to get up.'

'Poor thing. How awful for his owners.'

'Well, yes, understandably they were upset and scared, but he was lucky. It wasn't enough to kill him and he perked up overnight once he'd had IV drugs and fluids.'

'You know, you really should write your memoirs one day,' said Lily. 'It would make a fascinating read!'

'Hmmm, maybe one day…' laughed Janet. 'Perhaps you should, too?'

'I think I'll stick to painting,' said Lily.

The Black Dog slowly began to fill up whilst they chatted about Lily's plans for her new art gallery, of the auction, and the exciting discovery of a family album. She told Janet about the photo of Joe and her mother hidden in the back and how she planned to give it to him once he was home.

'How is he?' asked Janet.

'He's improving all the time, but I've heard nothing further from the police. I'll try the sergeant again in the morning, but I don't think they've got much to go on.'

'Hello!' said Timothy.

'Oh!' said Lily. 'What a nice surprise. Have you just got here?'

'Yes, I spotted you from the bar.'

'Why don't you join us? This is my friend, Janet.'

'Well, I don't want to impose,' said Timothy politely.

'You're not imposing at all,' Lily grinned, shifting slightly up the long seat of the booth.

Timothy beamed at Janet. 'Do you hail from Lostmor?'

Janet shook her head and smiled. 'No, although I have been here for fifteen years… I spend a lot of time in uncompromising positions with animals.'

Lily nearly choked on her drink. 'She's a vet!' she quickly added.

Janet, who was just being her quirky self, found herself uncharacteristically blushing.

'What a fascinating job. You must have some interesting stories,' Timothy said, completely unphased.

'Funnily enough, we were just discussing that,' said Janet. 'Lily has suggested I write my memoirs. Maybe one day, when I retire,' she smiled. They chatted amicably amongst themselves. Timothy got onto the police investigation and shook his head in despair when recounting the newspaper article.

'Dreadful. Have you been pestered at all by the local press?' he asked.

'Not at all,' said Lily. 'I think they probably don't know where I'm staying, or maybe it's just not that newsworthy.' She filled Timothy in on Joe's condition and of their looking after the aviary, which he also had not known existed.

'How amazing!' he said. 'The times I've visited the estate in the past and didn't realise. One day, I would love to see it. If Joe has no objections, of course.'

'Oh, it's enchanting,' said Janet. 'And it's full of the most beautiful orchids, too.'

'Really?'

Timothy knew nothing about Elizabeth's affair with Joe and of what Lily had subsequently learnt about her parentage. Perhaps one day she would explain, but now wasn't the time, especially when she hadn't yet told Joe. Lily caught Janet's eye, but she knew better than to mention family secrets.

Just then, the door to the Black Dog opened and Oliver walked in.

'Hi, everyone, sorry I'm late,' he said. 'I've been trying to fix the damn generator in the barn.'

'And did you?' Janet asked.

'I think so, yes. I don't use it that much, but it comes in handy all the same.'

Lily then did the introductions. 'Oliver, this is Timothy. Timothy, Oliver.'

'Ah, Timothy, Lily's solicitor,' said Oliver. 'Nice to finally meet you,' he smiled and shook hands. 'Would anyone like another drink?'

'Not for me, thanks,' said Timothy. 'I'm afraid I must be off. I have an early appointment with a new client, but it's very nice to meet you Oliver… and you, Janet,' he beamed in her direction.

'Okay,' Lily stood and gave him a quick hug goodbye. 'Thanks for all your help with the house so far.'

'My pleasure,' he waved, heading for the door.

'He was sweet,' said Janet.

Lily grinned at her.

'What?' Janet said, blushing slightly.

At the bar, Oliver ordered their drinks. 'Hey, Marcus, how are things?'

'Oh, you know,' replied Marcus. 'Business is not bad for March. Is it serious, then?' He nodded in Lily's direction.

Oliver grinned. 'It might be. That's Lily, she's opening up an art gallery in town soon.'

'She's an artist then?'

'Yep, a very good one, too – landscapes, that kind of thing. It was kind of random how we met. She found my dog, Flynn, roaming about on the coastal road.'

'That's funny,' Marcus replied. 'I've been seeing someone, too, and we only met because of Horace. She's just opened up a kennels nearby.' The pair laughed. Marcus didn't mention Douglas's stake-out at Oliver's farm. No point in worrying him now… Douglas would soon be history. 'I hope it works out for you, mate,' he smiled, passing him a half-pint of ale.

'You, too,' replied Oliver.

He sat back down, squeezing his legs under the table. 'I've been thinking, maybe we should mention Douglas Holt to Sergeant Weeks? Has he got a list of everyone who's been in and out of the place?'

'Yes, including Eastgate Skips,' said Lily. 'Do you think he might be involved?'

Oliver shrugged. 'It's possible. He's shifty alright and he's already proved that he can be violent. He lobbed a pitchfork at me and tried to land a punch.'

'Okay,' said Lily. 'I was going to ring the sergeant in the morning, anyway. I'll give him Holt's name and mention his attack on you. I don't think they have any other leads as he hasn't called me back.'

A short time later, Janet also made her goodbyes. She, too, had clients early in the morning, of the furry kind.

Now that they were both alone, Lily gazed out at the twinkling bay. She remembered wistfully how nervous she had been driving to her first meeting with Timothy and her initial shock at learning that Penwyth House had never been sold. Things had certainly moved on since then. She had found family, friends, and now love. Through the window, she watched as the ornate Victorian street lamps that ran the length of the curved promenade flickered on. All except for one, the light of which flared, then faltered repeatedly like some frantic Morse code signal.

CHAPTER 47

Marcus walked Horace across the drive at Fern Retreat. They were greeted by the deafening noise of excited dogs barking in unison. Business was booming.

'Hi, Julia!' he shouted over the din. She turned from shutting one of the kennel doors and waved.

'Hi, you two!'

He was slightly relieved to see she was smiling at him. Since the night at the pub when he'd dashed off leaving her all alone, and then later having revealed the truth about Rose and his real purpose for being in Lostmor, he'd sensed a change between them. Subsequently, she had twice made excuses not to see him. They may have been genuine reasons, he'd told himself. The kennels had got steadily busier since opening day.

'What a nice surprise,' she smiled, kissing him on the cheek and stroking Horace's head. 'I was just about to exercise two of my guests, Bertie and Coco. Do you want to tag along?'

'Sure,' said Marcus. 'I drove today, so Horace could do with a run, if that's okay?' He nodded in the direction of his parked truck. 'Got to get back for the evening shift.'

'Sure, I'll grab Bella, too. She's in the house.'

They stood watching as the two border terriers ran back and forth after a ball, while Horace and Bella belted off, chasing each other's tails.

'Are things okay, Julia?' asked Marcus, after a few minutes of silence.

'Yes,' she replied. 'I'm exhausted by the end of each day, but I'm loving it. Luckily, I have got a couple of people coming this week about the kennel hand position. Fingers crossed that at least one of them is suitable. That will, hopefully, give me a bit more time.' Julia paused for a moment before continuing. 'One is called Sarah. She's saving to go to university this October and already works a few shifts in a call centre, but prefers to be outdoors. She grew up on a sheep farm and is used to dogs. The other is Luke. He says he has previous experience, and wasn't put off by the low pay, either.'

'That's great,' Marcus smiled warmly at her. 'I always knew you'd make a huge success of this.' He gently took her arm so that they faced each other. 'But that's not what I meant. I meant are things okay between us?'

For a moment, Julia looked down at the ground, as if thinking what to say next. Then she met his gaze. Her pale blue eyes were completely mesmerising to him.

'Last time we met, I asked you to level with me, and I appreciate you trusting me enough to tell me the truth. But it was a lot to take in and I needed a bit of time to think. Also, I'm sorry, but I really have been busy with the dogs.' She turned to swing the ball thrower.

'I am sorry,' said Marcus. 'For leaving you like that and... well, you know the rest now.'

Julia turned back and looked directly at him. 'Look, I can't pretend that I agree with what you are doing, but I understand your reasons for wanting this man to pay for what he did. Christ, he killed your daughter. And I know you were trained to kill in the army... have killed... but this is different. Let's say you do find him. Can't you hand him over? I don't care what happens to him, but if you take his life and get caught, you'll go to prison. Your life will be ruined. Is that what Rose would have wanted? And what about me?'

'You know how much you mean to me… that's why I'm being honest with you. I promised I would.' He paused. 'I've already found him, Julia, and the only reason I haven't confronted him yet is to make sure I cover my tracks. I won't be caught. Besides, the police will have no reason to connect this person's death to Rose. That's if they're still even looking. They don't know what I know about him.'

Julia was shocked. 'How did you find him? Are you one hundred per cent sure you have the right guy?'

'Does it matter how?' Marcus replied. She didn't know of his trip to Douglas Holt's place where he'd found the missing part of the dragon's head chain. 'It's him, alright. I have proof.' He placed his hands on Julia's shoulders and gently smoothed her cheek. 'I don't want to involve you. At least, not any more than I already have,' he smiled grimly. 'I can't go to the police. I love you and I don't want to lose you, but I won't hand him over. In a matter of days, I promise you this will be over. Then, if you still want me… we can be together.'

Julia's heart sank because she knew that, even if she walked away from him, he wouldn't stop. She nodded her head slowly – because she loved him, too.

CHAPTER 48

'Miss Sanders? It's Sergeant Weeks. I'm sorry I haven't called sooner.'

'Hello. I was just about to ring you. How are your enquiries going?'

'We've nothing solid yet, but my men are going door to door as we speak. It can take a bit longer to contact some homeowners, especially if they are holiday homes. I understand you want answers, but we need to be thorough, which means sifting through a lot of information.'

'I appreciate that, sergeant,' said Lily. 'I wonder, can I ask about someone called Douglas Holt? He works for Eastgate Skips.'

Sergeant Weeks paused and there was a rustling of paper as he checked his notes. 'Yes,' he replied, 'an officer spoke to him earlier, and to Luke Holt.'

'Oh. Are they father and son?'

'No, it says here they're brothers, temporarily contracted for two weeks by the skip company. They both confirmed delivering a skip to Penwyth House. Why do you ask?'

'Brothers?' said Lily. 'Well, I don't know if this is relevant, but Oliver Bligh – I was with him at his farm when I first met you. He hired Douglas Holt as a farmhand a few weeks ago, but he turned out to be lazy and unreliable so he had to let him go. I know that isn't that big of a deal, but when Oliver asked him to leave, Douglas threw a pitchfork at him and tried to punch him. Oliver was shocked by his violent behaviour and it worried him a bit when he later saw him driving the skip truck at Penwyth House. He thinks he's trouble. It may be nothing, but Oliver asked me to mention him to you.'

'I see...' replied the sergeant. 'It says here that the brothers live together and were both at home all evening the night of the burglary. So, they are each other's alibi... Let me speak to the officer who called on them and check if either has any previous offences, especially for theft or violent crime. If something comes up, we'll pay them another visit. Having said that, you should be aware that there are a lot of "ifs". But thank you, we will look into it and I'll keep you informed.'

A few days later at Edhen Cottage, Oliver had stocked the fridge, chopped and stacked wood for the log store, and stoked a fire ready for Joe's return. Lily pulled up outside and helped Joe out of her car. His ribs were healing well and no longer hurt as much. When he was being discharged from hospital, he was advised it would be at least another three weeks before he would be free of pain and was instructed to rest as much as possible. His facial bruising was fading and the sight in his right eye was continuing to improve, despite Dr Lake's initial concerns.

'It's good to be home,' Joe said, walking slowly with the aid of one crutch. Lily carried his small case of belongings.

'Hello again, Joe,' said Oliver. 'It's really good to see you up and about and looking so much better.'

'Well, thanks for all your help, both of you,' said Joe. 'I don't know what I would have done without you.'

'It's the least we could do,' Lily said. She couldn't help feeling responsible in an indirect kind of way. She knew she was being hard on herself, but if she hadn't returned to Lostmor and had people coming to and fro at the house, it probably wouldn't have happened.

'Well, I may as well make myself useful and go tend to your aviary,' Oliver said.

'I wish I could come, too,' replied Joe sadly.

Lily smiled. 'Don't worry, we're taking good care of the birds and plants until you're ready.'

She walked outside with Oliver. 'Thanks,' she said.

Oliver slowly drew her to him and kissed her on the lips. 'Tell him,' he smiled fondly down at her. She nodded. 'See you later.'

After Lily had heated through some soup for their supper and added more logs to the fire, she told Joe about the recent auction.

'I met up with Mr Carne from Lostmor Antiques not long ago,' she said. 'His men helped take away some of the furniture in the house, and one of them found this hidden in an old desk.' She pulled out the treasured family album from her large shoulder bag. 'Here, take a look.'

Joe turned the pages slowly.

'Can you make out the photos okay?' she asked.

'Some of the faces are a bit blurry, but I can make out who people are,' Joe smiled.

'I didn't think there were any photos left of my family, so this was a lovely surprise.'

'They're wonderful,' Joe said, looking at the ones of Lily and Alice as children.

'And here, I found one at the back that I want you to have.' From her bag, Lily pulled out the black and white photo, now framed, and gave it to him. Joe stared in disbelief at the photo of himself and Elizabeth. They looked young and in love – as if they had not a care in the world.

'Thank you…' Emotion caught in his voice. 'Thank you, Lily,' he half-whispered. 'I only have one photo of her. I remember taking this. Setting the timer, us both laughing as I tried to get back to her in time before the camera flashed... but I never got to see the photo.' Joe's sea-green eyes glistened with tears. 'Until now,' he said, holding the frame to his chest. 'Before I was attacked, you and me talked about your mother and how she fell pregnant... you said that you would try to find out who your father was.' He looked at her hopefully. 'Did you? Find out, I mean?'

'Yes, I did...' replied Lily gently. 'Vincent is not my birth parent.'

Joe gazed at her, saying nothing.

'My friend, Janet, helped,' continued Lily. 'She explained that, because they were both blood type O, they could not produce a child who was A negative – that's me. It's not biologically possible. Which means...' She paused, the emotion building in her voice. 'I mean, I can't officially prove it to you... but, because you were honest with me about your relationship with Mother... and we know that you were the only one she was with... You must be my real father. My birth father.'

Joe's voice quivered. 'My child... I can't tell you how long I've wanted to hear those words.' He gently cupped her face in trembling hands and kissed her forehead.

They half laughed, half cried as they embraced, now as father and daughter.

CHAPTER 49

He was an hour early for his interview. Luke watched as a girl on a bicycle rode into Fern Retreat and then left half an hour later. He checked his face in the rear-view mirror of the van. He'd washed his hair that morning and tied it back in a ponytail. *Not too bad*, he thought. Clean-shaven for once and fresh T-shirt and jeans. He pulled out of the lay-by just past the kennels and turned left into the drive. He felt excited to be seeing her again after so many years. There she was, smiling and walking fast towards him in wellington boots and a mustard-coloured waterproof jacket. Her hair was still long. Not as long as she'd worn at school, though, and now it was partially tied back.

'You must be Luke, I'm Julia,' she offered her hand.

'Yep. Nice to meet you,' said Luke. He shook her hand and grinned his most charming grin. She had expected someone a bit younger, someone nearer to the girl Sarah's age who had just left. This guy was nearer thirty, but she guessed it didn't matter.

'So, Luke, shall I show you around? Then we can have a quick chat afterwards.'

They walked along the line of kennels to a crescendo of barking. Luke smiled and nodded and pulled sympathetic faces at the excited dogs. He feigned interest, asking Julia the obvious questions like how often she fed and exercised the dogs. Julia showed him the paddock and the hut where she received owners and took payments and discussed working hours.

'You know, you look familiar to me, but I can't quite place you,' she said back in the hut, where they perched on a couple of stools. 'Have you always lived in Lostmor?'

Luke played dumb. 'I don't think we've met… but yes, I was born and raised here,' he smiled salubriously. If anything, she had grown even more beautiful. He could imagine holding her, gazing down into those big blue eyes and kissing her soft, full lips. He leant forward slightly, feeling himself go hard.

'You know I can't pay very much and it's physically hard work,' Julia continued. 'There's a lot of mucking out and exercising to do, plus it goes without saying that you need to enjoy being with the dogs.'

He tried to focus. 'I understand about the money. My situation is that I run a farm with my brother. It used to be our father's and I'm just trying to subsidise our income a bit. I prefer outdoor work and I've always loved dogs. So, when I saw your ad, I thought, why not come along?' He was beginning to enjoy himself, but he didn't want to overdo it. 'I expect you have other people to see, but I would be very interested in the job.' He tried to look sincere and the right degree of humble at the same time.

'Your farm, doesn't it take up most of your time already?' asked Julia.

'It is busy, but we've reduced the number of livestock we have now, so my brother can manage it pretty well,' said Luke. 'You mentioned that the working day is eight until three, which is great because I could still help do the early milking. Even the later one, if needed… I'd just be splitting my time. If I get the job, that is…' He shrugged and smiled again. 'I'm not really a nine to five kind of guy. Ever since school, I've been working out in all weathers.'

Julia studied his face. School. Of course, that was where she knew him from.

'You're Luke from school! West Hill High School, right? My surname's Sutton. Julia Sutton. Do you remember? We used to hang out in the third or fourth year, I think. We met in the library.'

He feigned surprise and then broke into a broad grin that curled his lip.

'Julia Sutton! I should have remembered your surname in the ad! I'm sorry I didn't place you straight away.'

'Nor I you!' she replied. 'How have you been? Are you still an avid reader?'

'Wow, I can't quite believe this. Can you? Yes,' he lied. 'I read all the time. You?'

'Not so much these days. I've been too busy setting up this place. I've only been back in Lostmor a short time, and now that business is looking up... Well, that's why I need the extra help.'

'That's right, you moved away with your family?'

'South Devon,' she replied. Julia remembered now. Luke had shunned her after she had been flirting with some school kid. At the time, she had been shocked by his behaviour. She had only ever considered him a friend, but he had been jealous and angry. Their brief friendship and book discussions had come to a sudden end. Silly, teenage tantrums yes, but he had upset her, and being quite naïve she had not fully understood why. *This is all a bit strange*, she thought. Luke slid off the stool, sensing it was time to go.

'Well, thanks for coming,' said Julia. 'I've got your number, so I'll let you know in a few days if that's okay?'

'Sure,' he smiled. 'It's been nice to see you again.'

'What is your surname? I can't quite recall.'

'Holt. It's Luke Holt,' he replied, waving amicably as he sauntered back to his van.

CHAPTER 50

Moving into *Swan Song*, as it was shortly to be christened once the new signage arrived, went smoothly. Lily had set up her studio at the back and quickly made the upstairs apartment her new home. Oliver had helped and surprised her with a moving-in gift. It was a small sail ship softly crafted from aluminium with a half-moon and trail of clouds drifting horizontally from the top of its mast. She adored it.

'We should celebrate!' he said, looking around the shop front, admiring the artwork she had begun to hang and the tasteful basket of white lilies and trailing orchids in the front window.

'Well, we might be a bit premature,' she replied. 'I need to get on and paint a few more things, or I won't have anything to sell!'

'But not tonight?' he said cheekily. 'You did invite me to stay.'

'True, but as we have nothing here to eat apart from bread and butter, I nominate you to buy supper!'

'Cod and chips?'

'Splendid,' she smiled.

*

A few streets away, Marcus was upstairs in the Black Dog talking to Julia on the phone. The conversation was strained. She felt she was in an impossible situation. He asked her how the interviews had gone and she told him she was going to offer the job to Sarah. Luke, she had recognised from secondary school – not that that had mattered, she said, just that the girl seemed better suited. She didn't mention that there was something odd about him. That, now she had met him again, she realised there had always been something off about him. His manner with the dogs had been false; she could tell. At first, she thought he was just trying too hard to make a good impression; but, when he was leaving, Bella had come up to him and she had glimpsed, from the corner of her eye, him shoving her away quite hard. There was something maleficent lurking behind his casual words and manner and she instinctively did not want anything more to do with him. She had decided not to mention it, as Marcus had enough on his mind. Besides, she'd probably never set eyes on Luke again.

'I'm working tonight on a late shift,' said Marcus, 'but if you like I can pop over tomorrow evening?'

'I thought we were going to wait?' Julia replied. 'Until, you know… until this is over.'

'I know, I guess I just wanted to check you were okay.'

'I'm fine… And Marcus, be very careful… please.' She hung up.

He sat gazing at the television. The local news channel was on. A photo of a large mansion house and an image of a young girl flashed across the screen. He turned up the volume and caught the end of the report.

'Lily Sanders recently returned to Lostmor for the first time in twenty-four years since tragically losing her father and younger sister when they fell to their deaths from the roof of their mansion home, Penwyth House. On the 19th of February, an attempted burglary at the property ended in a brutal attack on the resident groundsman, Joe Newman.'

Marcus switched channels. There was a thin, balding man in a grey suit pointing at a map of the UK. He was explaining that a storm was due to hit the southwest tomorrow night. The area where Lostmor was located was covered with symbols of black clouds with raindrops and yellow zigzag symbols.

'That was delicious,' said Lily.

Oliver leant back, feeling comfortably full. 'Here's to you,' he said raising a glass of champagne. 'And to *Swan Song*, which I'm sure will be an even bigger success than *The Blue*.'

Lily's face lit up and he thought he'd never seen her more radiant.

'How did things go at Edhen Cottage after I left?' he asked. 'Do you think Joe will manage okay?'

'I think so,' replied Lily. 'He's a strong man – wilful. I just hope he doesn't try to rush things too much.'

'He's over the worst…' Oliver reassured her. 'Have you had a chance to speak to the police yet?'

She nodded. 'I forgot to tell you. Sergeant Weeks called me, anyway. I mentioned Douglas Holt, told him about his violent outburst at your place when you let him go, and your concerns when you later saw him at Penwyth House. You'll never guess what. He has a brother!'

Oliver frowned.

'Luke Holt,' said Lily. 'He was working with him at Penwyth House that day. He was in the truck, too.'

'What else did the sergeant say?'

'Not much. He was reading from some notes an officer had made when they were calling door to door. He said that the brothers live together and that they were in all night, the night Joe was attacked. He's going to take a closer look at them. If either has a criminal record, his officers will pay them another visit, but he did say there were a lot of "ifs". He's going to keep me informed, though, and he thanked us for the info.'

Oliver sighed. He couldn't quite believe there were two of them. It was feasible – there were two assailants and there were two brothers. They were probably both troublemakers. At least, he thought, the police were aware of them now. If they were to blame, they had hurt people he cared about and had no qualms about leaving Joe for dead. But, tonight was a celebration and he didn't want to worry Lily about the Holts. He put his arm around her and hugged her.

'And what about telling Joe your news?' he looked at her hopefully.

Lily nodded. 'He beat me to it and asked me. It was pretty overwhelming, but in a good way. I'm so glad he finally knows... I thought I had no family left when I first came here. Now I've discovered so much I didn't know about my mother... I have found my real father. And...' she said, kissing Oliver softly on the lips. 'You. I found you.'

However, that night, the first night in her new home, Lily awoke suddenly from a terrifying nightmare. She turned to look at Oliver. He was sleeping peacefully beside her. She quietly pushed back the heavy quilt and pulled herself into a sitting position. Strange echoes of dreams were chasing each other around her head. She sat with her eyes closed, trying to slow her breathing, but all the while voices were calling to her. Her mother chiding her over something, Alice giggling, Vincent's angry voice booming from a distance...

She heard an enormous clap of thunder and her eyes sprung wide open. She stared, unseeing, at the bedroom window. The voices faded, but now she could hear a howling wind. It was the familiar sound of the wind whistling down the chimneys of Penwyth House. She felt hot breath on her shoulder and slowly turned her head. Sitting next to her on the bed was the man she once thought to be her father. Vincent's distorted face leered in front of her. His words were calm and clear.

'Come to us, Lily. Join us. Alice and I, we miss you,' he smiled, but his mouth was just a black hole, moving like smoke.

This time, Lily awoke for real. Oliver was looking at her in alarm, and she realised she was screaming.

CHAPTER 51

7.00 am, Friday, 10ᵗʰ March 1995

Marcus parked his truck discreetly where he could still see the exit to Douglas Holt's place. Now all he had to do was wait for Douglas to leave and follow him. He didn't care how long it took — if not today, then tomorrow or the day after. He was used to waiting. In his past life, apart from the adrenaline-pumped moments of full-on armed combat, one was always waiting. Waiting for orders. Waiting for back-up. Waiting for the enemy. So, when late morning he saw the now-familiar transit van weaving up the lane towards the road, he was pleasantly surprised. Trees either side of the road were swaying slightly in the building wind and light rain was starting to fall. *Good*, he thought. A storm was blowing inland as forecast. Bad weather would make a fatal accident on a deserted coastal road more believable. He watched as Douglas turned left out of the lane, driving away from him. Marcus felt the reassuring metal of the Browning service pistol tucked in the small of his back. He turned the ignition.

Douglas had been angry with his brother. It was nothing new that Luke had disappeared without telling him. He had always been secretive. In the past, he had disappeared for weeks at a time without a word of explanation. No, what had upset him was that, at some ridiculous time of the night, he guessed not long before dawn, he had been woken by the roaring of his newly renovated Triumph Bonneville being ridden at speed away from the bungalow. For a moment, he thought someone was stealing it until he realised Luke's bed was empty.

He switched the wipers on and focused on the road ahead. His brother could be anywhere, but he couldn't just sit at home seething with rage. He hadn't even taken the bike on the road himself yet. Luke had stolen his moment of glory, after the weeks of hard work he had spent restoring it.

Cruising along the B-road linking Lostmor to St Oswald's, Luke couldn't go anywhere near the speed on the Triumph as the modern Kawasakis and Suzukis that he preferred. But, he had to admit that it was a pleasure to ride. Its 650cc engine purred like a cat, then increased to a satisfying throaty roar whenever he opened up the throttle. The journey had calmed him down. Ever since Julia's phone call yesterday evening he had been furious. He hadn't even got to speak to her. She'd left a hasty message on his mobile telling him she was sorry but she'd given the kennels job to someone else. Probably to the girl on the bicycle. Initially, he had been so mad that he had wanted to call her back and tell her what he thought of her, the little bitch. But then what?

When he had first driven out on the Triumph that morning, he had driven at break-neck speed, no helmet, skidding around all the bends. A cat had streaked across the road in front of him. He swerved and screeched to a halt, just managing to keep the bike upright. For a moment, he was shaken. He remembered that once a cat had run in the path of a van he'd been driving, then he had deliberately sped up and ran the poor animal over. It had been the highlight of his day. However, he knew he would be more vulnerable on a bike. He collected himself and pulled away, this time driving slower.

Grateful that he wasn't hurt, Luke started to think about him and Julia again. Maybe it wasn't such a bad thing. Just because he was not working at the kennels didn't mean they couldn't be together. Perhaps that was her plan all along? It might not be a good idea to get involved with someone who worked for you. Now, there could be no complications and she was free to step out with her old friend. Luke smiled. Of course, everything was clear to him now. He slowed again and did a U-turn, heading back towards Lostmor.

*

Marcus was finding it hard not to drive too close to Douglas. He was confident that Douglas hadn't spotted him yet. Transits didn't have the best rear visibility. Depending on which direction Douglas took, and if the opportunity arose, Marcus knew the best places to force him off the road. He had crisscrossed the area many times and knew the roads well. There was a steep descent just ahead. Marcus hoped the van's speed would increase slightly. The road was just wide enough for his truck to swing out behind him.

He put his foot down, then swerved left in a forty-degree angle in front of the van, forcing Douglas to follow suit before losing control and diving headlong into a six-foot ditch. Marcus jumped out and climbed into the ditch. It was unlikely another vehicle would pass by, especially as the storm was taking hold, but he still needed to act quickly. He peered in. Douglas was conscious. Marcus slid the passenger door open.

'I've been looking for you for a long time.'

Douglas looked at him dazed and bewildered. This crazy man had deliberately forced him off the road.

'Who the fuck are you?'

'I'm Marcus Cole, Rose's father. You killed my daughter and now I'm going to kill you.' Marcus was tempted to shoot him, there and then, but it had to look like an accident. The man had no seatbelt on. His forehead was bleeding where he had hit the windscreen and he was clutching at his chest where his body had impacted the steering column. It would be easy for him to embellish a bit. Douglas cowered, desperately trying to open the driver's door, but it was jammed solidly against the side of the ditch.

'You crazy bastard,' shouted Douglas. 'I don't know what you're talking about!' His voice was shrill, laced with fear.

Marcus slid in next to him. 'Well, I think you do,' he said calmly. 'It's a shame. If I had more time, I'd really make you suffer.'

'Look, mate,' said Douglas. 'I don't know who you think I am, but I never touched your daughter. Rose, you say?'

Douglas was a better liar than he had expected, but people would say just about anything when their life was on the line. Marcus reached into his jacket pocket and pulled out the wallet chain and dangled it in front of him.

'Are you telling me this isn't yours? I found it in your garage.'

Douglas stared at the chain. 'You stole it? That's not mine. That's Luke's.'

'Luke?'

'He's my brother. We live together.' Douglas wasn't sure he should have said that. He was scared and had blurted it out without thinking.

Marcus was remembering the voices he had heard that night when he'd broken into the garage. He had a bloody brother. Why hadn't he known that? How had he missed it?

'Luke hasn't killed anybody, either. I swear!'

Marcus studied the man's face. He had the wrong man.

'Where is he? Where's Luke?' he demanded.

'I dunno,' replied Douglas. 'He left really early. I was out looking for him cos he took my motorbike and I was mad at him.'

Marcus looked at him thoughtfully. 'Tell me… what were you doing that night parked outside Oliver Bligh's farm?'

'What? Nothing.'

Marcus punched Douglas in the face, hard. He shrieked and grabbed at his broken nose, pain searing through his already throbbing skull.

'Tell me...' said Marcus. He raised his fist and was about to hit him again.

'Alright, alright!' Douglas gurgled, swallowing blood. 'We never went near the farm. I knew Bligh, that's all.' He wiped away more of the blood streaming down his face. 'I worked for him, but not for long.'

'So?' said Marcus. 'That doesn't answer my question.'

'We were just keeping an eye on him. Luke and me... had plans to break into a really big place nearby. We saw him there and wondered why. We thought he might be seeing the woman who owned it.'

Marcus stared at him for a moment. Something was sounding familiar. 'What is this place? A house?'

'Umm, Penwyth. Penwyth House.'

Marcus suddenly remembered. It had been on the news, last night. Penwyth House and the return of its owner – a woman. Oliver was seeing her. She was the woman in the pub. Lily. Lily Sanders.

'You nearly killed the groundsman, didn't you?' Douglas stayed silent. 'My, you two have been busy.' For emphasis, Marcus pulled out his gun and pressed the barrel sharply against the side of Douglas's head. 'Unless you want to be looking over your shoulder for the rest of your life, this little meeting never happened. Do you understand?'

Douglas nodded vehemently, his eyes now wide with fear. The next blow, this time with the butt of the gun, knocked him out cold.

CHAPTER 52

By the time Luke got back to Lostmor, he was cold and soaked through. Not that that deterred him; he just needed to speak to Julia, then everything would be okay.

It was early afternoon and Julia was throwing balls for some dogs in the paddock. Her hood was turned up against the wind and rain that was steadily increasing. The gate behind her shook and rattled and she watched in surprise as a string of bunting that had been wildly flapping overhead flew off, getting stuck in a solitary tree by the house. She looked up at the storm clouds rolling in. The moist air was thick with salt. Overhead, gulls shrieked their warning of an incoming gale as they lurched and tumbled in its currents.

She called the dogs back and clipped them to their leads. She dried Ralph, a young boisterous Labrador, and the two cocker spaniels Treacle and Posie, refilled their bowls and settled them all down as best she could in the warm, sheltered rooms at the backs of the kennels. None of them were due to be picked up until tomorrow and she was worried that, if the storm got really bad, they would be frightened. She had visions of moving them all into the house for the night. For the first time since opening Fern Retreat, Julia realised just how exposed to the elements it was.

She was surprised to hear Bella barking in the house as she

rounded the corner. A large motorbike was parked right outside the front door. She looked around, but there was no one in sight. As she passed the side window she glanced inside. A man was sitting at her kitchen table. He was looking down – at a phone, she thought. What was happening? Was she being burgled? Whoever it was had walked straight into her house. She reached in her pocket for her phone, but she didn't have it. She silently cursed for leaving it in the house. She looked closer through the glass and realised, with a sickening feeling in her stomach, who it was. Not a burglar. It was Luke. Luke Holt.

*

Muddy water spumed out from under the truck's wheels as Marcus drove at speed along the uneven lane to the Holts' place. He drove past the bungalow, turned around in front of the garage, and jumped out. The darkening sky gave its first low grumble and the tar-black clouds released a deluge of rain. There was no sign of the motorbike. He lifted the overhead garage door a fraction. No bike. No one there.

He ran to the bungalow. The front door was locked, but the simple yale mechanism was no match for a quickly aimed heavy boot. It swung open, clinging to one hinge. Marcus quickly scanned the gloomy interior and what narrowly passed as a living space. Loads of shit piled up everywhere, about what he expected. Empty beer cans littered the floor and blackened ash from the now dead fire had spilled out onto the hearth rug.

He pushed open the door to what led to a small bedroom. Clothes covered the floor. A small table by one of two single beds held a photo frame. It was the first sign of anything remotely personal he had come across. It was a black and white photo of a middle-aged man standing proudly in front of a classic old Norton motorbike. A small boy with a thick shock of hair had been lifted onto the bike seat, his chubby legs dangling over the edge – it looked like Douglas.

The second bedroom was tidier. Clothes were folded in a pile on an old dining chair. Marcus sat on the unmade bed. A small clock and an ashtray full of cigarette butts sat on a low, wooden stool, a metal bin shoved behind it. He sifted through its contents comprising food wrappers and empty cigarette packets. He picked out a screwed-up page torn from a newspaper. He flattened it out on the bed and reached up for the wall light. A low-wattage bulb dangling from the ceiling dimly lit the room. It was part of the Jobs section of the local paper.

Marcus sighed. He didn't know what he was hoping to find. *A signed confession perhaps?* he thought dryly. He would either have to wait for Luke to come back, or go looking for him. He can't have gone far. Marcus tried to clear his mind. He had made a mistake. Julia's words echoed in his head, '...*are you one hundred per cent sure you have the right guy?*'

He pulled out the chain again and looked at the dragon heads. What could Rose have ever seen in someone like Luke? No doubt he was trash, just like his brother. Perhaps that was why? Rebecca had said she was rebelling. She took up with someone older than her. Someone reckless that she knew her parents would disapprove of.

Marcus looked down at the paper, skimming the jobs. Halfway down he saw: '*Fern Retreat, a recently opened kennels looking for a part-time kennel hand. Please call Julia Sutton on...*'

He remembered seeing in *Lostmor Gazette* the original news item and photo of Julia advertising the place, just a few short weeks ago, and his first visit there with Horace. He could picture Julia now, standing there in her wellies, her long blonde hair tied in a loose ponytail, a big welcoming smile on her face... *Why had Luke torn this out?* Marcus looked at the other jobs, but there was nothing obvious. No delivery or farmhand jobs. Sales reps wanted, call-centre work, and a kennel hand... What had she said? She was taking on the girl, she was called Sarah. The guy, it turned out, she had known from school, but he wasn't suitable. His name was... Luke.

Marcus grabbed his phone and dialled. It went straight to

answerphone. He tried calling three times, but nothing. He headed for the truck as fast as he could. The name Luke was coming up way too many times.

CHAPTER 53

Julia slid back from the window and tried to think what to do. She could confront him. Ask him what the hell he thought he was doing just walking into her home. But what if he didn't just apologise and leave? There was something deeply troubling about him that made her hesitate. She should run to the road. He hadn't spotted her yet. She should then just keep going until someone drove past. Her heart was racing, but she tried to calm herself. She could hear Bella still barking from somewhere in the house. He must have shut her in another room.

'Julia!' He was suddenly in front of her. 'There you are. What are you doing out here in the rain? Are you coming in?' He was grinning from ear to ear. 'I've been waiting for you.' He was drenched. His hands hung loosely by his sides and long, wet strands of hair clung to his face. He was acting like he lived there, she thought, or as if he were a regular fixture around the place. His behaviour was scaring her and she instinctively tried to humour him.

'Luke! What a surprise,' she half-smiled, hoping she sounded convincing. 'I've been in the paddock, but got rained off.' She walked slowly towards the door.

'Is this your bike?' she asked lamely.

'Kind of,' he said, cheerily. 'I borrowed it.' He gently placed his hand on Julia's back, directing her in through the open door.

'I can hear Bella?' she said, trying to keep her voice casual.

'Hmmm, she wouldn't stop barking, so I shut her in your bedroom. Don't worry,' he smiled amicably, rolling his eyes. 'I know how you are about dogs. She's fine. Let's sit, shall we?' He pulled a dining chair out for her. 'Oh, let me take your coat. It's soaking wet.'

Saying nothing, Julia slipped her coat off and sat. On the table, there were two glasses and a bottle of wine he had taken from the fridge. He sat down beside her.

'How about a drink?' he asked. Without waiting for a reply, he poured them both a large glass each. He smiled affectionately. 'I'm sorry to turn up unannounced like this, but you don't need to be nervous. I just need to talk to you – about us.'

He really is bat shit crazy, Julia thought, but he didn't seem to wish her any harm. Maybe she could find a way out of this. She glanced at the wall clock. It was 2.30 pm. After her conversation with Marcus last night, she knew he wasn't coming over anyway. Luke casually pulled out her car keys, then her phone from inside his leather jacket.

'Someone called Marcus seems keen to get hold of you,' he said casually. 'He's rung three times.'

Julia's heart sank. It was worrying enough that Luke had walked straight into her home and started talking to her as if they were old friends. He had already crossed the line. But happily showing her that he'd taken her means of escape and her communication with the outside world suggested something worse... But there was a glimmer of hope... Marcus was trying to contact her.

'Marcus? Oh, he's just a client. I look after his dog sometimes.'

'I see.'

'Is this about the job?' she said, changing the subject. 'I'm sorry, Luke... perhaps we can talk about some other role for you? What do you think?'

'That's exactly what I had in mind, too,' he grinned. He turned his chair to face her and gently touched her face. Julia put her hand on his and slowly removed it. She smiled and took a sip from her glass.

'Here's to us,' she said raising her glass. He raised his glass and took a large swig. Outside, the rain lashed against the glass and the old sash windows juddered. Maybe she could cook something for them? That would waste some time.

'Are you hungry?'

'Hmmm, no,' he replied. Heavy-lidded eyes scaled her body up and down.

'Okay, well I am. Do you mind if I make something quick?'

'Let's drink these first, eh?'

She took another sip and swallowed. 'What is it you wanted to chat about?'

'Well, I admit I was a bit disappointed by your telephone message the other day,' he began. 'But then I got to thinking... we go way back, don't we?'

'Yes, I guess we do.'

'I wanted to say sorry for the way I treated you back then.'

'We were friends, weren't we?'

'Yes, but I got upset over one of your friends – Josh.'

'I can't remember him,' Julia said flippantly. 'It was such a long time ago.'

'Well, never mind, it doesn't matter now,' said Luke, placing one hand on her thigh.

Julia tried to rise, but he placed his hands firmly on her shoulders. 'Don't be so jumpy! We're celebrating, after all.'

'What are we celebrating?' said Julia, her voice shaky.

'You and me, of course!' Luke replied pleasantly. 'It's okay that you gave the kennels job to someone else. You did find someone, right?'

'Yes.'

'Well, then! That means you'll have more time for yourself now. Which means?' he said cheerily.

Julia was perplexed, trying to work out where this was going.

'You and me, silly!' said Luke, not waiting for an answer. 'We can get to know each other again. We can talk about books, just like we used to.' He drained his glass and lifted Julia's to her lips. 'Drink,' he said, softly. Julia did as she was told. He reached over for the bottle and refilled their glasses, then rose and casually walked to the window. He looked out at the rain, his expression bland.

'Are you sure this Marcus is a client?'

'Yes. Yes, he is,' replied Julia. 'He's probably phoning to say he's on his way... to pick up his dog... Ralph.'

'You know, I was waiting forty minutes for you to come back from the paddock,' said Luke softly. 'So I had a little wander about. Your appointments book in the hut looked busy for the next few weeks... but I didn't see anyone called Marcus. I could have sworn good old Ralph was not being picked up until tomorrow... by Caroline?'

He slowly turned to face her. Something dark and unreadable flickered across his features. Julia returned his gaze. She was much closer to the door now than him and impulsively she leapt for the door handle. But he pre-empted her. He got to her seconds later. Grabbing her from behind, he threw her headlong back into the room. As she landed, her head hit the brick edge of the inglenook fireplace. She heard a strange, whimpering noise leave her throat. Dazed, Julia raised her hand to the side of her head and felt blood. She tried to focus, but the room was swimming.

Luke pulled her roughly to her feet and sat her firmly back on the chair. He knelt in front of her and tugged at her jeans. Ripping her leather belt off, he used it to bind her wrists behind her. She was hardly aware of what was happening. Pain was blooming in her temple and she struggled to stay conscious.

'You shouldn't lie to me, Julia,' he hissed. 'You're seeing this

Marcus, aren't you? I was hoping we could make a fresh start, but now you've spoilt everything.' His face was inches from hers. She could smell sour wine and tobacco and felt nauseous. He grabbed her chin and moved her face from side to side. 'Shit, you're a mess. You shouldn't have made me do that.'

Julia tried to speak, but the words wouldn't form. Her whole face felt numb.

'Why do you keep whoring yourself out to other men?' he whispered, maleficently. He sighed. 'If that's what you are, then I guess I'll have to treat you like one.' Walking to the units, Luke slid a kitchen knife out of the wooden block, came back and knelt in front of her. He turned the knife's edge in his hands and smiled. He used the blade to roughly flick the top button off the front of her shirt.

'You know, even when you're a mess, you still look sexy.'

She managed to whisper. 'Please don't... you wanted to talk.'

He slid his hand inside her shirt and gently stroked her breast. Julia cringed at his touch, but remained silent.

'Talking's over,' he said softly. He put the knife in his pocket and drew her chair closer to him. Her phone lit up. She had a voicemail. Swearing, he picked it up. Marcus again. He went to put it down, then had second thoughts. He listened to the recording, then put the phone back in his pocket. 'Well, it seems your hero is on his way, so I guess playtime will have to wait. Still, nice of him to give me forewarning.'

CHAPTER 54

Marcus drove like a bat out of hell towards Fern Retreat, his mind racing. Luke Holt was responsible for Rose's death, he was certain of it. Douglas had recognised the wallet chain as his brother's, and Ellie had found the missing links on the road where Rose was killed. Julia had interviewed someone called Luke, who she had recognised from high school. Marcus had no way of knowing if it was the same person, but he had found the Jobs page, showing her advert, in Luke Holt's bedroom – a big coincidence. Luke did not know Marcus was looking for him and they had never met. But they both knew Julia. He might have applied for the kennel job, not realising that he knew her from school – or, he only applied because he did. Maybe he once had a crush on her, or just remembered she was pretty and fancied his chances.

Marcus gripped the steering wheel harder. He knew the man was also capable of extreme violence, as demonstrated by the attack on the groundsman at Penwyth House, when he and his half-witted brother had tried to rob the place. And, he thought grimly, Julia had no idea how dangerous he was. He stared at the road ahead and prayed that everything was fine. That the person she had interviewed was either a different person or that Luke Holt was elsewhere and he was overreacting. That the reason why she wasn't answering her phone was because she'd left it in the house, which she often did when she was busy with the dogs.

*

Luke dragged Julia to her feet. He pushed her outside and shoved her against the wall while he kick-started the motorbike. He pulled out the kitchen knife again and shouted at her to get on. She was sliding down the side of the house.

'Fuck!' He lifted the bike onto its centre-stand and dragged Julia to her feet.

'GET ON!'

'Can't…' she managed to say.

'Christ,' he muttered, quickly unfastening the belt and lifting her on to the back. She looked in danger of passing out.

'Don't try anything,' he said, wielding the knife. 'Hold on to me. We're not going far, just back to my place. Once we're home, I'll clean you up.'

Julia clung to him, partly to protect herself from the driving rain and partly because her vision was blurry and she was terrified of falling off. She was instantly soaked and the sluicing wind and biting cold shocked her back into cognisance. After a few minutes, the pain in her head started to fade to a dull throbbing. She could vaguely make out lights coming towards them.

Luke switched off his headlight and quickly pulled in to a lay-by, where they were partly concealed by a hedge. He grabbed Julia by the hair and pulled her head down in an attempt to hide her. A new wave of pain screamed in her temple. When the vehicle passed, he let go. They were straddling the bike, its engine still running. He turned slightly, still holding the knife.

'You have to hold on tight!' he half-shouted through the rain. He switched the headlight back on, geared up, and accelerated. Julia wasn't sure how long they had been driving, maybe only five minutes. The road looked wider and the hedgerow had disappeared. She guessed they were in open pastureland now and nearer to the cliffs.

Coming from the opposite direction, Marcus saw a single headlight. When it had oddly vanished, he slowed a little and peered through the windscreen. As he drove past the lay-by, he glimpsed the back end of the stationary motorbike. Something was off. It had to be Luke. Who else would be hanging around in this weather? He was not far from Fern Retreat, either. Marcus's instinct told him to go back rather than carrying on to the kennels.

He reversed as far as the lay-by, but the bike had gone. He swung the truck around and sped up. As the road widened, he could see a tail light up ahead. He drove faster to catch up with it, switching to full-beam, cutting through the gloom and driving rain. He could see a woman on the back. She turned slightly. Marcus couldn't make out who it was at first, but then he saw her. He was horrified. Julia had no helmet, no coat, and was swaying precariously. Luke reacted by speeding up.

Marcus had thought that nothing could ever scare him more than the day he learnt of Rose's death. But now, by some sick twist of fate, here he was watching history repeat itself and he felt powerless to stop it. Fearing for Julia's life, he drew back, hoping the bike would slow, too. It made no difference. He followed from a distance, keeping the bike's rear light in view.

Luke was hunched low and he shoved the knife back in his pocket so he had better control. He guessed it must be Marcus who had passed them earlier. He had spotted the bike and now he was following them. Damn it! The night was not going as planned.

Julia had guessed it must be Marcus, too… She had to try and stop the bike. They might crash – but, at the speed they were taking the bends, they were bound to, anyway. Her hands were so cold she could barely move them, but she let go with one and quickly fumbled for the end of the knife sticking out of Luke's pocket. She managed to grab hold of it and, before she had time to think about it, drove the knife down into his upper back.

She heard him cry out and felt the bike wobble. They left the road, bumping onto uneven grassland. Luke half jumped seconds before the bike connected with a large log. On impact, Julia was catapulted onto the grass. Luke landed headlong in some bushes, where he lay with his head and shoulders embedded in thorny brambles. He groaned and tried to pull himself free. He screamed with pain, his face and hands ripped to pieces. The thorns, like dozens of tiny barbs, gouged his skin and became entangled in his hair. He slowly tried again, firstly pulling his arms out, then using his hands to manoeuvre his head clear. He crawled free and stood with the knife still sticking out of his back.

'JULIA!!' he yelled.

The bike's headlight was still on, its beam half illuminating where her body lay motionless. He scrambled to her, dropped to his knees, and pulled her over on to her back. She screamed and was filled with fear at the sight of his ruined face, looming over her. Red hot pain kicked in and tore through his upper back. She had actually tried to kill him. With renewed fury, he straddled her and tried desperately to reach the knife in his back.

Julia could hear the sea raging below, and she realised they must be close to the edge. She couldn't fight any more. Everything hurt. She was falling into a peaceful, dark place and she welcomed it. But, just before she passed out, she vaguely heard Luke scream and Marcus's voice speaking calmly to her as he gently drew her up into his arms.

He laid her across the back seat of the truck and covered her with a blanket. He could see she had taken a blow to the head – her shirt was covered in blood and she was icy cold. He looked up and was shocked to see Luke, who he thought he had just knocked out cold, pressed up against the window and smiling at him. Streaks of blood oozed down his punctured forehead, into his eyes and mouth. Marcus got out slowly and closed the truck door. Luke took a step back.

'You must be Marcus.'

'And you must be Luke.'

'How do you know who I am?'

'Because I've been looking for you.'

'I thought you were here for Julia?'

'I am, but I've also been looking for you… for a long time.' Marcus pulled out the wallet chain and threw it at Luke. He caught it and looked at it curiously.

'You fixed it,' he said, matter of factly. 'Where did you get this?'

'Well, part of it I took from your garage,' replied Marcus. 'The other part came from a little girl, called Ellie?'

'I don't know anyone called Ellie,' Luke said, scornfully.

'No? But you did know someone called Rose.'

Realisation dawned and Luke's smile dissolved. He thought he'd been the only person alive who knew about him and Rose, but this man knew.

'Are you the police?'

'You wish,' Marcus said calmly. 'Rose was my daughter.'

Luke fidgeted. 'You're Rose's father?'

'Yes, genius.'

Luke looked at Marcus, standing unmoving in the rain, his face lit by the bike's headlight.

'And you're seeing Julia. My Julia?'

'You don't get to ask any more questions.'

Luke smiled mockingly. 'That's pretty fucking trippy!'

Marcus had heard enough. He drew his gun. Luke's eyes widened.

'It wasn't my fault… it was an accident! I got hurt, too! My leg still aches all the time!' he shouted, his voice shrill.

Marcus couldn't quite believe what he was hearing. Rose had been killed by a deranged idiot.

'Quite accident prone, aren't you?' he replied, nodding at the motorbike.

'I loved Rose and she loved me,' Luke said defensively, eyeing the gun.

Marcus stared at him. 'Don't even speak her name,' he scowled. 'You are not worthy. You took her life. Just threw it away. And then, like the low-life coward that you are, ran off leaving a little girl and her injured grandmother alone… and now Julia, too. Are there others? Other women that you've hurt?'

'No,' said Luke. 'Like I said, it was an accident. I know I shouldn't have left, but she was dead. There was nothing I could do. I know I should have stayed and looked after the little kid. Ellie, you say, and the old lady too, but I was scared and I ran.'

'Bullshit. You could have still come forward later, but you didn't. At least that might have given Rose's mother, and me, some sort of closure. For losing our only child.'

Luke said nothing.

'I met your brother Douglas earlier today,' Marcus continued, with a steely-eyed gaze.

'Douglas! He doesn't know anything,' said Luke. 'I took off not long after the accident. He covered for me when the police came. He didn't even know I'd been seeing Rose… sorry, I mean, your daughter. He just does what I tell him. He told the police we fell out. That I was abroad somewhere.'

'And where were you really?'

'I was abroad. In Spain. I stayed there until things had calmed down. Then I came back. I'm being honest with you, man. I'm sorry. And Douglas, he didn't do anything.'

'He'll live, which is more than I can say for you,' Marcus said, slowly raising the gun.

Luke knew he had nothing to lose. He reached for the knife in his back and, with effort this time, pulled it out, all the while staring at

Marcus. Without another word, he raised it above his head and suddenly ran at Marcus, screaming like a banshee. Tempting though it was to simply shoot him, Marcus resisted. He deflected the knife, easily knocking it out of Luke's grip, then brought the butt of the gun round and hit him a glancing blow on the cheek. Luke fell to his knees.

'Don't even think about picking that knife up, or I will shoot you dead,' Marcus hissed. He nodded at the motorbike. The engine was still running. 'Pick it up and get on,' he demanded.

'What...? Why?' asked Luke in confusion. 'Are you letting me go?'

Marcus bent down and picked up the knife, not taking his eyes off of Luke. 'Kind of,' he smiled. 'You're going to get on it and drive that way...' He waved the gun in the direction of the cliffs and sea beyond. 'If you don't, I'll shoot you anyway.'

Luke laughed. 'You're fucking crazy!'

'You better believe it,' said Marcus and fired the gun, just left of where Luke stood.

Luke glared at him, his long sodden hair half covering his shredded face. Silently, he dragged the bike upright and swung his leg over. He jutted his chin up and laughed again, defiantly. Whatever he did next, he knew he was dead. He gazed at Marcus one last time.

'I'll be seeing you.'

He squeezed the clutch lever and accelerated. Marcus watched the bike go. A few seconds later, he heard the engine screeching as it shot over the cliff's edge and dropped into the tumultuous black water below.

CHAPTER 55

'Are you okay?'

'Yes, I think so. Do you have any water?' Julia whispered. Marcus passed her a small bottle and helped her sit up. The movement caused her a sharp pain in her shoulder and her head throbbed like hell.

'Luke?' she asked with a trace of fear in her eyes.

'Luke won't be troubling you ever again. You're safe now,' Marcus said, gently stroking her hair. He could see that she had a deep gash to her temple, but it had stopped bleeding. 'I'm taking you to the hospital.' Julia closed her eyes. The terror he had felt just minutes ago when he thought she might be killed was replaced by a massive sense of relief. She was still with him. She was going to be okay.

By the time they reached St Oswald's Hospital, Marcus had devised a cover story. Julia had rushed out of the house in the storm after hearing a loud crashing noise coming from the kennels. Part of its roof had lifted off in the gale. She was up a ladder trying to secure the felt, when she lost her balance and fell, landing heavily on her shoulder and hitting her head on the corner of the decking. If asked, that would also explain her wet clothes – alarmed for the dogs, she had acted quickly, on impulse. Julia nodded that she understood.

The severity of the storm meant a quiet evening for the A&E

department. So far, only two minor injuries and three drunks. Two nurses saw a man carrying a semi-conscious woman into reception; she was wrapped in his coat and a blanket. A trolley got to them just as they reached the doors. Julia was whisked away and Marcus was despatched to the waiting room.

A nurse came out to take some details. He gave her what he hoped was a feasible version of events, explaining that, luckily, he had been on his way to see Julia. When he found her, he could see she was badly hurt. As the kennels were quite remote, and worried that they may have to wait a long time for an ambulance, he had decided to drive her to the hospital himself. The nurse looked him up and down. Marcus knew he was a mess, but he figured he would have looked that way being out in the storm with Julia.

Several hours later a doctor emerged.

'Hello, I'm Dr Williams,' she said. 'And you are?'

'Marcus. Marcus Cole. How is Julia? Is she going to be okay?'

The doctor nodded. 'She has received a nasty head injury, but the MRI scan shows no trauma to the brain. She has a fractured collarbone and some superficial cuts and bruises. We'd like to keep her in. Just to keep an eye on her... I think for a couple of days.'

'Thank you, doctor,' said Marcus. 'Do you think I could see her now?'

'Yes...' The doctor paused. 'It is lucky you turned up when you did, isn't it?'

'Thank God, yes.'

Dr Williams studied his face, then gave him a brief smile. 'Please don't keep her too long, she's had a mild sedative and needs to rest.'

Julia's head was bandaged and her right arm was in a sling. She was hooked up to a monitor and a saline drip. Marcus was used to hospitals, albeit military ones, both as a patient and as a visitor. As a result, he disliked being anywhere near them. Back in the day, many of his army friends' lives had been saved by skilled medical teams, but others had been beyond help, including his friend Jack who he'd known since joining up. Images of men he had known well over the years, their bodies mutilated and broken, dead or waiting to die, still haunted him.

He gently held Julia's grazed hand. She turned her head and opened her eyes.

'Hi,' she smiled weakly. 'You look tired.'

'I'm fine,' he whispered, drawing closer to her. 'You're the one who needs looking after now.'

'Bella… can you check on her? And there are three other dogs in the kennels. They're all alone…'

'Don't worry. I'll pick up Horace, then go stay at yours. I'll take care of everything and we'll talk in the morning. Now, try and rest. I love you,' he smiled, squeezing her hand and wishing he could stay.

'Love you too,' she murmured, before drifting off into a heavy, dreamless sleep.

*

Fern Retreat had taken a pounding. Several fence panels at the front of the property were down, but at least the rain had finally subsided. Marcus swung the truck into the drive. The house was lit up like a Christmas tree.

'Stay here, Horace. I'll be right back.'

He stepped onto the porch. Julia's belt was on the floor and the front door wide open. Rain had soaked the entrance and the room was freezing. *What the hell has happened here?* he thought, looking around apprehensively. A chair was turned over and there was half a bottle of wine and two glasses on the table. And Julia's phone. He picked it up; he saw his unanswered calls and a voicemail. Either she had told Luke he was coming, hoping he would leave, or maybe he had listened to the message and fled. Unfortunately, he had taken her with him. Marcus leant down and picked up Julia's car keys from the floor.

'Bella?' he called. He could hear the dog barking excitedly. Despite his leg niggling, he took the stairs two at a time. She leapt at him enthusiastically as soon as he opened the bedroom door. Checking all the upper rooms, he was relieved to see nothing was disturbed. It looked like the bastard had only got as far as the kitchen.

He cleaned up downstairs and returned the knife to the wooden block. The Aga was cold, but a big old Victorian-style radiator was on full blast. In a few hours, it would warm up. He noticed blood on the brickwork. Was it Julia's or Luke's? He sighed. It looked like she had tried to escape, or to defend herself from him. One of them had taken the knife. Either way, in the end, Julia had somehow stabbed him when she was riding pillion.

Marcus grabbed the torch by the door and went back outside. It was 10.00 pm – it felt more like the early hours of the morning. Fatigue was setting in. He looked up; the black sky was suddenly illuminated by lightning that ripped across the sky in crazy zig-zags, shortly followed by thunder cracking directly overhead.

He unlocked the kennels. The dogs were quiet and afraid. Ralph was sitting in the corner, refusing to move. Marcus climbed through and comforted him, then persuaded him out on his lead, likewise with Treacle and Posie who were huddled together, whimpering. Next, he fetched Horace and settled all the dogs in the kitchen. He lay down on the couch in the lounge. He didn't want to sleep in Julia's bed without her. The lightning soon stopped and the thunder became a distant rumble. Fat raindrops hit the window, a slow patter at first that turned into a steady drumming. He closed his eyes and drifted off within seconds.

The next morning, Marcus was greeted by clear, bright blue skies and sunshine. He took all the dogs for a run. There were two sheets of corrugated iron in the paddock area that had blown off a small lean-to. One of the sheets had landed on the fencing that he and Julia had erected. The posts weren't broken, but leant right over.

He phoned Susie, whom he had already spoken to the evening before at the pub when he had picked up Horace. She was her usual amenable self, reassuring him that, between her and Andy, they could cover for a few more days and would be sure to lock up each evening. Bernie was due at lunchtime to cover in the kitchen and Debra the following two days. Marcus thanked her and hung up. Next, he called the dogs' owners, Caroline, and Joanne and Tom Nash, and asked if they could pick up their dogs late afternoon, explaining again that Julia had had an accident. Then he cancelled all the bookings listed for the coming week. Lastly, he called Rebecca. Luckily, she was alone.

'How are you?' she asked.

'Okay… you?'

'The same,' she replied. 'What do you want, Marcus?'

He paused. 'I got him, Rebecca.'

There was silence. She knew him well and she knew what that meant.

'Thank you… now, please, don't call me again.' She quietly hung up the phone.

*

As Marcus left Fern Retreat, he noticed that the green swing sign was hanging from one hinge. He smiled; it was all stuff that could easily be fixed. He was going to be busy for the next few days.

'Hey, how are you?' He was pleased to see Julia was sitting up in bed, sipping a cup of tea.

She smiled at him. 'Glad you're here.'

He leant over and studied her head bandage. 'Quite a bump,' he said, kissing her gently on the cheek before taking a seat next to the bed.

'It's not hurting so much now,' she said. 'I've had painkillers. How are the dogs?'

'They're all fine. Bella and Horace are back at the house. Ralph and the terriers are being picked up later on today, and I've cancelled your bookings for the next week. And there's no need to worry, people were more concerned about you than their bookings.'

'What have you told them?' she asked. Her face was cut and bruised, but her brave blue eyes melted his heart.

'The same as I told them here. That you fell off a ladder trying to fix the kennel roof in the storm. You landed badly, hitting your head and breaking your collarbone. Sorry to involve you in more lies, but if I'd told the truth – I would have been arrested by now.'

She nodded and looked at him curiously. 'How did you know? How did you know I was in trouble?'

He took her hand. 'It can wait. We'll have plenty of time to talk when you're feeling better.'

'I know my face looks like I've been hit by a bus, but I'm okay… honestly… thanks to you. Please, tell me.'

Marcus got up, closed the door and returned. He explained as best he could how he had tracked Douglas down, convinced he was Rose's killer, only to discover it was his brother, Luke, who was responsible. How he had found her job advertisement on a page torn out from the newspaper in Luke's bedroom.

'I knew he had killed Rose and that he and Douglas had attempted to burgle a nearby mansion house, seriously injuring a groundsman. I didn't know for certain he was the same person you interviewed and knew from school, but I wasn't taking any chances. When I couldn't get hold of you, I drove straight to your place… and, well, you know the rest. I saw you on the road before I even got there.'

'He just turned up,' Julia explained. 'He was unhinged. He was waiting for me in the house when I got back from exercising the dogs, and started chatting to me as if I was his girlfriend. When I could see he wasn't going to leave, or let me leave, I tried to get away. He grabbed me and threw me across the kitchen. That was when I banged my head on the fireplace.'

'You don't have to relive this now...'

'I want to,' said Julia. 'I want you to know what happened. He did try to come on to me, but your message stopped him in his tracks. He had my phone, so he knew you were coming. I don't know what he was thinking by making me leave with him. He was driving us to his home. Probably, he couldn't face the consequences of what he'd done, or else he was plain delusional, thinking we could stay at his place and everything would somehow be okay. By then, I was in no fit state to argue. He threatened me with a knife and I was struggling to stay conscious...' Her voice broke, emotion getting the better of her.

Marcus looked at her with concern. 'It's okay. You were brave to face up to him. You tried to get away and he hurt you... badly. He could have killed you. All that matters now is that you are safe and here with me.'

'And Luke?' she whispered. 'What happened out there?'

'He met with a tragic accident,' replied Marcus. 'Or, at least, that is what will be assumed if his body and possibly bits of his bike wash up farther down the coast. They will say that he was probably driving too fast, in a storm, on an unlit road that, in places, is little more than a track and only feet away from the cliffs. Like I said,' he whispered, 'he won't be troubling you anymore.'

CHAPTER 56

1.00 pm, Friday, 10ᵗʰ March 1995

'Would you come to Penwyth House with me? Tonight?'

Oliver looked at Lily's drawn face. Yesterday evening, they had celebrated the imminent grand opening of *Swan Song*. She had been relaxed and happy, yet last night she had had the most dreadful nightmare. She had told him about her bad dreams, her flashbacks, but up until now he had not seen the effect they had on her.

'If you think it will help,' he replied. 'But you didn't get much sleep. Perhaps we should wait until you're less tired?'

'Honestly, I'm fine. There's a storm coming… just like the night of the accident. Maybe if I can somehow recreate that evening… who knows, maybe I can finally remember everything.'

Oliver looked at her, concerned.

'I'm getting closer to the truth,' Lily continued. 'I know I am… my parents argued that night… what happened after that is in here.' She pointed to her head. 'I just need to unlock it and… who knows, being there at night may trigger something.' Her eyes implored him. 'I have to try.'

He shrugged. 'I'll go with you, of course I will… What about Joe?'

'I don't want to upset him. Besides, he won't be anywhere near the house. He promised me he would not be doing his evening rounds for now, and I'm pretty sure he wouldn't even try yet, let alone in a storm. We'll go later, then. Say around nine-thirty?'

At 9.45 pm they pulled up outside Penwyth House. The deluge of rain that had fallen for most of the day had slowed, but an icy wind screamed around the mansion's walls, rushing inland like some unleashed demonic force from the watery depths beyond. Lily gazed up at the roof. It was so dark she couldn't make out the familiar chimneys and spires.

'Come on,' said Oliver. 'Let's get inside before something falls on us.' His torch cast an eerie light around the hallway. Shadows jumped out at them and the house creaked so loudly under the strain that he could imagine the whole place being lifted up and carried away. 'Are you sure you want to go up there? The gale is so strong. Half the roof might be missing.'

Lily nodded and stopped at the bottom of the grandiose staircase. 'We can use the torch to see what the damage is like before we set foot out there. The surveyor's report said it was much worse in the west wing, but the roof access is in the east wing so I'm hoping it's not as bad.'

He raised his hands. 'Okay, but we stay together.'

As they reached the top of the staircase, it felt like the whole house was vibrating. Oliver swung the torch upwards and saw fragments of plaster falling from the ceiling and heard the sound of the chandelier's thousands of crystals tinkling.

'This way,' said Lily. She placed one foot on the first step of the roof stairs. Last time she had been here, she had heard her father whispering in her ear. She had been so frightened she had fled the house. Now, strangely, she felt nothing, apart from the eeriness of being in the dark and the sounds of the storm, but no flashbacks and no gut-wrenching feeling of dread. She tried to focus on that fateful night twenty-four years ago.

'Can you shine the torch on the door?' She banged hard on the horizontal metal bar and it budged. Another shove and it opened.

'You okay?' Oliver asked. She nodded, looking in awe at the carnage. A smaller chimney close to the entrance had fallen and lay half-submerged in a pool of rainwater. Chunks of concrete, and broken bricks and tiles, littered the floor.

'We won't be able to see where we're standing in all this water,' said Oliver, shouting to be heard above the wind. In the distance, thunder rolled inland. 'We can only go a few steps,' he continued, 'or we'll be blown away. Stay low and in front of that wall.'

They moved around the fallen debris. Lily gazed ahead at the spot where Vincent and Alice had stood, shortly before they fell to their deaths. In the torchlight, right by her feet, she could see something small that was filthy, wet and vaguely blue. It was Alice's favourite blue bunny, Hoppy. She picked it up and edged towards the turrets at the far ledge. Oliver grabbed her arm, just as a powerful gust of wind flattened them against the wall. They had no choice but to kneel down, huddled together.

'You okay?!' said Oliver. Thunder rippled across the sky, this time closer.

'Yes.'

'We're going back, now!' he shouted. Lily nodded her agreement. Seconds later, white-hot lightning lit up the entire sky like a camera flash. They watched as a silent pattern of light crisscrossed downwards, followed by an eruption of noise. One of the two largest turrets collapsed, falling partly onto the roof and partly onto the drive below. A sonic boom of thunder exploded overhead so loudly it felt as if the sky was being ripped in two. They had no choice but to wait until the chaos stopped.

Oliver shone the torch across the charred remains of the collapsed column. The air was filled with the smell of ozone and alive with static electricity. They looked at each other in disbelief. Heavy raindrops began to fall that fizzed and popped on the scorched rubble and the storm slowly moved away.

Back inside, Oliver looked in concern at Lily. 'Did it help? Being out there?'

'No,' she sighed. 'After all that... I'm sorry, I really hoped it would. But I did find this. Alice's favourite toy, Hoppy. She must have dropped it just before she fell.'

He put his arm around her. 'Come on, let's get out of here. We can always try again... but not tonight... the wind's too strong. Christ, we nearly got hit by lightning.'

Lily nodded, disappointed and upset. Back downstairs, Oliver swung open the front door.

'It's pelting down again. Why don't you come out in a minute when I've turned the car around? And watch out for the fallen rubble. Here, you have the torch.'

She sat on the low windowsill by the door, watching him run through the rain. Swinging the torch around, she glimpsed something jammed behind the radiator next to her. Gingerly, she reached for it with her fingertips. It felt dusty – whatever it was had probably been there for decades. Lily slid it out and brushed away the filth. Her heart leapt into her throat. It was the face she had seen a hundred times in her nightmares. It was a mask, an African mask. *My God, it used to be on a stand in the window.* Then it happened... the final piece of the jigsaw slotted into place and someone was calling to her...

Lily was nine years old. She was standing in the doorway, on the roof of Penwyth House. She watched as Alice ran through the storm to her father. He swept her up in his arms; they were swaying in the wind and the rain.

'Lily! Come here!' Vincent gestured towards her, his voice half lost in the storm. She peered out at them, silhouetted by lightning in the night sky.

'Lily!' her mother called from below. 'What are you doing up there?'

'Daddy and Alice are up here! Mummy, they are right by the edge and he's calling me!'

'No! No, Lily.' She could see her mother now, standing at the bottom of the stairs. *'You come back in, right now. Do you hear me?'* Lily nodded and climbed back down the stairs. She could still hear her father shouting. Her mother grabbed hold of her tightly. *'It's very important that you listen to me. Go downstairs and wait for me in the main hallway. Okay?'* Lily solemnly nodded. Her mother's face was deathly white. *'Go! Go now!'*

Lily ran as fast as she could down the main stairs and stood breathlessly waiting. After what seemed like an age, her mother too came running down the stairs. She looked terrified.

'Where's Daddy and Alice?'

Her mother didn't answer. *'He won't come down. I have to fetch Joe. You stay right here, okay? Your father's had a bit too much to drink, that's all, and needs help. Don't worry. Joe will know what to do. Promise me you'll stay here.'* Lily's eyes grew wide with fear.

'I promise.'

Her mother ran out into the storm, leaving the door wide open. Lily wandered over to the window and picked up the African mask from its stand on the sill. She ran her fingers over the slits for eyes and the grooves of its harsh features… then… something dropped right in front of the window. She slowly looked up… she dropped the mask, which fell with a clatter behind the radiator. With feet like lead, she walked through the front door, down the steps, into the rain and stared at the crumpled heap on the floor. Vincent was still alive and reaching out to her with one hand. A trail of blood trickled from the side of his mouth. He was trying to speak. She could see one of Alice's tiny hands. It was motionless, protruding from underneath her father's broken body. Lily started to cry.

'Daddy, what do I do?!'

He was still trying to speak. She knelt and put her ear close to his mouth.

'Why did you run away, Lily?' he said with effort. *'You should have come with us.'* Then he smiled at her. His eyes froze over and his hand flopped to the ground. She heard a man's voice yelling and got to her feet. Her mother and Joe

276

were running towards her...

'Lily! Why didn't you come out?' called Oliver. Then he saw her face, drained of all colour. She dropped the mask on the floor and looked in bewilderment at Oliver.

'He jumped,' she said flatly. 'It was never an accident... he jumped.'

CHAPTER 57

'Hello, Miss Sanders. It's Sergeant Weeks. I have some news for you.'

'Oh? Is it regarding the forensics?'

'No, but I thank you for your cooperation. However, you'll be pleased to hear that, following a police search of the Holt brothers' residence, we have retrieved a firearm that we believe to be Mr Newman's.'

'Really?'

'Yes. I've not had a chance to inform Mr Newman yet. There's no phone at Edhen Cottage, so I'll go and see him in person.'

'Good grief! I guess Oliver's hunch was right.'

'I'm confident Mr Holt's criminal record would have come to light shortly, as we were checking all offenders in the area. But your and Mr Bligh's concerns certainly brought him to our attention more quickly. He has a string of previous minor charges brought against him including theft, common assault and drunk and disorderly. In this instance, he is charged with burglary and causing grievous bodily harm.'

'What about his brother?'

'Luke Holt? He is still something of a mystery. He has no previous convictions and his brother insists that he acted alone. However, going by Mr Newman's statement, he is quite clear that there were two assailants. Unfortunately, Luke Holt seems to have vanished so we are unable to question him. He was last seen on the morning of the 10th of March when, according to Douglas, he left home on an old Triumph motorbike that belonged to their late father. That same day, there was a particularly bad storm… perhaps you remember?'

'Yes… yes, I do.'

'Well, it is possible that he had some sort of accident. Some of the coastal roads around here are treacherous, especially when there's poor visibility. He could have left the road, even gone over the cliffs and smashed into the rocks. If he ended up in the water, a body may wash up along the coast in a week or two. It wouldn't be the first time. Or, the other explanation is that he absconded, but it seems unlikely. The brothers appeared to be living a pretty frugal existence and Douglas Holt confirmed that they had very little money. Plus, Luke's belongings are still in the house.'

'I see… is Douglas Holt still in custody?'

'Yes, for now. He may make bail, unless the court decides he is a danger to the public or a flight risk, but I don't think that you or Mr Newman need be concerned. It almost seems like he wants to stay imprisoned. Oddly, when myself and a colleague were on our way to the Holt residence, we happened to receive a radio call requesting we attend a car accident en route. A young family had reported passing a van that had come off the road and landed in a ditch. When we reached the scene, the driver gave his name as Douglas Holt. He had suffered some minor injuries, but when later questioned about the burglary he voluntarily confessed, as well as to the assault on Mr Newman and the gun theft.'

'So, he just happened to come off the road?'

'It was a stormy day, but yes. It was bizarre that we happened to be driving to question him at the time. He explained that he was out looking for his brother. He was angry that Luke had taken the motorbike because he had just spent weeks restoring it and was hoping to take it out first himself.'

'Well, I can't tell you how relieved I am to hear you've made an arrest,' said Lily. 'And, of course, Joe will be, too. Thank you for calling, Sergeant Weeks. Oh, I was planning on seeing Mr Newman later. Is it okay if I let him know?'

'That would be fine, Miss Sanders. Perhaps then you can also let him know that we will need him to come to the station to identify the retrieved firearm? It will be held as evidence until the court case is over.'

*

Joe was sitting outside Edhen Cottage. He waved as Lily pulled up. He looked better – his face was healing nicely and, when he got up to greet her, she could see he was moving more easily.

'Come on in,' he smiled.

Lily noticed the photo she had given him, proudly placed next to the one of her mother.

'You look so happy together,' she said, picking it up.

'And young!' he added.

She laughed. 'Well, you certainly seem better. How are you feeling?'

'My jaw doesn't ache as much,' he replied. 'I've been able to eat some softer foods – omelette, baked beans, that sort of thing. It's an improvement on soup and liquids through a straw! Ribs are still a bit sore, but I'm getting there.'

'And your eyesight?'

'I've got an appointment in a few weeks at the hospital, but I think the right one has improved a bit. Enough, I think, for me to take care of my birds now.'

She smiled, relieved for him. 'Have you been to the aviary yet?'

'Yes, and I bumped into your friend, Janet, the vet, there. Nice lady. We had a pleasant chat by the waterfall. I thanked her for all her help, but said that I thought I would be able to manage from now on.'

'That's great,' said Lily. 'I know how much it means to you to be back caring for your birds and plants. While you were in the hospital, Timothy drew up papers for me signing this place and the land we mentioned over to you. When you are ready, I have them here for you to look at. I can leave them with you?'

Joe shrugged and smiled. 'I trust you, Lily. Tell me where to sign.' She showed him the deeds again that outlined his property boundaries, but it was all just formalities and he willingly signed the documents making him the new owner of Edhen Cottage.

'Congratulations! Edhen Cottage is yours and always will be.'

'Thank you,' said Joe. 'You've made an old man very happy.'

Lily smiled. 'I have some other news, too… about the people who attacked you.'

'Oh?'

She repeated her conversation with the sergeant. Joe was relieved to hear that someone had been caught, and even more so that he had confessed.

'Those Holt brothers sound like a nasty business,' he said. 'Let's hope we can put it behind us now.' He sighed. 'What will you do now? Are you going to stay in Lostmor?'

'Yes,' said Lily, taking his hand. 'Everyone I care about is here. Why would I leave?'

He smiled, relieved to know that his newly found daughter wasn't about to be lost to him for a second time.

'Where will you live?'

'I've opened an art gallery in town,' she said. 'It's just a small shop, but it has a flat above it. I'm going to stay there for now.'

'And Oliver? You two courting?'

She smiled and nodded. 'He's already asked me to move in with him at Bligh Farm.'

'You like him a lot, don't you?'

'Yes, I do… In fact… I love him.'

Joe smiled. 'Then I'm happy for you both. He seems a good man.'

'There's one more thing…' said Lily. 'I've decided not to sell Penwyth House. I'm going to renovate it. After that, I'm not quite sure, but I'm afraid it may be a bit noisy around here for some time to come.'

'I'm not bothered by a bit of noise,' said Joe. 'It's been quiet for the past twenty-odd years – apart from my birds! Besides, I'm glad it's you restoring the old place and not some stranger. It's your home, Lily. I've done my best with the estate, but the house has been neglected for decades. It's time to return it to your care.'

'I will do my very best.' She paused. 'Talking of birds… have you ever rescued a seagull or been visited by one?'

'Mike, you mean? Fixed his claw when he was a chick. He's massive now, though. Have you seen him, then?'

'Several times, most memorably with you…' said Lily, grinning. 'The day I found you injured by the woods. He stood guard over you. At first, he blocked my way, but he seemed to sense I meant you no harm and eventually let me pass. Even then, he stayed on patrol right up until the ambulance came!'

'My word, that is something, isn't it!?' said Joe laughing. 'Good old Mike. He flies in and out, but I haven't seen him for a while. Next time I do, if he hangs around long enough, I'll treat him to a fish supper.' He paused for a moment, gazing at Lily with his sea-green eyes. 'How about you and me go visit Alice sometime soon?'

Lily smiled and nodded. 'Yes, I would like that. I would like that very much.'

The headstone simply read:

Alice

1965-1971

Forever in our hearts

Lily placed a small bunch of yellow roses, along with Hoppy, on Alice's grave. They stood quietly together under the cedar tree.

'I miss you,' she whispered to her sister. She then turned to her father. 'I finally remembered what happened that night. You were there, weren't you?'

Joe slowly nodded. 'But it was too late,' he said sadly. 'There was nothing any of us could have done, Lily. It was just a tragic accident.'

He never knew the truth, nor did my mother.

'Yes,' said Lily. What was there to gain by telling him what Vincent had whispered to her that night? That he had tried to take her, too.

They held hands and gazed out to sea, lost in their thoughts. Above them, a gentle breeze rustled the leaves, bringing with it the promise of spring.

CHAPTER 58

9.00 pm, Saturday, 24ᵗʰ June 1995

'It seems strange… to be here just as a customer,' Marcus smiled, looking around the busy bar and nodding at Tom, who was in his usual corner. 'I may forget in a minute and start pulling pints!'

Julia laughed, her fingers lightly touching the now fading scar at her temple.

'Does it bother you?' he asked.

'What? Oh no, not at all,' she smiled.

'Good. It hardly shows, anyway. What about your shoulder?'

'It's holding up okay,' said Julia. 'I threw balls for the dogs overarm today instead of relying on Sarah to do it, and it didn't hurt. The hospital did say that I should be back to full strength in three months, so I think I can start pulling my weight a bit more now.' She sighed. 'We're lucky that Sarah turned out to be such a diamond… I'm going to miss her when she goes to university this autumn.'

'She's been a great help alright,' said Marcus, 'and offering to doggy sit tonight was thoughtful… I guess we ought to advertise for someone else nearer the time.'

'Yes, but I'll be a bit more selective with the interviewees this time,' she said wryly.

Ever since Julia had been discharged from hospital, Marcus had been by her side. He took no pleasure in what he had done, but neither did he have any regrets. He had avenged his daughter's death. If he had gone to the police and Luke had gone to prison, he knew the sentence could have been anything from two to fourteen years, depending on the court's assessment of the accident, and Luke would most certainly be out in less. In the eyes of the law, Marcus had committed murder and his actions wouldn't bring Rose back. But he could now rest easier.

As for Julia, strangely tangled up in this whole mess with Luke, he had worried that the events of that night would come between them. She had suffered a violent attack and, although he was not to blame, the coincidence of him hunting down this man could have made him a constant and unwelcome reminder of what took place that day. And she was carrying the knowledge of what he had done to Luke Holt.

But he need not have worried. As soon as Julia was discharged, she just wanted to get back to normal and help with the dogs as much as possible. He had witnessed post-traumatic stress disorder before and she showed none of the signs. They had talked over what had happened that day, but not dwelt on it. Instead, as the weeks went by and Julia gradually recovered, she had told him she loved him and asked him to move in with her. Marcus had not hesitated. Taking her in his arms, he had told her how much he loved her, too. Not long after, he resigned as landlord at the Black Dog Inn.

Julia looked at Marcus's face, his features now so familiar to her. The haunted look he had worn all those months ago was gone and, in his intelligent grey eyes, she saw only kindness.

Marcus felt a firm hand on his shoulder. 'It's been a while. How are you?'

He got to his feet and shook Oliver's hand and smiled at the woman by his side.

'I'm good,' he replied. 'I'm not sure you've met Julia. Julia, this is Oliver. And you... must be Lily?'

'Yes!' she replied. 'Of course, I know your face. You used to work here!'

'For my sins, yes,' he grinned. 'I don't want to impose, but you're welcome to join us?'

Oliver looked at Lily, who was already being beckoned to sit by Julia. 'Thanks, why not?' he said, also sitting. 'What are you up to now then, Marcus?'

'I'm helping Julia run Fern Retreat Kennels.'

'And how's Horace?' Oliver asked.

'Horace is having the time of his life,' replied Marcus. 'He spends his days tearing around the exercise paddock with the other dogs. And he has taken a shine to Bella, Julia's springer spaniel.'

'I remember seeing Horace in here,' Lily said. 'A big soppy Labrador?'

'That's him,' Julia smiled. 'What do you do, Lily? Do you work in Lostmor?'

'Yes, just around the corner from here. I run an art gallery called *Swan Song*. Do you know it?'

'No,' said Julia, 'I'm afraid I rarely get a chance to go anywhere since I bought Fern Retreat. We're only here tonight because our kennel hand offered to doggy sit!' She laughed. 'Not that I'm complaining. Business is booming and I'm really enjoying it. And it's easier now that I have help.' She glanced happily at Marcus, who was chatting to Oliver about his farm. 'I only moved to Lostmor earlier in the year. I was brought up locally, in West Hill, but my family moved to South Devon when I was a teenager.'

'Well, I guess we're both newbies then,' said Lily. 'My family come from Lostmor, but I only moved down from Bristol this year, too.'

'Is that why you moved here? To open up *Swan Song*?'

Lily leant back and smiled. 'No, that came later. I moved here because of Oliver... We met by chance, thanks to a Jack Russell called Flynn.'

Julia looked at her curiously. She remembered that she, too, had only met Marcus by chance when he had brought Horace to Fern Retreat. 'It sounds like an interesting story!'

'Lily, do you want a refill?' Oliver asked. 'And can I interest anyone else?'

'I'm definitely interested,' Marcus smiled. 'But we told Sarah we'd be back by ten.'

'Some other time then?' said Oliver.

'Why don't you and Julia come to the farm one evening?' Lily suggested. 'We could cook for you?'

'That would be lovely,' Julia grinned at Lily. 'Then you can tell me all about your chance encounter with Oliver and a Jack Russell called Flynn.'

Oliver laughed. 'That may take some time!'

CHAPTER 59

'That was a busy afternoon!' Julia said over dinner at Fern Retreat. 'Lots of people picking up on a Sunday, but at least tomorrow's pretty quiet.'

She paused for a moment and looked at Marcus. 'They were a nice couple... Oliver and Lily... last night, in the pub,' she said.

He smiled and stroked Horace's head that was nudging him for food under the table.

'Oliver's a good bloke,' he replied.

'How do you know him? I mean, by your own admission you've kept to yourself ever since you arrived in Lostmor.'

'True,' said Marcus. 'But when you're running a pub, people chat to you, a lot! That's how we met. But he's one of a small number that I actually enjoyed talking to. And Lily... she's Lily Sanders. She recently inherited a big old mansion house and estate on the edge of Lostmor. I think it has a bit of a troubled past, though.'

'Goodness, really? Some people do have interesting lives!'

Marcus remembered the news report – the attempted burglary and assault involving the Holt brothers at Penwyth House. He didn't want to mention it now. Some other time. If they did go to Oliver's farm for supper, then he would forewarn her, in case they mentioned it. Otherwise, there seemed little point in digging up their unwelcome names.

'Well,' he remarked. 'I wouldn't say ours were exactly run of the mill… would you?'

Julia laughed and reached for his hand across the table. 'There's something I have to tell you…'

'What?' he looked expectantly at her.

'What if I were to tell you that our lives are about to get a whole lot more interesting…' She paused.

Marcus gasped. 'You're pregnant?'

Julia nodded. 'I know we haven't even talked about children… but yes… I am.'

Marcus rose, pushing the kitchen chair back and went to her. Julia wrapped her arms around his neck. He looked at her with tears of emotion in his eyes.

'I could not be happier,' he whispered.

'Are you sure?' said Julia. 'I mean, we're so busy with the kennels and things have already moved so quickly between us…'

'It's true, things have happened quickly for us,' said Marcus. 'But I'm glad. I only want to be with you… and with our baby,' he smiled, gently placing a hand on Julia's tummy. 'You couldn't have given me any better news than this, and the kennels will be fine. We can always hire more staff, and you don't have to worry about money. Working at the pub was only ever about Rose. Twenty-odd years in the army and not a lot to spend it on has left me pretty secure financially.'

'That's good,' she smiled fondly at him and kissed him softly on the lips. 'Because it's twins.'

*

At Bligh Farm, Oliver sat on the oak bench gazing at the horizon. It was a warm summer's evening. The long hours of daylight lingered into twilight and, beyond the cliffs, gentle waves glittered like sequins.

'There you are,' Lily smiled, sitting down next to him. 'I have something to show you.'

'You do?'

Lily nodded and handed him the one remaining photo of her grandparents, Alfred and Jeanie. 'I took this out of the album to frame it, and look what I found on the back.'

Oliver turned it over. 'It's a recipe… for whiskey!'

She nodded. 'This is my family's legacy. It is the ingredients for the finest single-malt Cornish whiskey ever produced! And, as far as I know, the only one in existence.'

He looked at her in surprise. 'This is unbelievable! But it begs the question – what will you do with it?'

'I'm not sure yet, but it's another piece of Sanders' history reclaimed. A handwritten list… just found by chance!'

'Perhaps the gods are moving another chess piece.'

'Perhaps,' Lily laughed. Her long hair fell gently over her shoulders and Oliver thought she had never looked more beautiful than she did at that moment. Above them, birdsong floated down in the evening air. Skylarks. He couldn't remember the last time he'd heard skylarks. He leant in gently towards Lily and kissed her.

'Looks like it's your move.'

EPILOGUE

A curious lad and his father discovered a large exhaust and part of the casing of a fuel tank washed up at Penny Cove a few weeks after the worst storm in Cornwall's recorded history. The police later confirmed that it was from a Triumph Bonneville motorbike.

Douglas Holt was found guilty of burglary and causing grievous bodily harm. He is currently serving a ten-year sentence. Luke's body was never recovered.

Julia and Marcus are now the proud parents of twins, Jacob and Paige. They continue to run Fern Retreat Kennels, and Bella and Horace spend their days messing about in the paddock.

Lily no longer suffers nightmares. The following summer, she married Oliver on the cliffside at Bligh Farm, with her father by her side and surrounded by friends – and, of course, Flynn. She continues to paint and spends most of her days at *Swan Song*.

Oliver diversified… *Lostmor Legacy: Single Malt Cornish Whiskey: Chapter 2* was born, courtesy of one of Bligh Farm's barns that he'd converted into a distillery. In the summer, the fields are filled with acres of swaying golden barley.

Joe Newman remains at Edhen Cottage and visits his aviary daily, where he tends to his beloved birds and orchids.

Mike appeared briefly at Lily and Oliver's wedding, perched on the roof of Bligh Farm. Most of the guests had no inkling – except for Joe and Lily.

And as for Penwyth House? It is a work in progress...

The End

Watch out for the equally spellbinding suspense sequel,
'Penwyth Hotel' coming soon...

ABOUT THE AUTHOR

Ann Smythe grew up in Bristol where she worked in the editorial world of publishing for many years before finally taking the plunge with this, her first novel, The Aviculturist.

She moved to beautiful North Somerset with her husband and son seventeen years ago and spends her days writing and walking her dogs.

Thank you for taking the time to read this book. If you have enjoyed it, please consider using your skills to leave a short review on Amazon.

You can find Ann online at https://www.annsmythe.com

on Twitter @AnnBSmythe and

on Facebook at www.facebook.com/ann.smythe.uk

Printed in Great Britain
by Amazon

80718317R00173